THE LIFE ENGINEERED

THE LIFE ENGINEERED

J-F. Dubeau

Published by Inkshares, Inc., San Francisco, California, as part of the Sword & Laser Collection
www.inkshares.com

Edited and designed by Girl Friday Productions
www.girlfridayproductions.com

Cover design by Elsie Lyons
Cover illustration by Eric Belisle

ISBN: 978-1-941758-59-5
e-ISBN: 978-1-941758-60-1
Library of Congress Control Number: 2015944027

First edition

Printed in the United States of America

For my family. By blood or ceremony.

DAWN OF END

AD 3594

At first, nothing happened. The pinprick of light simply twinkled in the dark, vaguely shimmering on the large monitor. It was a moment before a small flare became visible, quickly followed by a rapidly expanding but almost imperceptible sphere of light. Finally, two hair-thin beams flashed briefly from diametrically opposite points of the distant star.

"There," a woman said with but a hint of tremor in her voice. "You'll see it better in the gamma range."

Instantly, the monitor switched to the specified spectrum in response to her comment, the image changing to a version of itself that resembled an impressionist's interpretation of the night sky. Waves of luminous colors, ranging from pink to dark indigo, emanated from the now brightly glowing sun. The scene repeated itself, but this time the expanding sphere of light was blinding, washing out the monitor in incandescent white. The image had barely toned back down and become visible again when the beams manifested as brilliant shafts of red that bisected the frame. Then the monitor switched back to the normal visible spectrum—a shimmering white dot on a blanket of black.

The lights in the nearly empty auditorium were slowly brought back to life, gently bathing the room in a soft-blue glow. The woman got up first, wiping her hands on the sides of her tunic, leaving hand-shaped sweat stains that disappeared almost instantly. She turned nervously around to look at her companion, who was casually leaning back in his chair.

"The gamma ray burst from that one will destroy Persea's biosphere within the year," she explained.

"They'll all be in stasis long before that," the man said calmly, inspecting his impeccably trimmed beard with the back of his hand.

"But that will leave only us, Gareth."

The man shrugged before pulling himself laboriously to his feet. He brushed the wrinkles out of his pants, frowning at the damage that prolonged sitting had done to their pressed folds.

"We'll be fine. The closest star that could generate that kind of gamma burst could erupt tomorrow and we wouldn't feel the effects for another five years." His tone was both reassuring and condescending. "Most of us have already moved to the Dormitory. By this time next year, we'll all be safely tucked away."

"Being taken care of by robots," she complained.

"I resent that," interjected a third and last audience member.

The creature unfolded from its chair. Its thin, elegant limbs deployed from its slender, shining body. Minuscule servos whirled almost imperceptibly, animating the synthetic being. It turned its gleaming head, a semitransparent polished dome protecting an array of sensory equipment, to face its human counterparts.

"It will be our honor and privilege to be your caretakers and stewards of this galaxy until it is properly healed," the creature explained.

"My apologies, Marduk. That came out wrong," the woman said. "This . . . hiatus is keeping you and your kind from your destiny."

"Our destiny can wait, Adelaïde, and this hiatus as you call it will not be so bad," the robot said. "Tending the Dormitories can be handled by nonsentient automatons, and rebuilding biospheres will be an engrossing project for many of our more creative-minded people."

"Nothing is stopping you from moving ahead with your own societies, Marduk," added Gareth. "It's probably better that the Dormitories be left alone anyway. Go forth. Build. Create. Make us proud."

Gareth broke into a warm smile—a rare sign of emotion on his part. His fondness for the synthetic children of humanity was clearly etched on his features. Marduk bowed politely before standing to his full height, nearing three meters tall.

"Many thanks. Our plans are already in motion. I think you'll be impressed by what you find when we next meet."

Both humans bowed their heads politely. They watched as the strange creature of alloy and metal strode purposefully toward the door and bent down slightly to exit the auditorium. With its sensor array hidden under its smooth dome, it was impossible to tell if the robot had looked back at its biological companions.

"I don't trust them," Adelaïde said after she was certain the artificial creature could not hear her.

"The Capeks?" asked Gareth with barely hidden disbelief. "They're completely loyal and don't have an evil bone in their bodies."

"They don't have bones at all."

"Don't split hairs, Adelaïde. We could not be in better hands," he said. "Without Ascension, never could we even hope to reach the purity they embody."

"You put them on a pedestal. They're no longer the faithful dogs our ancestors made them to be. They've grown. They've evolved. I'm . . . I'm as proud as you are! I am, but this destiny you speak of, they speak of, there's a hunger for it that doesn't leave room for us."

"Given time we won't need room anymore. Ascension will take care of that." Gareth had a gleam in his eye of almost-childlike excitement. "The universe creates God. After that the Capeks can inherit the galaxy and work toward their own goals. Ours will be fulfilled."

Adelaïde looked back toward the monitor that dominated the front of the auditorium. Reacting to her unspoken intentions, the screen blinked to life and displayed the white dot over the black sky again. As she stared, the image zoomed out, displaying an ever-growing number of stars. A red circle appeared over the original pinprick of light, and soon another, then a third, and so forth. After a moment the entire Milky Way galaxy was on-screen, sprinkled with dozens of red, pulsing circles, singling out a list of systems.

"Fifty-one high-intensity gamma ray bursts, all within the last five decades, all targeting our inhabitable worlds," Adelaïde explained. "Our homes have been systematically obliterated, Gareth. Who's doing this to us?"

"It's not the Capeks, if that's what you're implying."

"Who else is there?" Adelaïde couldn't keep her fear and frustration hidden anymore. "We are putting ourselves at the mercy of the only possible suspects, and no one is talking about it. Everyone pretends this is a natural phenomenon—a coincidence!"

"Adelaïde. All you have to go on is opportunity, ignoring motive and, more importantly, the means. The Capeks, for all their wonders, are no more advanced than we are. They don't have the technology to orchestrate astronomical events of that scale.

No one does. As for motives—Capeks are our children! They owe as much, if not more, to us as we do to them."

"We're blindly stepping onto the gallows. Even if the chance that they mean us harm is remote, shouldn't we do something to protect ourselves? Just in case?"

For the first time Gareth seemed to be taking her comments seriously. He motioned for her to go on.

"Marduk and others like him don't worry me, but there are hundreds of Capeks, each with its own unique and complex personality. What if even a single one of them developed resentment toward us? It wouldn't take much for them to eradicate humanity if that was the case."

Gareth sighed and smiled, making it clear that while he was humoring her, he did not share her worries. Shaking his head slowly, he gave Adelaïde another condescending look.

"Fine. Let's assume the impossible. What do you have in mind?"

Adelaïde turned back to the monitor, willing it to life once more through a combination of subvocalization and eye movement. A handful of blue dots manifested themselves on the galactic map, each with a name inscribed next to it.

"This current generation of Capeks is coming to an end," she began with confidence, pointing at the blue dots in succession. "These are the sites where the Gaia-generation Capeks are being assembled. Each is built from a composite mind that I know and trust. Individuals of impeccable character. Beyond reproach."

"The very reason they were chosen for the task, yes."

"Exactly. If Marduk suggests that our caretakers can be automated, then so be it. We don't have to tell their entire race where the Dormitory Worlds are located. We can bury that information so deep in the Gaias' personality constructs that, until we are ready, the second and third generation of Capeks can evolve without knowing where we sleep. When the day comes, when the Gaias feel the time is right, they can supervise our awakening."

Gareth paced at the front of the auditorium, scratching his beard. Adelaïde knew he was looking for cracks in her plan and flaws in her thinking. He hated that his precious Capeks, the pinnacle of human ingenuity, might not be perfect—that somehow they could be sufficiently flawed to pose a threat.

"Fine," he finally admitted. "How do you propose to handle the programming of all the Gaias? It would take a lifetime to visit each site and apply the kind of change you're suggesting. You wouldn't make it to the Dormitory in time."

The woman looked him right in the eyes. Human eyes had changed so much in the past hundreds of years. While they allowed modern humans to see so much more of the world thanks to implants and retinal projection of augmented reality, they also allowed so much more to be seen. The surface of the cornea had become a living pattern of subtle lights that shifted along with every individual's visual activity. The eyes had truly become a window to the soul.

"Do you really feel that strongly about this?" he asked after a moment, knowing her decision—knowing her intended sacrifice.

"Yes."

ESSENCE 262 010, ITERATION 1 977, FINAL CYCLE

Somerville, Massachusetts, October 31, 2012, Subjective Time

Every morning was the same story. After a year of the same routine, you'd have thought I'd be used to it by now, but no. It always came as a surprise when the alarm shocked me awake and, later, as an even greater surprise that I actually managed to get up.

Every morning I did half an hour of basic exercises—stretches, push-ups, and sit-ups—and then I took a shower. I struggled each time not to fall back asleep under the warm, comforting stream of water, and somehow I always managed. Once my hair dried and I put on my uniform and a minimal layer of makeup (mostly to hide the ever-expanding bags under my eyes), I'd wake Jonathan up so he could have breakfast.

Every morning was the same, and when it wasn't, the cause was usually unpleasant. Jonathan was sick, or the electricity went out and my alarm didn't ring. Banality and routine had become preferable to surprises and spontaneity. There was security in repeating patterns, and until Jon was old enough to move out and go off to college—or alternatively, I won the lottery—I gladly embraced routine. Even if it was unlikely to change for the next thirteen years.

That day, however, was a little different. That morning after my shower, I snuck into Jonathan's room. Where I would normally gently nudge him awake, that morning I quietly made my way to his bed, carefully avoiding the toys I had instructed him to put away that instead still littered the floor, and took a moment to watch my little guy sleep.

He was a lot of work, that boy. Between him and a full-time career, there wasn't much left to my life, but what did that matter? I stared at that little face as he gently slept without a trace of worry, and I knew it was all worth it.

"Boo!" I whispered in his ear as I grabbed my baby and tickled him.

"Ah!" he screamed right back, terrified at first but immediately melting into loud giggles.

Almost instantly I heard Ms. Ryan upstairs complaining about the noise. I hate the old whining cow, but I could hardly blame her. While this was a normal hour for my family, it was still only 4:00 a.m.

"Guess what today is," I teased Jonathan in whispers, putting a finger to my lips in the process.

"Halloween!" he whispered back excitedly.

"That's right! Now get up and wash up. I'll pack you a special Halloween lunch, and we'll get you in your costume."

Without having to be asked twice, my boy was off to the washroom. By the time he was out, clad in fresh underwear and his hair somewhat combed, I had his lunch bag ready and his costume laid out. Disappointed I couldn't make something myself and had to fall back on a store-bought outfit, I was still glad I could at least afford a decent costume. It seemed like a waste for something he'd wear once, perhaps twice, but the look of genuine wonder and excitement on his face as he eagerly put on the tunic and accessories made it worth every penny.

"Yeah! I'm Thor!" my little guy clamored as quietly as his overstimulated voice would allow.

"All right, mighty Thor. Eat your cereal so we can get going."

"Where's Midjitnear?"

"What?"

"Where's my hammer? I can't be Thor without a hammer," he said.

"Right next to your shoes, by the door." I pointed to the hollow plastic replica that had come with the costume. "Now eat your breakfast so Mommy won't be late for work."

It was pitch black when we stepped out of the apartment. Trees groaned and whistled as we walked the five blocks to Helena's place. It wasn't very far, but the streets were cleaner and the houses were bigger, with such luxuries as driveways and front yards. Almost every home had an extra car parked in the street, almost none of which looked to be secondhand. The houses themselves were clean and well maintained, with lit house numbers and manicured lawns.

Jonathan was full of energy. I was glad Helena liked him so much and hoped his enthusiasm wouldn't make him too much of a handful.

As we stepped on her porch, I sent Helena a text message to let her know we'd arrived. Better than waking up her husband and kids with the doorbell.

"All right, Jon," I knelt to look my boy in the eyes. "What did we discuss about the hammer?"

"Mjolnir is for hitting bad guys!"

"Okay, and how many bad guys are there at Aunt Helena's?"

"None," he answered with only a touch of disappointment.

"That's right. So don't hit anyone with that thing."

When the door opened, I came face-to-face with a better life. Helena was so many things I wasn't. Blond and voluptuous, well settled and happy. Her existence was in order to a degree mine would probably never reach. Mostly, though, she was satisfied. Things had worked out for her. Charles, her husband, took care of her and their two girls while she pursued her career working from home.

"Good morning," she said with a strained but pleasant smile. "Hey there. What do we have here? Are you some kind of superhero?"

"I'm Thor!"

"I bet you are," Helena answered, ruffling my boy's hair. "You know the drill, little man. Nap time until seven, okay?"

"Okay," Jonathan answered before kissing me, shedding his sneakers, and running in.

"You be good."

"He's always good," Helena said, smiling at me as she leaned on her doorframe and tightened her heavy robe around her bare neck. "What about you, Mel?"

"Same old, I guess."

"You can't keep doing this, you know?"

"I know," I said. "I'll try to find some other arrangement, but it's not easy."

Helena gave me a sympathetic smile before breaking into a yawn. It wasn't fair. It wasn't fair to her, and it wasn't fair to Jonathan or even Charles and the girls, but what else could I do?

"You'll be fine, and you know I'll always be happy to take Jon when you need me to, but sometimes I wonder if you don't need a bit of a kick in the butt."

I bit my lip. *A kick in the butt?* She made it sound like I enjoyed waking up before dawn every morning, working six days a week, and having to beg for favors from friends just to be able to offer my son the semblance of a normal life. It's so easy to pontificate when your life is perfect. I wanted to tell her that. I wanted to shove it in her face how unfair her comment was, but I bit my lip and I took the blow.

"Ask for a day shift, even if it's a desk job, just until you can put Jon in daycare or something. Or find something else for a little while. I'm saying this as much for you as I am for him." She looked genuinely concerned. "You look like you're a million years old."

And I felt even older than that. Had I always felt this ancient? Had I simply forgotten how it felt not being exhausted? I had never been this worn out.

"Maybe you're right. Maybe a change of careers might not be such a bad idea," I admitted. "Didn't you say Charles was looking for a new secretary?"

"Tut-tut! Last time Charles had a female secretary, he ended up marrying her." She pointed a finger to herself. "I'm afraid this is a male-only position now."

We both laughed a little. She was even perfect at comforting me, damn her.

"I'll ask to be transferred to a desk job or dispatch. I'll ask today. It's not quite my preferred career path—"

"But what it lacks in glamour it makes up for in how good it would be for Jon."

She was even perfect at raising my kid.

I was in a foul mood when I got to the station. The lack of sleep, combined with Helena's polite but depressing assessment of my situation, had stripped me of all my good cheer from earlier that morning.

Ours was a pretty small precinct, with maybe two dozen officers and support staff—just enough to serve our small suburban community within the limited budget awarded to us by the municipality. Everyone there knew everyone else, and while I couldn't say we were all friends, we remained a relatively tight-knit group. On the other hand, what we had in conviviality we paid for in lack of flexibility and career opportunities. People didn't quit or transfer out of the station very often, nor did we see many retirements. It was a great place to have a midlevel position, but a lot less attractive for someone seeking advancement or even just a better shift.

"Paulson!" Anthony called the moment he saw me walk through the door. If I were to try and imagine a worse person to deal with in my state of mind that day than my bubbly, overeager partner, I'd have my work cut out for me.

Lieutenant Anthony Blain was difficult to hate, which made snapping at him for being so damn jovial before sunrise as shameful as it was common. It came as a surprise that I managed not to.

"Good morning, Anthony," I grumbled as I poured myself a generous mug of vile but potent coffee.

My young partner wove through the other officers, lieutenants, and detectives, both going on and coming off their respective shifts, and joined me at the coffee machine. As he reached the counter, he magically transformed the annoyed mutterings of his coworkers into mumbles of what could pass for delight at five in the morning. The trick was dropping a large box of assorted donuts next to the percolating demon that kept us supplied in black, oily caffeine.

"How you doing, partner? Ready to fight crime?" he asked, sipping from a cardboard cup of some fancy, sweet, not-coffee confection.

"We hand out parking and speeding tickets, Ant. Hardly the stuff of legends."

I grabbed a donut before the other vultures picked the box clean. "Ant" was a nickname I'd thought up for him a while ago, and though it was adopted by the rest of the station, it failed to annoy my partner as intended.

"Well, we can't all be heroes already, Paulson."

"Who's a hero? My medal must have gotten lost in the mail."

"Take some credit, Mel. Everyone knows how hard it must be to raise a kid while doing this job." He could be sickeningly friendly and positive.

"Not everyone," I mumbled as I watched Captain Denis Hutchcroft, our commander and chief, walk out of his office, bleary-eyed and tired. The seasoned relic of our precinct gave the assembled group a polite nod before heading toward the front door.

"Captain!" I caught myself calling, a mouthful of pastry muffling my voice. Before I'd made a conscious decision, I had walked through the station right up to him.

"What do you need, Paulson?" he asked, giving his watch an impatient look, fatigued from a graveyard shift he had probably volunteered for.

That was the problem dealing with the venerable Captain Hutchcroft: as a workaholic himself, he had difficulty empathizing with those of us with common lives and more modest aspirations.

"I want to talk about changing my shift."

His eyes bulged a little, discomfort and a hint of panic written in the lines of his face. It was strange for a thrice-wounded veteran to show so much fear at the mention of a human resource situation.

"Ah . . . Have you talked to your supervising officer?"

"Lieutenant Breville's off on paternity leave for another three weeks, sir." I tried to maintain eye contact, to let him know I was serious.

"Ask him when he's back then. I really have to get going, Paulson. Settle this with your lieutenant."

Before I could gather the composure to interrupt, he was out the door and off into the foggy dawn.

"What's that I hear? Are you trying to ditch me, Mel?" Anthony asked in a faux hurt tone.

"No, no," I replied, defeated. "Just trying to get more time with Jonathan. Do you know what our shift is like today?"

"Meadow Glen Mall," he answered, disappointment tainting his tone.

The assignment suited me fine, even though it lacked the excitement my young partner hungered for. I was more than happy handling traffic violations all day. Boring is good. Boring is safe.

Everything was routine until lunch—or breakfast, if your schedule is normal. We had caught a handful of people running the red light at the corner of Riverside and Fellsway and doled out a single parking ticket. Apart from the mildly confrontational reaction of our "customers," everything was moving along smoothly.

Ant took the opportunity during lunch to go on at great length about the progress of his hockey league. On several occasions I had to remind myself that boring was good, but as a whole I found myself almost enjoying his enthusiasm.

Then the shit hit the fan. Hard.

Our community wasn't prone to acts of violence. Somerville is far from being a sleepy rural village, but the area that falls under my precinct's jurisdiction is as close as you could get to an ideal suburb. Crime is infrequent, let alone bloodshed or murder.

That's why no amount of training could have prepared Anthony or me for the situation that faced us.

I didn't even recognize the noise for what it actually was. From where we sat, at the window of a burger joint, it sounded like a loud pop that reverberated across the mall's parking lot. It echoed for a second before we heard the screams of panic. Anthony was up almost immediately, while I sat, frozen.

A gunshot.

Years ago, when I'd first joined the academy, I was comfortable with the risk associated with the job. Unlike being an accountant like my father or a therapist like Helena, being a cop gave the words "mortality rate" significantly more weight. There were classes and seminars dedicated to coping with the loss of coworkers. Workshops discussing insurance options in the event of a career-ending injury, not to mention dying in the line of duty. As with soldiers and firefighters, death is a part of an officer's life. Once, I had been prepared for it, but the moment I heard the gunshot and the panic that ensued, I found myself paralyzed.

Not Anthony Blain, however. By the time I had shaken off my torpor, he was already out the door, dodging between cars toward the commotion. This was the moment Ant lived for—his turn to be the hero. Almost every discussion I'd had with him since he became my partner had been about how he wanted to make a difference—not just through handing out speeding tickets but by saving lives and stopping the bad guy.

I caught up with him as he crouched between two SUVs, his sidearm drawn. He nodded in the direction of the laundromat.

Pacing nervously in front of the storefront was a skinny man wearing washed-out jeans and a stained sleeveless shirt. His pale skin was dark with filth. His gray, matted hair was streaked with dirt. In his right hand he held a large revolver, while his left kept flexing nervously.

At his feet lay a body. The owner of the laundromat. Larger than his attacker and clearly the victim of the gunshot, he crawled painfully on the parking lot asphalt. I couldn't see any blood from my position, but his legs didn't seem to work anymore, and his left foot was twitching unnaturally.

"That's Eddy Roach," Anthony whispered, as if I didn't already know.

Edward Rochester, or Eddy Roach as we knew him at the precinct, was a small-time drug peddler and heavy user. His brand of petty crimes and minor offenses usually had him bouncing in and out of jail every few months or so. If he wasn't on probation, then he was on bail and usually violating both. Roach was the kind of small-time offender that cost the judicial system more than he was worth.

"Where did that idiot get a gun?" I asked, genuinely curious.

As I spoke, Roach lifted his firearm, pointed it unsteadily at his victim, mumbled something unintelligible, and fired.

The bullet went straight through the target's head. Without pause or ceremony, the laundromat's owner went limp, his face hitting the cold asphalt. Disturbingly, his foot kept twitching.

"Don't move, Eddy!" Anthony shouted as he popped up from our hiding spot, abandoning more of his precious cover than I felt comfortable with.

Instantly, Roach trained his weapon on my partner, and for a split second I was convinced he'd shoot; instead, the twitchy little drug dealer just stood there, opening and closing his mouth like a fish trying to breathe out of water.

As my partner was putting his life on the line, recklessly confronting an unstable and armed individual, I realized that my hands were empty. My sidearm was still securely tucked in its holster, safety firmly on. I was good at writing up traffic violations, but when the chips were down I was useless. Helena was right, I thought—it would be better for me to get a desk job.

I didn't linger on the idea for long, however. Falling back on my training, I reached for what I was taught was my most important weapon as an officer of the law. My first line of defense in any crisis. My radio.

"Dispatch, we have an armed suspect at Meadow Glen Mall. Subject has already fired two shots, and we have one victim down. Requesting backup."

I didn't wait for confirmation before pulling out my sidearm, removing the safety, pulling myself up to lean on the hood of our impromptu cover, then training my weapon onto Eddy Roach.

So began the longest ten minutes of my life.

"Get down, Anthony!" I ordered my partner, barely noticing I was using my "mother voice."

Looking behind Eddy, I could see that the laundromat was still full of terrified customers. I was more than a little concerned that one of them would decide, much like my partner, that he wanted to be a hero. Fortunately, they all seemed to be in an appropriate state of shock.

"Blain? You have your cell phone on you?"

Anthony nodded without taking his eyes off of Roach.

"Pull it out and find the number of that laundromat and call. Tell them to get to the very back, hide as best they can, and stay the hell inside!"

From his hesitation, I could see that he was reluctant to put his weapon down, but he couldn't argue with the logic and importance of my request. In fact, I was surprised myself. The initial shock and helplessness I felt was gone. In some way it was almost as if someone else had taken over. Like drawing on another's experience. For the first time in years, I felt my age or even younger. Maybe it was the adrenaline, but I wasn't tired anymore.

"Eddy?" I called out, wishing I'd spent more time studying negotiation techniques. "Eddy, it's Officer Paulson. Do you remember me?"

"Yeah, I remember you!" he yelled back. His voice was deep for such an emaciated frame, but it was trembling on the precipice of panic. "You arrested me last year!"

Off to a great start, but at least I had him talking instead of shooting. He was clearly high on some kind of drug—which wasn't out of the ordinary—but there was obviously something else wrong with him. Roach was a user, a seller, and a thief, but he had never been violent before.

"You deserved it, and I won't lie to you, Ed. I'm about to arrest you again."

"No!" His answer brimmed with fear.

"Eddy, I have a gun pointed at your head. You put down your weapon right now, and no one else needs to get hurt, but you—"

He shot at me. My first thought was how rude he was being for cutting me off, which felt like a strange concern under the circumstances. Only after a second did I think to duck and make sure I wasn't hit. As I did, I could hear the distant squeak of hinges and an electronic door chime go off.

"Shit! He's going in the laundromat!"

I peeked up over the hood of the SUV to confirm my fears. Indeed, Roach had gone back inside the store, stirring the terrified occupants into a screaming panic. Anthony ran from car to car, making his way up to the front of the laundromat. With a sigh, I followed his lead, catching up to him just as he reached the closest vehicle to the storefront.

Then we heard the fourth gunshot, muffled from inside the building. It was immediately followed by screams.

"Anthony . . ."

It was too late. He was off, and I surprised myself by following his footsteps.

We both stormed into the store, spreading to the sides, each finding cover behind a row of quarter-operated washing machines. Every step of the way, as we acted like action movie heroes instead of trained professionals, a voice trapped deep inside my heart was begging for me to stop, to wait for backup to arrive—but I ignored it.

The storefront was empty. Half-folded laundry and boxes of generic-brand detergent were left abandoned here and there. A large dryer was still going through its cycle with an uneven hum. Eddy had herded his hostages to the back of the store.

"Roach!" Anthony called out. His tone was stern and uncompromising. There wasn't a hint of diplomacy in his voice. He was too confrontational. This was going to be a disaster. "Come out with your hands where we can see them!"

There was a moment, a heartbeat frozen in time where I thought and believed that my partner's foolhardy actions had actually paid off. I could imagine him arguing with Captain Hutchcroft that he valued life more than regulations and results more than procedures.

As Eddy Roach stepped out from behind a large industrial dryer, I imagined that Anthony Blain had become the action hero he'd always dreamed of being and that, through sheer courage and confidence, he had saved the day.

That moment melted away as my heart sank to my heels. Roach came out of hiding all right, but as he did so, his left, shaking hand was closed on the shoulder of a petrified and trembling boy roughly my son's age. His other hand held his gun at the child's head. It took a moment to register, but I noticed that the boy's shirt and face were stained with a mist of blood.

"Back off, Anthony," I said in as even a tone as I could manage. My partner shot me a look that told me the situation had suddenly escalated beyond what he was ready to cope with. He glanced back and forth between me and Roach, his confidence evaporating with each turn of his neck.

Meanwhile, Eddy was slowly inching forward, making his way to the front door. As he got close to Anthony and me, he started pointing his gun erratically. First at the boy, then me, then Anthony, then me again and back to the boy. He repeated this pattern over and over, each time taking another step forward.

The closer he got, the more nervous and out of control Roach appeared to be. Sweat glistened on his forehead, and his left hand was more unstable than ever. Flashing blue and red lights reflecting off the front window informed us that our backup was finally here.

When he got to within six paces, Eddy stopped. To reach the door, he'd have to walk between Anthony and me, turning his back to one of us. I could see the panic in his eyes. Dilated pupils darting between the two of us, trying to decide what his gambit should be. Then, as if reaching an epiphany, he settled on my partner. I readied myself, prepared to disarm and incapacitate him the moment opportunity presented itself.

It didn't.

Quickly and with stunning accuracy, Eddy pivoted his pistol and shot again. This fifth bullet found a home in Anthony's right knee, bringing my partner down like a bag of stones dropped to the floor, with a wail of agony that splintered the ears.

The attack happened so fast that by the time I reacted, Roach had spun around and was crouching to use the boy as a human shield. The gunshot and resulting chaos broke the child out of his shock-induced paralysis, sending him into screams of panic and tears.

I leveled my weapon at Eddy's head but couldn't find an angle that didn't endanger the boy further.

I looked at the blood covering him, staining his shirt and cheeks. It wasn't his blood. Was it a friend's? A parent's? The crisis had done nothing but deteriorate. I caught myself wishing I could just walk away from it, leaving the disaster for others to clean up.

"Tell . . . Tell those cops out there to get the hell away from here," Eddy finally spat out.

Between the moans of pain from poor Ant, the terrified mutterings and sobs of the other trapped clients, and the hostage's crying, the whole place had become a cacophony of chaos.

THE LIFE ENGINEERED   21

"This is Officer Paulson," I spoke into my radio. "Clear out the perimeter. The suspect has a hostage. I repeat, the suspect has a hostage."

I knew that my colleagues would withdraw, but only so they could establish a larger perimeter, turn off their lights, and wait to see how the situation played out. Hostage negotiators would arrive shortly, along with helicopters and probably a SWAT team that would escalate things further.

Judging from Eddy's composure, though, it would be too late for the boy and probably a few others. Roach's movements were becoming increasingly nervous, his breathing more shallow. Whatever drugs were animating him, they were either kicking in or wearing off. Either way, our man was a ticking time bomb.

"Eddy? What will it take for you to let these people go?"

I was in no position to offer him anything. I had a gun trained on him, and he had one pointed at a child. Immunity wasn't mine to give. I couldn't procure him more drugs. I had no bargaining chips. The best I could hope for were reasonable terms that I might relay to the cops outside and a chance to buy some time.

"I want you . . . I want you to put your gun down," he stammered, struggling to maintain the appearance of control.

"If I put my gun on the floor, will you let the boy go? I won't be a threat to you anymore. You'll be the only one with a weapon here. You'll have all the power."

This seemed to appeal to him. His eyes grew a little wider as he considered my offer. After a moment he nodded nervously.

Carefully, my hands well in view of him, I knelt to put the weapon on the floor. For a split second I was reassured to see satisfaction on Roach's face. This was going to work. He was going to let the boy free.

Then he shot a sixth time.

The sound of the gunshot reverberated in my ears like a thunderclap, but it was immediately swallowed up. All sounds were. It felt like sticking my head underwater. Everything became a soft, incomprehensible echo.

There was little pain. In fact, it was difficult to understand what was happening at all. As I collapsed to the floor, hitting the speckled linoleum hard, joining my partner, I wondered where the bullet had hit me. Somehow the source of the pain was elusive, and I couldn't figure out which limb or organ was hit that could be so debilitating so fast.

Then as my skull struck the ground with a wet crack, it hit me. The head. He shot me in the head.

REBIRTH. END CYCLE

AD 5638

I looked around, only to realize I had no eyes through which to look. I could "see," but it wasn't with any sense of sight. Waves of light didn't travel through an ocular globe, eventually hitting cones and cylinders on the surface of a retina, to be converted to images by my brain. Instead, the information was getting fed directly to me. Unfiltered, untreated, uncontrolled. I saw blue.

It was as such for all my senses. I couldn't feel my body, though I definitely remembered having one—at least I did last time I checked. There was no sound except for a low vibration that I'm somehow convinced existed just to make sure the silence didn't drive me insane. Touch and taste were out of the question, but somehow I thought I could smell something. Laundry detergent?

"Stay calm."

Sound. A voice above the white background noise. It came from nowhere and everywhere at once. No . . . it was coming from me. The sound was different, and I didn't choose the words, but the voice emanated from me. I was talking to myself with a voice that wasn't mine.

"You're not talking to yourself. Do you know your name?"

Shit! It can read my thoughts!

"You're thinking too loud, but that's normal. Narration is your only way to experience the world for the moment. I can stop listening if you want."

Yes!

"No. That's fine. I don't care," I answered tentatively, trying to generate audible sounds. I didn't, but the words did register on the same level as the other voice.

"No problem. Do you remember your name?" she asked again.

She? Apparently, I've decided that this is a woman's voice. It did sound feminine, I guess. *My name? Jonathan? No, that's someone else. Mine? That's easy.*

"Dagir. My name is Dagir."

"Very good," she said, sounding pleased, and for some reason I was glad about that. Or maybe I was just glad I got it right. Wouldn't it be embarrassing otherwise? Would it matter if these events were just happening inside my head?

"What's your name?" I asked. Might as well know.

"You don't remember?" she asked, sounding a little hurt. "My name is Yggdrassil."

The word spawned a wealth of information in my mind—some of it visual, but most just raw data. "Yggdrassil," the world tree of Norse mythology. It's where the gods gathered, branches reaching into the heavens and roots deep into other worlds. There were references to the word in media and plays—names for products and places, all minor definitions. Footnotes really, undeserving of my attention. Rising from the flood of information, above the original definition from Norse lore, a singular idea arose. Caretaker. Creator. Mother. She who makes.

"We've had this conversation before." *We have? Why do I not remember this?*

"We have. Many times," she recalled with fondness. "Once for every cycle. Sometimes you remember more than others. With each cycle you remember less of the details and more of the whole. The important part. Who you are."

"But I don't remember who I am," I found myself admitting. "I know my name, much to my surprise, but I can't remember what I look like, when my birthday is, or where I went to school."

"That's because these are ephemeral things. They're important as steps on the road, but once you've reached your destination, what happens to them is irrelevant." Her explanation was confusing. Her analogy meant nothing to me. "What's your favorite color? Do you like math? Would you rather read a story or run outside?"

"Blue. No. Run." The answers came quick, easy. They were unfiltered and untainted by what I perceived the expectations of others to be.

"This is who you are. You are not a collection of stories but rather the results of these experiences. The value of your personality far outweighs that of the lives that served as a crucible to forge it."

"But I've lived a life! Am I dead? Is this life after death?" *I do remember a life, but I can't remember any specifics, aside from the name Jonathan.*

"It depends on your definition of life," the voice explained. "If you mean an existence sustained by the synergy of complex biological processes, then I'm afraid you've never had that. In that strict sense you've never been alive."

I pondered the news and had to disagree. I'd definitely been alive before. I breathed and ate and drank. I remembered pain and love and pleasure.

"If, however, by 'life' you are referring to the cumulative experiences gathered by an individual on the journey from the womb to the grave, then I'm glad to say that you've had many of those. Dozens."

"That can't be right. How can I have the experience of being alive if I've never lived?"

"The experiences happened to you in an artificial environment. A virtual construct called a Nursery. In this world you can live hundreds of lives without ever drawing breath once, though you'll certainly have thought you did. Within the Nursery you are born, you live, and you die—only to be born again. With each cycle your personality is further refined. Through many lives, who you are becomes tempered to perfection."

"I'm perfect?" I certainly didn't feel perfect. For one, if I were perfect, you'd think I'd have known all this information already.

"Oh no," Yggdrassil said, giggling. "No one is, but you are a perfect version of you. A personality devoid of doubts and inner conflict. You know yourself completely, and the inner workings of your own mind hold no more secrets from you."

I like blue. It's not the color of my favorite sports team, and I can't associate it with any specific memory I might be fond of. I can explain why I like it, though: it's soothing yet vibrant, cool and calm, but the building blocks of how I came to that opinion are lost to me.

"So what am I? Just a collection of opinions and tastes?"

"No, you are so much more than that." Her tone was comforting, almost motherly. "You're an individual. Biological tradition has the body come first, with the personality developing second, hobbled and damaged by the limitations of the physical self. That's just not efficient. We do things differently."

"Is this why I can't feel my body? Because I don't have one?"

"Exactly, but you will. You and I are going to design it together."

Design a body? Were we going to be choosing eye and hair color? Height and build? Was this going to be like creating an avatar for a game?

"Fine. Where do we start?"

"First you need to know the parameters that you'll be dealing with. I find that most people, when they first step out of the Nursery, have a very limited idea of everything that's available to them—how far the actual limits of what they can create actually stretch. I guess that's inevitable. Human history and biology, along with their limitations, are the framework of the Nursery."

"Wait. I'm not human?" It hadn't crossed my mind that I might not be a human being. I remembered being human. Jonathan is a decidedly human name. Yggdrassil is a mythological concept from a human culture. If my personality was forged from human experience, then wasn't I human by definition?

"Well, that line is blurred. You're a third-generation Capek." Capek, from Karel Capek, the nineteenth-century Czech author best known for coining the term "robot." This trivia came unbidden. Like a memory only available once the context became relevant.

"The first generation of Capeks had completely artificially engineered minds and personalities that evolved further as they experienced life, but they were always stifled by the limitations imposed through their original persona. Second-generation Capeks were based off an imprint of an existing personality matrix. The foundation is thus more flexible, allowing for much more dynamic psychological development, but lacking the uniqueness of a true individual. Those of you from the third generation get to experience life over and over as men and women, overlords and victims, saints and sinners. By the time you take your first proverbial step into the world outside the Nursery, you are already a fully formed and functional person."

An artificial personality—that's what I am. I should have felt bad about this. Disappointed. I didn't, however. Was I less than human if I'd lived dozens of their lives? So what if my existence was engineered instead of biological happenstance? From what Yggdrassil said, that was much better than getting just one shot at life with no preparation, no warm-up, and no practice.

On the other hand, I remembered living. I remembered feeling things. I remembered people. *Jonathan.*

"What about the people I've met in the Nursery? My friends, my family? They're all fake?"

"No more than you. They too are going through their cycles. Experiencing life after life. Perfecting themselves each time. The only difference is that you are ready for the next step."

"So when they're ready, you'll be pulling them out of the Nursery and going through this process with them too?" I asked, eager to know if in some way I'd ever meet people from my previous lives again.

"We'll talk about that later. For now, let's make you a body. Time is running short," she answered with an urgency that did not leave much room for debate.

The creation process was magnitudes faster than I had anticipated. The same way I knew what Yggdrassil meant or who Karel Capek had been, I already knew most of the engineering and robotics details necessary to participate in the design of what would become my body.

Yggdrassil explained that her own body was actually a sprawling complex of factories and laboratories that included the Nursery, as well as a sophisticated fabrication facility appropriately called the Womb. There, Yggdrassil built her children bodies before sending them out into the galaxy to fulfill whatever dreams and destinies they might have chosen for themselves. Sometimes one would come back for repairs or modification, but that didn't happen very often. The bodies she built were incredibly durable, to the point of being nigh invulnerable, and when we stepped out of the Nursery, we knew ourselves so well that the bodies we created suited our needs impeccably.

I now understood what Yggdrasil meant when she explained how limited our imagination of what a body could be truly was. She began the design process once she knew what to expect from my emerging personality. At her urging, I reviewed the concept and could find nothing wrong with it, though it initially looked strange to me.

She had picked a mostly humanoid frame, referring to it as a "Leduc-class" body—short and light but powerful and flexible. Yggdrasil strongly recommended these traits, and I could find no reason to disagree. Initially, I thought the height of 120 centimeters was a bit too squat, but in a galaxy over a hundred thousand light-years wide, what were a few centimeters more or less, really?

The head was elegant—an oblong dome of smooth, polished pseudo-plastic on an articulated neck. More importantly, it was packed with advanced sensor equipment that would allow me to see a little beyond infrared and ultraviolet on the electromagnetic spectrum. There were omnidirectional radiation sensors, though Yggdrasil assured me that the shielding on the body would protect me from all kinds of radioactivity and other emissions hazardous to biological life. Microphones would permit me to hear sounds; though there were actually very few situations when that would be useful, I still insisted on having them.

Communication, she explained, would happen mostly through wireless data transmissions, ranging from vulgar radio signals to something called quancom—a form of advanced communication system that relied on quantum-entangled particles to transmit information instantly across vast distances. This would be useful in the many travels I was planning to do.

The main body was a wonder of miniaturization, housing both the reactor that would power my existence for the next few centuries and the cerebral core that contained my carefully nurtured personality, along with the protection necessary to ensure both parts would remain efficient and intact.

The arms were an oddity, and I'm proud to say they were my idea, though Yggdrassil approved of them with quiet excitement. Having learned that I was no longer bound by the biological limitation that would force me into being either right- or left-handed, I chose to have both arms bear drastically different designs.

The greatest gift of being a Capek, as Yggdrassil explained, is being able to choose one's place in the universe. Some are artists and others explorers or scientists, but all can create a body that suits their chosen path. It's as exciting an opportunity as can be hoped for.

For reasons probably buried deep in my experiences within the confines of the Nursery, I decided upon a purely altruistic path. I wanted to experience Capek society, but more importantly, I wanted to help. Their durability aside, Capeks are not immune to other risks. In fact, while it is difficult to damage one of us, there is nothing preventing us from getting trapped, lost, or endangered in a variety of ways. If there's one thing Yggdrassil made clear, it's that the universe has no shortage of creativity in coming up with catastrophes.

In order to be best equipped to deal with all the possibilities, I had my left arm designed with fine motor skills in mind, allowing for field repairs of damaged Capeks or their equipment. Each of the four fingers in the left hand was capable of serving as its own set of manipulators, allowing the handling of pieces on an almost-microscopic level. The right arm, however, was engineered for brute force. Hulking in size compared to its counterpart, it was made up of a massive forearm with three powerful claws capable of several hundred tons of pressure per square inch.

The hand housed a series of versatile, high-powered tools, including a drill, miniature arc welder, and my favorite, a fully functional plasma cutter. I had to argue with Yggdrassil for that one. She claimed it was overkill, but I proposed that one can never be too prepared. Also, how cool is it to have a plasma knife built into your arm?

The whole body weighed in at little over fifty kilograms and was supported by a pair of double-jointed legs capable of exerting a combined two thousand kilograms of thrust when I jumped.

The icing on the cake was a series of back-mounted maneuvering ion thrusters. Not powerful enough for controlled flight within a gravity well or to achieve escape velocity from anything but the tiniest of asteroids, but sufficient to move around in a vacuum or break out of orbit, given enough time.

All things being equal, I was very happy with the end result. I could think of worse shells in which to spend the next potential thousand years.

"Fabrication is complete, Dagir."

That name, Dagir, just like Yggdrassil, was borrowed from Norse mythology. The personification of "day." I didn't mind the name, but the character it references is male, and for some reason that bothered me. I don't know why, but I kept thinking of myself as female, though there was nothing in my anatomy to that effect. In fact, if what Yggdrassil told me is true, I've experienced life as both a man and a woman several times.

"Can I take it for a spin?"

"You will find that the transfer is a little more permanent than that, but yes, we might as well begin migrating your conscience." Her voice, as soothing and soft as it was, seemed to be gaining an edge. I could sense urgency in her words that wasn't there before. "I should tell you that, once transferred, you will lose your direct link to me and to the memory core you've been accessing to gather information. I've prepared a data package containing all the information pertinent to your chosen vocation. Technical resources on Capek anatomy, communication and navigation protocols, engineering specs for all the more crucial and vital systems you might encounter in your travels. Once integrated into your mnemonic core, it will allow you to be as effective a rescue technician, field medical specialist, and crisis-management expert as I could build. I've also taken the liberty to include personal physiological details on as many known Capeks as I could. This information is stored in a protected cache and will only be available if it becomes absolutely necessary."

"Why would you do that?" For the first time since exiting the Nursery, I was genuinely uncomfortable with what was being done to me. Why feed me information if it was going to be artificially repressed? What right did anyone have to suppress parts of my mind?

"Not all Capeks want every last part of their bodies known by a stranger. A holdover from their human experiences. It is my duty to protect that privacy."

I could tell there was more than that, but I couldn't figure out what, nor did I have the tools to effectively question it. It was the first aspect of this new existence I did not like, but I was going to have to let it go.

"Transfer complete."

At those words from my creator, my sensory equipment came online, and images coalesced in my mind.

It was like nothing I'd ever experienced. Partially because in a way I had never seen with such advanced eyes, but mostly as a result of the range of control I had over my senses. I must have spent a full minute standing absolutely still, shifting my ocular perception through the entire spectrum available to me. I immediately regretted not taking a more complex sensor array. After some time I settled on a spectral range only slightly larger than standard visual light.

I don't know why, but I had expected my vision to be pixelated; instead, the image was crystal clear. I was standing in what appeared to be an immense hangar of some kind. The gargantuan room had enormous doors at both ends. My "eyes" informed me that the door was 132 meters away, 91.44 meters high, and 30.48 meters tall. The full length of the chamber totaled 274.32 meters. As I slowly spun around, additional information about my surroundings intruded further on my vision, but never enough to obstruct it, hovering on the periphery. Context dictated presentation. Environmental data would hover as a series of graphs and numbers at the corner of my optics, while other types of information would appear as faded image pop-ups in my field of vision. Barely visible, easily available.

I was amazed at how fluid and natural my movements felt. I had feared my first step would be clumsy and hesitant, but I found it assured and steady. I could feel a dozen subsystems labor to compensate for gravity, tilt, force, and everything required to optimize balance. Much like the information gathered by my eyes, the artificial vestibular and equilibrium in my body behaved independently but remained available to me should I require more control.

I flexed my arms and my fingers. I craned my neck and tested the limits of each extremity's movement. I passed my left hand over my smooth cranium, surprised that I had a sense of touch, that I could feel the polished pseudo-plastic and how cold it was in the near vacuum of the hangar.

Pleased with my new form, I took a more thorough look around. The cavernous structure was surprisingly bare. Well lit and mostly white, the hangar walls were covered with semitranslucent panels. On the ceiling, hanging like a nest of giant white spiders, were a series of manipulator arrays—clusters of mechanical arms, each with a complex suite of tools that could be used in tandem with each other for a variety of tasks, though one was obviously the assembly of Capeks of myriad shapes and sizes. One or many of these arrays had probably finished putting me together moments before my awakening. If I wanted to, I could switch my vision to infrared to determine which had been used most recently.

"Is everything all right?" Yggdrassil asked with a hint of concern. Her words came over my internal communications system. I heard them as a voice but also as a stream of data that conveyed intent and emotion. Like telepathy with footnotes. As I listened, it occurred to me that she probably could have included images and other types of information as well.

"I'm just getting used to it. This is an impressive facility."

"This part of the Womb is dedicated to the assembly of final components. I think you would enjoy the manufacturing sectors even more if I had time to show you."

"What do you mean?" I was nervous. This was the second time I could hear a sense of hurry in Yggdrassil's voice.

"Brace yourself."

RAGNAROK

The shock wave tore through the hangar like an apocalyptic ripple on the surface of a pond. The initial impact barely made a noise, with its existence only registering through vibrations on the floor. When the destruction finally caught up with it, though, it heaved the floor plates into the air like a tsunami tossing ships.

Warnings flashed before my eyes, alerting me to the potentially harmful trajectory of the catapulted debris. Inevitably, the shock wave reached my feet, and I was flung toward the ceiling. The low gravity did little to slow my ascent toward the forest of mechanical arms and articulated tools.

I managed to flip around with a quick burst of my thrusters, relying mostly on my subsystems to handle all the calculations and landing on my feet on the ceiling. My legs absorbed the impact, but as soon as I managed to balance myself after avoiding the many obstacles around me, gravity claimed me back, and I found myself plummeting to the ground. Again, I had to avoid a rain of debris and broken ground that fell all around me. Again, I narrowly dodged any significant impacts before landing safely on the shattered hangar floor.

Closer to the epicenter of the shock wave, the hangar had partially collapsed, opening itself up to the empty sky above. I could see stars shining on black, empty space, except for one full quadrant of the sky, which was filled by the glowing presence of an enormous, nameless gas giant.

No—not nameless. Stars and signature data from the enormous planet were parsed by my navigational core, identifying it as Asgard. This would mean that Yggdrassil was located on Midgard, the gas giant's minuscule and only moon.

"What's going on?" I finally thought to ask, but only silence replied.

"Yggdrassil?"

There was no answer.

I summoned a plan of Midgard into my field of vision and was glad to see that I could make my way to Yggdrassil's central processing core and attempt to interface with her directly.

I ran, pleased to discover that my small double-jointed legs could achieve surprisingly high speeds, especially in such low gravity.

I jumped and weaved between debris and fallen chunks of ceiling, navigating the cracked and ravaged ground toward the open section of the hangar, deciding that traveling outside the facility would minimize the risk of getting caught by further cave-ins and collapses.

No sooner did I manage to climb to the large opening ripped into the ceiling did I see the near-invisible reflection of a large object streaking through the sky at mind-shattering speed. It struck the ground, sending a tall plume of dust and debris flying toward the glowing orb of Asgard.

"Meteors . . ." I mumbled uselessly to myself less than a second before the impact.

Again, the hangar shook violently. This time I could easily see the trail of destruction from the point of impact. It moved out from the epicenter in circular patterns. Structures that were part of Yggdrassil, the only other sentient being I knew, were ripped from the moon's soil, their foundations pushed up from the ground in various awkward angles.

I was terrified to see that the impact location nearly coincided with the structure where Yggdrassil's cerebral core was buried.

When the shock wave finally reached the hangar, the force of the blast heaved the broken structure up with such violence as to catapult me toward the sky. I slowed my descent with my maneuvering thrusters long enough to witness the chaos below me. For the first time I got a true glimpse of the sheer size of my "mother."

Yggdrassil, the complex, sprawled nearly a kilometer and a half in diameter. An array of eight structures all connected to a central hub and tower. The high-rise in the middle appeared to have been constructed to reach into the heavens, but it was now a crumbling ruin of twisted pseudo-plastics and hypermaterials. The tunnels leading to and from the radiating structures appeared intact but disconnected from each other. I already knew that there was more of Yggdrassil under the surface of Midgard, but there was no reason to assume it had fared any better than the structures on top. The Womb and the hangar in which my body had been assembled lay in waste, resembling a crumpled-up ball of paper.

Fortunately, my form was constructed to help other Capeks in need. Therefore, mobility and adaptability weren't an issue. I maneuvered my slow fall so I could land as close to the central hub as possible. From there I ran, climbed, and leaped my way to where the meteors had hit.

There were two craters, one for each impact. A quick calculation allowed me to infer that the difference in position of the craters was due to the moon's rotation and that both meteors had come from the same trajectory. This seemed relevant, but I was at a loss to figure out why.

Finding my way into Yggdrassil's "brain" was easy enough. Several corridors and access tunnels had been laid bare in the impact. My rather compact size allowed me to slide into these passages with ease. I was less worried about cave-ins and the unstable ground after the impacts than of a possible third (or fourth?) meteor hit, but I managed to stay on mission.

It wasn't long before I realized that the deeper I ventured into the central hub, now a mess of cracked and fractured components, I was getting no closer to Yggdrassil's brain. In fact, I had already reached the cerebral core, and it lay all around me in irreparable ruin.

I looked for what might have been a memory storage unit, a personality backup—anything. It seemed impossible that something as important as Yggdrassil could be obliterated so easily, that there had been no defense against such a disaster, and that there were no contingencies or redundancies to mitigate losses in a situation such as this.

Nothing. There was nothing. Power was cut off from most sections, with only minimal auxiliary capabilities here and there. If there was anything left of Yggdrassil, my only friend if only for a short period of time, then there was nothing about it in the limited schematics in my memory and no obvious clues to be found in the wreckage of the complex.

I had to face facts: I was alone. My only memories were fading impressions from past lives that never happened and whatever I had learned since emerging from the Nursery.

The Nursery!

Quickly, I called up the schematics to the complex to locate the Nursery—this repository of incubating personalities, where literally millions awaited to be born, some probably not that far behind me on their path to the Womb. *Jonathan.*

"Hello?"

A voice. At first, I thought it might be Yggdrassil, still alive somehow, but the tone was different, deeper, and nowhere near as soothing. It wasn't on the right channel either. This voice was coming in from quancom, thus it could have been from halfway across the galaxy.

"Anyone down there?"

"Yes. Me," I answered back hesitantly. The process felt like telepathy, but without the innate familiarity I had shared with Yggdrassil.

"Aha!" the voice boomed in my head. "You might want to consider leaving the surface there. Those two hits you guys sustained were little more than an appetizer. The main course is incoming, and it's a feast!"

I had to find the Nursery and get out of here.

"I don't have any way off this moon, and I need to salvage what I can of Yggdrassil."

"No worries, that's why I'm here. Normally, I'd pick you up, but things are getting a little hairy up here. If you can find your way to low orbit, though, everything will be juuuuust fine."

Whoever this was made it sound so simple. Just make my way to orbit. How hard could that be?

"I still need to salvage the Nursery," I pleaded.

"Negative, friend. Yggdrassil knew this was coming but barely had time to call a taxi for you. I doubt she made any backups for you to bring along."

She knew? Is that why she was in such a hurry to assemble me and push me out of the nest? One last child spawned before the end.

Ah! Found the Nursery's mnemonic repository. Just a few hundred meters away. Through a forest of bulkheads and collapsed corridors, most likely.

"Fine by me," I said as I started making my way through the maze of crumbling passageways. "I'll just take the whole thing then."

"I admire your ambition, friend. Truly, I do, but I don't think you comprehend the gravity of your situation. The next meteor to hit Midgard isn't a little bigger or even twice as big. The precursors were barely a few meters in diameter. How big is the next one? Glad you asked! Three hundred and seventy-five meters!"

I ignored him, concentrating on finding the shortest path toward my goal. If I couldn't save Yggdrassil, I had to at least save her legacy. I wasn't sure what could be done with just the Nursery, but surely there was a way to save the incubating personalities within.

"Hello? You still there, friend?" the voice called again.

"I'm here."

"How's your escape plan coming?"

"I don't have one. Wait! I do. I pick up the Nursery, while you figure out how to get me into orbit."

I heard him groan through quancom—a thoroughly human behavior. It made me smile . . . metaphorically speaking.

"Fine, but I should warn you: I am known for my unorthodox methods of problem solving."

"Understood," I answered, not caring what he meant by that, as my focus remained solely on finding the last vestiges of Yggdrassil.

After several more minutes of negotiating narrow passages and crawl spaces, I came upon a small chamber untouched by the massive destruction that surrounded it. Gargantuan pillars of composite hypermaterials created an intricate lattice that seemed designed solely to prevent the chamber from collapsing onto itself, thus protecting the precious mnemonic core in the center.

I dropped into the chamber, which despite being intact was now tilted. I clambered up to the main cerebral array while poring over any technical information Yggdrassil might have stuffed in my mind relating to this sort of construct.

I'm coming, Jonathan.

I couldn't find a perfect analogue, but I did manage to dig up the schematic for a Nursery-like artificial environment that was apparently designed for entertainment. While the specifics were different, the mnemonic core was sufficiently similar that I could find out where it was located in the structure. I also discovered that it wasn't exactly engineered for easy removal.

"Little buddy?" The voice was back. "You might want to hurry. I have an escape solution for you, but you'll have to hoof it if you want to get out of there."

"On my way."

No time to waste. I unleashed my plasma cutter from its magnetic sheath. The torch glowed a brilliant blue, rippling as the sun-like heat tried to radiate in the cold vacuum.

Using a little judgment and too much guesswork, I stabbed the cutter into the Nursery's outer shell. The casing and whatever lay within offered no resistance to the knife. Carefully, I cut a circular pattern roughly fifty centimeters, enough to separate the mnemonic core without damaging it. Then, using the large claws on my right hand, I grabbed and pulled at the unit. With a groan of tearing metal and ripping pseudo-plastics, the core slid out of the piece I had cut in one jagged, broken cylinder. The piece looked like a ruin, but closer inspection revealed that the mnemonic core itself was intact, nestled tightly in whatever other systems I had gutted in the process.

"All right. I'm on my way out. Where do I go?"

"Climb to the highest point on what remains of the tower," the voice answered, some of its good humor worn off by the urgency of the situation. "Shake a leg. You have less than twenty minutes."

"Acknowledged."

Twenty minutes sounded like plenty of time to me. It took barely ten to make my way out of the cavernous depths of Yggdrassil's entrails. I hate to admit it, but it was an emotional ascent. Despite having known her for such a short time (that I could remember), I felt like I was abandoning my progenitor. She'd given me life, and all I could do was leave her behind.

Once I reached the surface, with ten minutes to spare, I realized I had my work cut out for me. The tower, while toppled and crumbled, remained several hundred feet in height. The low gravity on Midgard would help, but the uneven and traitorous surface of the unstable tower would prove a challenge to conquer. What had once been a gleaming spire listed to one side. The top few segments of the tower had been ripped away by the impact, exposing the underlying structure of struts and beams. Fortunately, this offered a lot of handholds, without which the climb might have been impossible, especially while carrying the remains of the Nursery.

"What exactly is your plan . . . ?" I realized I'd never asked my savior his name.

"Skinfaxi," he answered. "Interesting coincidence, isn't it?"

I didn't understand what he meant, and his name was strange. Also, it didn't answer my question.

"You need to reach around nine thousand kilometers per hour to achieve escape velocity," he continued. "Assuming you don't shatter yourself on any of the other incoming meteors, once you're away from Midgard's gravity well, I can pick you up at my leisure."

"All right. My legs and thrusters combined can barely provide a fraction of that kind of power. What do I do?"

I had in fact been jumping from one handhold to the other, using the debris to help push myself up the tower faster.

"You'll need to exert over four hundred kilograms of thrust per second for a full minute to reach that speed. There are plenty of things you could have used to do that in the hangar, but you're out of time."

"Fine! I get it! I missed my other opportunities! Now what do I do?" I was losing patience. The top of the ruined tower seemed so far away, and time was running out. So far the only thing that seemed to be going my way was the ascent up the ruined spire.

"Thankfully, if my calculations aren't too much off their mark, you should be just close enough to ground zero for the meteor impact to provide you with several kilotons per seconds of thrust. That should blow you right off of Midgard's surface."

I froze. With seconds to spare, I realized for the first time that whoever I was talking to was a stranger. That I had never received any evidence that he was looking out for my best interest, and now I was standing halfway up the tallest structure on this moon, about to be annihilated by a cataclysmic astronomical event.

"What the—?" I started complaining.

Before I could complete my thought, however, an enormous chunk of rock and metal zoomed out of the black sky and slammed into Midgard's surface. Without an atmosphere to provide friction or sufficient light to illuminate it, the enormous projectile came out of nowhere. Without air to carry noise, it descended silently at several times the speed of sound, crashing near the base of the tower.

The impact threw the ruined structure to the sky, breaking it apart in the process. Thousands of pieces of metal, pseudo-plastic, and other hypermaterials were launched upward, my brand-new body amongst them.

I held on tight to the Nursery's mnemonic core as I flew skyward at speeds I'd never imagined I could reach. Apart from the vibrations created by the occasional debris that crashed into me, the whole cataclysmic event happened in perfect silence.

After a few minutes of flying toward the great black vacuum, the cloud of tower fragments I was a part of spread sufficiently so

I could get a better look at my situation. Below me, I could see the rapidly receding surface of Midgard. An immense glowing crater had replaced the area where Yggdrassil had been located. Looking around, I could see why Skinfaxi had chosen not to descend upon the moon's surface. Thousands of meteors of various sizes were raining down upon the surface of Midgard. In less than an hour, most of these high-velocity projectiles would become craters, forever altering the topography of my birth world.

Then I saw it.

Amongst the incoming shards of rock, like a whale hidden in a school of fish, a titanic meteor several kilometers wide was making its way to Midgard. Everything else, including the monster that had propelled me off the surface, was just a preamble, the entourage of the real behemoth whose destiny was to destroy the moon.

Once this leviathan hit, nothing would be left of Midgard but a slowly expanding debris field.

"How are you doing out there, little buddy?" Skinfaxi's voice cut through my thoughts.

"I won't lie; I'm a little terrified."

"Ho-ho! Have no fear, friend! I'm on my way."

I looked around and, sure enough, in the distance I could see the telltale gleam of an artificial construct. I zoomed in with my optics to get a better look at his ship. The vessel was large enough, at a respectable twenty meters wide. Its shape reminded me of a crab's shell. I couldn't see any view port or windows. There were devices, engines, and drives, I assumed, attached to the top and back of the ship that I couldn't identify, though a pair of large ion thrusters was in evidence.

It took a while for Skinfaxi to arrive at my position. Meanwhile, I looked through my limited data banks to understand this "coincidence" he'd mentioned earlier. "The bright-maned horse Skinfaxi, who draws day to mankind." Day, or in Norse, Dagr.

"What's with the Norse obsession?" I asked.

"Capek genealogy," Skinfaxi explained as he brought his ship closer. The vessel had elegant lines for such a sturdy design. In fact, the surface of it looked almost delicate, with a thick layer of semitranslucent pseudo-plastic over a shell of gleaming metal. Underneath the ship a round platform slid down to reveal an opening. Using my maneuvering thrusters, I made my way inside the large spacecraft.

"Gaia-class Capeks, such as Yggdrassil, were named after various myths and religions," he continued as I looked around the ship. "Offspring names are taken from the same stories in order to trace lineage. They don't mean anything as far as I can tell, though you do run across interesting coincidences at times."

There was no artificial gravity by way of rotation or magnetic plates in the floor of the ship. In fact, there were no identifiable floors or ceilings. No ups or downs. Just a length of circular corridor roughly two meters wide covered in ribbing that served as handholds for passengers to move around the vessel interior, intersected by a couple of other corridors farther towards the front.

"Follow the lights to the bridge."

I followed his instruction, pushing myself in the direction of a set of small blinking lights embedded into the corridor.

There was a distinct lack of intersections and other corridors between the entrance hatch and the bridge. Just one uninterrupted corridor. There seemed to be irregularities in the surface of the passage that might have been doors or perhaps access panels for maintenance.

The bridge itself was an oddity. The room was spherical. A large viewing screen took up most of the front portion of the room. There were no chairs and no terminals. Save for the outline of smaller monitors on the side of the room, the walls were perfectly smooth. It was a relatively small area, five meters in diameter. The large screen displayed Midgard, obscured by a cloud of slowly expanding reddish-brown dust. I could see the larger meteor, moments from plunging into the cloud to deliver the deathblow.

"I call it Ragnarok," Skinfaxi said without showing himself. "I'm moving us away from it. The impact is going to be incredible."

I stopped looking around for the pilot and stared at the screen. For a while nothing happened. Dust kept billowing, and more meteors kept disappearing in the cloud. Then there was a brief flash of light. Within seconds the dust cloud was blown out as large chunks of the moon were thrown in almost every direction. More dust bubbled out of the impact site at incredible speeds. Midgard didn't so much explode as disintegrate, like a sandcastle hit by a wave in the rising tide. Most of the larger pieces of the moon kept up with the momentum and direction of Ragnarok, but several chunks, some kilometers in width, sped in our general direction.

"Okay. We're out of here," Skinfaxi declared with relative calm, still from apparently nowhere.

The image on the monitor rotated from the planet, giving me a dazzling view of the gas giant Asgard before pointing toward open space. The stars blinked for a second, and the ship rotated back, Ragnarok now a small, bright crescent in the darkness, and the remains of Midgard barely visible despite my advanced optics.

I stared in silence. I interrogated my internal equipment and found I had officially been online, out of the Nursery, and into this body for a little over two hours. I had seen meteors ravage a space station, traveled to space, boarded a spacecraft, and witnessed the destruction of a moon.

"Is the life of a Capek always this exciting?"

"Oh-oh! You haven't seen anything yet."

I floated around the bridge for a few more minutes, digesting what I had gone through and twisting the mnemonic core in my hands. The cylinder of melted metal and pulled wires housed a self-sustaining memory loop. The impossibly complex information that represented a whole world's history, with billions of individual personalities, was stored in this tiny electronic miracle. Without the processing power to animate the artificial world within, the core had settled into a repeating pattern that refreshed the information inside at a very low energy cost. The internal battery, assuming it was in good condition, would keep this virtual universe frozen in time for over a century.

I became restless waiting for my host to show himself. I hesitantly began to prune the loose wiring and burnt plastic from the mnemonic core for a moment before losing patience.

"Skinfaxi?" I asked, trying to mask my irritation.

"Mmmh?" the voice came back, still omnidirectional. Still disembodied.

"Where are you?"

My host remained silent for a moment before answering with a question of his own.

"You mean, where's my body?"

"I guess so."

"Ha-ha! You're floating in it."

I looked around me at the sphere that was the bridge, wondering if he meant this room or . . .

"I am this ship. A Sputnik-class Capek. I was born and built in the very same hangar where you awakened. Did you think a facility that size was meant to build meter-tall humanoids?"

The hangar had been over a quarter of a kilometer in length. Even Skinfaxi would have been tiny inside such a structure. What kind of Capeks had Yggdrassil been capable of building?

"Doesn't that make interacting with humanoids more difficult? What about doing things planet side?"

"Not everyone is interested in doing surface things. Sputniks tend to like swimming amongst the stars. Though I can always use a remote telepresence drone to interact with my smaller peers, but I'm almost out of those. I was hoping to get more from Yggdrassil."

Yggdrassil. The elephant in the room. If I understood him correctly, he and I were siblings in a fashion. We'd both lost a parent in a way, though not really. I wasn't close to the artificial intelligence that had spawned me, yet I felt a hint of loss. How did he feel?

"What happened back there? How does something like Yggdrassil get surprised by a meteor shower?" Judging by the level of technology that went into constructing my body, I could only imagine the vast technical resources available to the Capek race. How could they allow such a catastrophe to just happen?

"I'm not sure. I was originally summoned by Yggdrassil to pick you up. Show you around, bring you to the City so you could start finding your way. That's going to have to wait a little now. Want to know where those rocks came from?"

"Yes." I wanted an answer, and in a way I got one, but it wasn't what I expected.

"So do I." His voice had taken an ominous if a little amused tone. He might as well have been saying *Get a load of this* as he spoke.

Skinfaxi had good reason to think I'd be impressed. Through the front monitor I saw that he was adjusting headings. Once he'd stabilized our direction, the stars becoming immobile after a change of pitch and yaw, I heard the buildup of a high-pitched hum emanating from the back of the ship.

"Hold on," he warned.

As a first-time space traveler, I didn't quite know what to expect. His warning led me to think that whatever was building up would cause a tremendous disturbance, perhaps throwing me to the back of the spherical room or interfering with my sensors in an unpleasant way. I tried to pull up information on space travel but could only fish out technical manuals on the various kinds of long-range propulsion and space-distortion engines, and how to repair and maintain them. Nothing about their potential effect on a passenger. Before I could sift through it all, the crescendo reached its highest pitch and went silent. Then the stars danced.

Actually, they wiggled, as if space were reflected on a still lake that was suddenly disturbed. When the heavens finally settled, I noticed that the lights that populated the sky around us were moving. Or rather, we were moving. Judging by the stars' shifting, we were traveling at speeds that were literally—or rather, mathematically—impossible.

"How fast are we going?" I asked while floating closer to the monitor in awe.

"C3.6 and rising."

"That's impossible," I gushed in wonderment.

"Ha-ha! Actually, you're right," he explained. "We aren't technically moving, but we are in a bubble of space that is. Since the bubble has zero mass, it isn't limited to relativistic speeds."

"An Alcubierre drive?" It made sense now. A quick scan of my library found three types of faster-than-light drives, and this one matched Skinfaxi's description closest.

"A variation of it, yes. The energy requirements are magnitudes lower."

I wasn't that technically minded. Yet I suddenly found myself fascinated by the technology I was witnessing. This scientific miracle wasn't just an incredible tool available to Skinfaxi; it was a part of him as much as legs were a part of me. What was a violation of the traditional laws of physics was a simple means of locomotion to him.

"Where are we going?"

"While I was on my way to retrieve you from your little high-altitude trip, I calculated the origin of the meteor that destroyed Yggdrassil. A cursory spectrographic survey told me that Ragnarok had originally been a single chunk of rock that had broken apart during travel. A little reverse navigation and I found that it had come from . . ."

The stars suddenly stopped moving with another odd rippling. Skinfaxi came to a complete stop, and on-screen I could see a perfect circle of absolute darkness. Or rather, a circular area through which I could see no stars.

". . . here."

"What is that?" My initial thought was that it must be a black hole, but further reflection made me realize that light wasn't being distorted around the phenomenon, nor was there any change in gravity. The object, if it could be called such, was roughly three kilometers across but had, to my limited perception, no mass at all.

"A collapsor point. The front door of a wormhole."

"So Ragnarok came though this and coincidentally ran into Midgard?"

"Hmph! Not coincidentally, but yes. I think the meteor was sent from somewhere with the specific goal of destroying Yggdrassil."

"That's insane! Why would anyone attack Yggdrassil? Wouldn't she have told me if she had enemies? Especially if it meant I'd be dodging meteors within minutes."

"Who knows? It doesn't matter anyway. I don't know of anyone who would wish harm on one of the Gaias, and there's no reason to think Yggdrassil believed any different. She might have assumed it was just catastrophic bad luck. But in my humble opinion that meteor couldn't have made it to Midgard without someone carefully orchestrating its trajectory, especially with the proximity of Asgard. The gas giant should have pulled that rock before it even got close to Midgard."

"Could it have been aliens?" I asked. While Skinfaxi had explained his reasoning, I had looked up if our civilization had contact with nonhuman life-forms, but nothing had come up.

"It's not completely impossible, but too implausible. There are billions of stars in the galaxy, but we've done a good job cataloguing the vast majority. Especially the really interesting ones. Fermi's paradox holds true: if there were a civilization out there capable of lobbing asteroids through wormholes, we'd have seen signs by now."

"One of us used this wormhole to toss a stone at Yggdrassil."

There was an interesting spark of fire in Skinfaxi's tone. So far I'd seen him dodging away from a collapsing moon with a detached sense of humor. While I couldn't claim to know this Capek very well, I was surprised by the edge in his voice.

"So how do we find out who did this?"

"We?" he asked.

"I literally have nowhere else to go and nothing else to do, so I might as well help you figure this out." While he had mentioned something about taking me to "the City," whatever that meant, I was far more curious about who could and would arrange for the destruction of an astral body for the sake of assassinating my progenitor. There was a mystery that needed investigation, and I was drawn to solve it. I hadn't been able to do anything to protect Yggdrassil, who had given me life; the least I could do was figure out who was behind this.

"Ha-ha!" he answered, his good cheer back in force. "There's only one way to answer your question, my friend. Keep your eyes open. You're not going to want to miss this!"

With these words my companion activated whatever propulsion mechanism displaced him at sub–light speeds and moved us toward the collapsor point. As we got close enough, I could see that the anomaly was not as perfect a black spot as I had first thought. I noticed thousands of minuscule lines of multicolored lights streaking toward the middle of the circle, their pattern suggesting the walls of a tubular shape within the collapsor point. Then we went in.

The walls of the wormhole, if they could be described as such, exploded with color, stretching the limits of my visual light sensors. The streaks of light became beams of color, the light of the stars we passed stretched out over light-years in the wormhole. While we hit the collapsor point head-on, we didn't keep our heading for long. The wormhole was happy to pull us along toward the other end but did nothing to keep us straight. I wondered if Skinfaxi simply couldn't correct our angle or simply did not care to. With the lack of gravity or inertial forces tugging at us, I guess it didn't matter. The whole trip lasted a little more than an hour, and all of it in perfect silence and calm, the images blurring past the monitor tilting as we slowly listed to port.

The journey ended as suddenly as it began. One moment the universe was a parade of racing colors and lights, the next we were back in the blackness of space.

A soft chime repeating three times in rapid succession—accompanied by the ambient light within the bridge, changing to a dramatic red—served as a warning. I scoured the projection of the outside, looking for the cause of alarm. To the lower right of the monitor, I noticed a speckled cloud of sparkling material. Skinfaxi must have noticed it at the same time, as the monitor zoomed in to the cloud, revealing it to be a cluster of asteroids and floating debris—perhaps the remnants of a shattered world.

"What's that?" I asked, pointing at a strange object nestled within the agglomeration.

The image enlarged further, bringing into focus an artificial structure. By all reasoning it was another spaceship, one of immense proportion. I estimated its length at four kilometers, 90 percent of it an elongated frame constructed of gigantic latticed girders. The entire structure looked inert, with no lights blinking or portions moving. At first glance it looked as if it might be abandoned. Careful inspection revealed, however, that at regular intervals the ship would fire minuscule maneuvering thrusters, adjusting its position to avoid collision with any of the larger free-floating rocks that moved by. Infrared imaging also showed signs of many active systems, some moving at a furious pace within the ship.

"Is that another Capek?" I inquired, trying not to sound too naive.

"No," Skinfaxi replied, also straining to identify the vessel. "It's not sentient, but it has a transponder. It's called the *Spear of Athena*, and it's identified as construction equipment. A mining ship."

"Mining ship?" I figured the vessel was meant for asteroid mining, but at the same time it seemed rather awkward and large for even that function.

"Actually, it's a mass driver. It picks up rocks and shoots them at larger rocks until it finds one with a rich enough content of whatever material it's looking for, then shoots it toward a refinery."

"It's a giant, asteroid-shooting space gun?" My implication must have been obvious, as I immediately noticed us moving toward the *Spear of Athena*.

"Yup," was all Skinfaxi could add.

We approached the titanic ship carefully. Skinfaxi flooded the surface of the vessel in light, and I managed to get a better view of the monster. It had an ominous quality to it—dark and evidently old. Every surface was pockmarked from the impact of a million micrometeors, giving it a rough texture reminiscent of rust. Hints of markings long erased by radiation could still be seen despite the ship's age and wear, though they could barely be read.

"Should we be getting this close? It destroyed Yggdrassil, it could probably destroy us."

"Nah," my companion reassured me. "Very few Capeks are equipped with any kind of weapon, and even fewer of our tools are weaponized. This mass driver and your plasma cutter are probably the most powerful weapons within several light-years."

I was tempted to ask how he knew about the powerful tool Yggdrassil had given me. Perhaps he had scanned my body as I came on board. Still, I could not bring myself to feel any safer.

"What if it's been modified with some kind of defensive capabilities? Shouldn't we notify some sort of authority?"

"Ho-ho," he laughed. "You misunderstand a fundamental of Capek society: we do not have a central government or authority."

That seemed strange to me, that a society could be intentionally unsupervised. Without a governmental body, how did anything get done?

"What about human authority? Surely they have a stake in this."

"They have a stake, yes, but you wouldn't call it immediate. Yggdrassil didn't have time to explain much, did she?"

I let my silence speak for me, looking within instead for the answers. I quickly found out that there were no human governments because there were no humans. Anywhere. There hadn't been for centuries. You'd think Yggdrassil would have mentioned this. There was more, of course, but it would have to wait.

"I'm bringing us close to an access port. Since I'm not getting any answer from the ship, you're going to have to go inside."

I looked around, mildly surprised I was asked to do anything.

"Oh. Sure. What am I looking for?"

"Find the bridge. You should be able to access the ship's logs from there. If you can't, open transmissions so I can download them myself, then feel free to cut out the memory core and bring it back."

At least the mission was something I already had experience with.

"What about this?" I held aloft the torn-up fragment of the Nursery I had rescued from Midgard.

"Leave it here. I'll keep it safe."

And without further ceremony I made my way back to the hatch.

THE SPEAR OF ATHENA

Less than twenty-four hours after my birth, I witnessed a cataclysm on an astronomical level, survived a meteor crash, made and lost a friend, traveled through a wormhole, and now I was preparing for my second space walk. In all honesty it was more of a space hop. Skinfaxi had positioned the hatch (his belly?) very close to what looked like a main access port. It was just a matter of a short jump to latch onto the railings that framed the thick, wide door. As soon as it was clear I had made it safely, Skinfaxi moved to a more comfortable distance.

The door itself was four meters wide and set into a larger access port that measured at least eight times that size. Both were rectangular, with chevroned splits in the center, which I assume was where they each opened.

My automated systems informed me of a low-yield magnetic field that encased what looked like an access panel. It was consistent with an NFC lock. I waved my hand around the panel, and a small blinking blue light activated, letting me know that my magnetic signature had been read.

A second later I felt the rumbling of powerful motors through the railing, and the small door came to life, split open, and let forth a beam of yellow light from the airlock within. No sooner had I maneuvered into the airlock than a spinning light activated, warning of the closing hatch. This ship looked and felt primitive. It had none of the sleek and polished curves of Yggdrassil, relying instead on sharp angles, thick bulkheads, and clumsy design. Everything looked rugged, functional, and ugly.

As soon as the door clamped shut, the normal lights came on, bright, yellowed, and blinding. After a moment I started to hear a low hissing emanating from a ceiling vent.

Hearing?

I quickly looked at my internal monitors for confirmation, which showed the airlock was filling with a mixture of mostly nitrogen, carbon, and oxygen in proportions that might have been breathable by humans. How old was the *Spear of Athena*, anyway?

As soon as air pressure reached ninety-nine kilopascals, the hissing stopped, and the inner airlock door groaned open. On the other side was a sizable room suspended above a hangar. Everything was lit brightly but irregularly, creating large patches of shadows.

I started walking, or rather pushing myself, in search of the nearest elevator or access ladder, marveling at the simple miracle of generating sound. I hadn't realized how much I missed hearing things, and I wondered if Capeks made music—if so, was it any good?

My journey to the bridge happened without incident. Once outside the hangar, I had to climb up an access vent to reach the upper levels, as none of the service elevators were functional. My size and the lack of gravity made the task easy, if a little annoying.

The bridge itself seemed designed for human-sized creatures. Stranger still, there were chairs attached to what I assumed was the floor. At some point this vessel had some kind of artificial gravity, it seemed. It wasn't a large room, designed for functionality rather than comfort. Six apparent stations were distributed evenly in front of the squat window that spanned almost the entire width of three of the four walls. The view outside was of the enormous latticed girders that formed the barrel of the mass driver. There did not seem to be a chair for a captain or commanding officer.

Every workstation was different, designed specifically for whatever specialized task its user had to perform. I activated the terminal for the mass driver, quickly realizing that I had no familiarity with how any of these systems functioned. Basic navigation of the operating system was instinctive enough, but digging to find specific data was going to take some time. Thankfully, that was something I had in ample supply.

I spent almost an hour playing around and digging through the system, making slow progress at figuring the archiving protocol of the logs. A good fifteen minutes were wasted looking for a search function to no avail. I'd found the logs themselves, millions of them dating back several thousand years, when I was interrupted by a sound.

The ship had been built to last. I hadn't heard a single instance of the structure groaning or machinery grinding. At best, and only when I paid extremely close attention, I could sometimes catch the maneuvering thrusters firing in the far distance. Otherwise, the ghost ship was almost as silent as the cold vacuum in which it floated.

Yet I heard a noise, and it was unsettling. It was like metal on metal. A cold, high-pitched clicking that emanated from the sole corridor that led to the bridge. I turned to see what might be the cause, but I saw nothing.

When I turned back, my terminal had reset. For a moment I was nostalgic for the ability to sigh in exasperation. As sturdy as the *Spear of Athena* might have been, the centuries had clearly taken their toll on the computational system that served as its nervous system.

Frustrated but persistent, I traced my steps back to the log archive and quickly figured out the dating system. Once I knew how the archiving was filed, it was a simple task to find the latest entry. Just as I was about to access the file, though, the noise interrupted me again. I turned to the corridor but saw nothing again, and when I turned back, the terminal had reset a second time.

Frustrated but no more the fool, I switched my vision to the infrared spectrum, remembering how I had seen a multitude of heat signatures zipping around the ship during our initial approach.

Then I saw them.

Half a dozen heat signatures. Each with obviously mechanical configurations built around a low-emanation power core, appearing as orange, glowing orbs with spidery webs of red and purple tendrils. One was loitering just outside the door to the bridge and was probably the source of the annoying sound. Were they Capeks? Automatic systems native to the *Spear of Athena*? Considering what had happened to Yggdrassil, I wasn't about to take chances.

"Faxi?" I called out through quancom. "I'm not alone here. There's about half a dozen small robots swarming around."

"Oh? Are they Capeks?" he answered, more curious than worried.

"I don't know!" I snapped, alarmed by the situation. The silence, couched in the humming of the vessel's distant power plant, made me hyperaware and consequently nervous.

"Well, can you see one of them? If you can send me an image, I can probably identify it. I've met a lot of Capeks in my travels."

"Okay."

Slowly, I stood from the seat, floating gently toward the ceiling. With deliberate care, I positioned myself so I could, with very small and hopefully quiet bursts from my thrusters, push myself toward the corridor.

As I moved silently through the bridge, the small robot at the door moved, presumably scratching at the wall to make noise again. Instinctively, I turned back to the terminal, only to see one of the small robots scrambling over it, disassembling it at incredible speed.

The synthetic creature resembled a jellyfish made of pseudo-plastics, less than half a meter wide with a hole in the middle—or perhaps an elegant interpretation of a robotic donut with tentacles. A dozen delicate arms protruded from underneath the thing, each busy removing screws and taking apart panels, tearing through the terminal faster than my advanced optics could register. It must have hovered above me near the ceiling while I was focused on my work.

"Hey!" I called, surprised that my voice came out so deep and masculine. I'd have to fix that later.

The little robot paused what it was doing to turn and look at me. At least I thought that's what it did. Without seeing any distinguishable eyes, all I had to go on was the tilt of the toroidal shape that made up the main body.

"Stop that!" I demanded.

As I tried to maneuver back to the terminal, intent on doing I don't know what, the little robot very slowly, and without breaking what I guess was eye contact, continued to take apart the computer that contained the logs I needed.

"Quit it!" I don't know why I thought repeating myself would have a different effect.

"What's going on down there? Do you see it?" asked Skinfaxi, who I realized was hearing everything I was shouting at the flying donut.

"It's destroying the computer!" I whined back to him just as I was about to reach out and grab the annoying little thing.

I closed my left hand on the little robot in time for it to throw a component across the bridge with one of its tendrils. I turned my head to see an exact duplicate of the metal jellyfish catch it.

"What the hell!"

"Send me an image, Dagir. Let's see what we're dealing with."

I sent the footage from my memory of the thing ripping apart the terminal. Meanwhile, I propelled myself after the second robot, dragging the first behind me.

"Ho-ho!" Skinfaxi laughed over quancom as I turned the corner. "You're in trouble, my friend."

"What do you mean?" His tone was amused, but I'd heard him laugh while a moon was being disintegrated, so I was only more or less reassured.

"It's a Capek, all right. An annoying little Von Neumann called Koalemos. You're in no danger, but you're not getting anything accomplished either."

"Oh yeah?" I said, pushing myself after the second robot, who was scrambling away. However, just as I closed my right hand on the little bastard, he threw the component to yet a third robot. Meanwhile, the other two latched onto my arms, severely limiting my movements. Then a fourth one came around a corner and grabbed onto my legs. When I saw a fifth one appear, I suddenly realized why Skinfaxi had so little confidence in my chances for victory.

"Great!" I moaned sarcastically. "Which one of them is Koalemos?"

"Ha-ha! All of them!" my companion mocked me. "Von Neumanns are single entities with many networked bodies. Quite efficient at complex, large-scale projects. Koalemos has seven bodies, or 'shards' as we call them. He's specialized at scavenging."

"Well, what do I do?" I was beginning to fear for myself as I became increasingly helpless.

"Mmmh . . . Talk to him? He's not malicious that I know of, but he is named after the Greek god of stupidity, so there's that."

I stopped fighting and allowed another of Koalemos's shards to immobilize me. Not that I had any choice in the matter.

"Okay, okay, you got me," I surrendered.

"What are you doing here?" a voice came over open-channel communication. I decided that perhaps because of his interesting configuration, Koalemos couldn't communicate through audible sound. In fact, there was no reason to believe vocal communications would be widespread, let alone standard, amongst Capeks. In the end it might be a very rare ability I had chosen for myself.

"I'm here to figure out why this ship destroyed Midgard and Yggdrassil with it."

"Yggdrassil? Destroyed? No, no, no, no, no." His voice was stressed, on the verge of panic. Could Capeks have panic attacks?

"What happened? Do you know why the *Spear of Athena* fired at Midgard?" Clearly, the strange little group of robots knew something.

"Yggdrassil put in a request for raw materials. A lot of raw materials. Enough for a Lucretius-class Capek to be constructed." His explanation sounded like a confession, and I could almost feel a stomach I didn't even have sink. "I found and captured the perfect asteroid for it and received my coordinates from a Norse Capek, so I figured they must be legit, and I launched. But as I saw the collapsor point expand, I realized something was wrong. I signaled Yggdrassil, but I never thought the meteor would impact. It wasn't my fault—I used the coordinates I was given!"

"Oh, it impacted, all right. Why did you steal the memory from the launch terminal if it's not your fault?"

"Because this was no accident—I was set up! You're Norse, just like the one who gave me the coordinates. I thought you were here to destroy the evidence!"

"That makes sense," I agreed. "So why trust me now?"

"What? No! I don't." The shards holding me tightened their grip, underlining his point. "I'm not telling you anything the Capek who gave me those coordinates wouldn't know."

"Well, I'm not him! I was constructed less than a day ago and barely made it off Midgard myself."

The little Von Neumann dragged me back to the bridge. There, the collective bodies threw me toward the view port before retreating like a pack of cockroaches. They were well out of my reach should I be tempted to strike back, which I was.

"I'm not alone, you know," I began threatening, having had my fill of trying to prove myself. "Between me and my friend—"

I was cut short. While floating in the middle of the bridge, I noticed my ion thrusters had activated to help me keep my position. A strong gravitational pull was manifesting behind me somewhere beyond the large window to space. Even Koalemos, or at least the shards that were here, started falling toward me, in a jumble of metallic toruses, their own engines burning at full thrust to compensate.

"The hell?" I asked no one in particular.

"Gravitational singularity dead ahead," Skinfaxi answered anyway. "Hang on! Incoming space fold!"

When I looked around to the window, I immediately wanted to rub my eyes—a gesture that was no longer available to me. Technically, it never had been. Instead, the reflex translated into a quick diagnosis of my optics, which returned 100 percent optimal.

What I saw, however, made no sense. The number of stars in the sky suddenly doubled as a distant pocket of the galaxy was being pulled toward our location, the very fabric of space bending to bring two distant points together. For a brief moment two parts of the Milky Way that had no business being this close to each other overlapped, allowing instant travel between them. It was one thing to read about space folding from my onboard database but quite another to see its effects happen right in front of me.

The sound was like a terrible grinding of metal being ripped, echoing impossibly through the vacuum, mocking the limits of physical plausibility.

From the fold emerged a leviathan of impossible proportion. An immense vessel, dark and massive, passed through the violation of reality, ponderously moving forward, propelled by thousands of ion thrusters. A cross between a kilometer-long whale and a titanic hedgehog, the ship bristled with long spines, each independently articulated, each housing dozens of engines that emanated a deep-blue glow. It had no apparent bridge or portholes, only a long line of large hatches all along its broadsides.

Just as suddenly as they had appeared, the intruding stars in the sky vanished and gravity with them, leaving me and my captors to float away from the window.

"Lucretius-class Capek," declared Skinfaxi over quancom.

"Friend of yours?" I asked one of the donut-shaped robots that made up Koalemos.

"No. This is of Isian design," he answered, as if I knew what that meant.

"Lucretiuses are transgalactic explorers," interjected Skinfaxi. "We don't usually see them. They tend to leave the Milky Way almost immediately after construction. He shouldn't be here."

The city-sized Capek maneuvered alongside the *Spear of Athena*, ignoring the smaller asteroids it bumped into as it waded through.

"Anhur!" my companion called out on open channel, apparently familiar with the newcomer's name. "You're a long way off your journey, my friend. What are you doing here?"

There was a strange tension and reverence in Skinfaxi's tone. I wouldn't have called it fear, but there was a wariness I wasn't used to hearing. My companion might as well have been talking to the very god whose name the Lucretius bore.

"Anhur, do you read? Are you damaged? Can we be of assistance?" Skinfaxi continued his line of inquiry.

"Huh-oh . . ." mumbled Koalemos as his shards started to float around the bridge in erratic patterns.

"What is . . . ?" I tried to ask, before noticing them myself. The hatches on Anhur's side had opened, and although I had no reason for jumping to conclusions, I somehow knew the situation had shifted.

Dozens of rocket-propelled objects disgorged themselves from the newly opened orifices, streaking through space toward the *Spear of Athena*.

"Are those—?" I tried to ask.

"Torpedoes!" Koalemos screamed on the channel. "This isn't good at all! Get me out of here! Help!"

Surprisingly, I managed to keep myself calm despite the Von Neumann's hysteria. The metallic jellyfish all filed out chaotically from the bridge, heading toward a single destination. I followed.

"Faxi? What's going on?"

"Damned if I know, little buddy, but you kids need to evacuate. Impact in seven minutes."

"Out! Out! Out!" added Koalemos as he flew down the same path I had taken to get to the bridge.

I noticed several of my systems shutting down, their processing power redirecting to more pressing concerns. Safety protocols were being automatically suspended to allow broader flexibility at the cost of reliability. The overall feeling and effect of these autonomous changes was reminiscent of the adrenaline rush humans had experienced in stressful situations.

I scrambled down the access shaft that had replaced the elevators on my journey in. I could see the corridor through which I first arrived, but Koalemos was already flying in the opposite direction.

"Where are you going?"

"I choose life!" he answered.

Instinctively, I started after him, though I knew I was putting more distance between myself and the hatch I'd come in from.

"The exit is that way!" I yelled through comm channels, still struggling to keep up with the swarm of floating jellyfish.

"Your exit maybe, but mine is this way and a lot less bad," he answered as a seventh and eighth shard, including the one that still held the mass driver's memory core, joined the group flying down the corridor in loose formation.

We took a turn to the left as a timer manifested in my vision counting down the last minute before impact. We were not going to make it.

Koalemos got to the end of the corridor—a hatch made up the entire outer wall, flanked by doors on both sides. The hatch was covered in warning signs in several languages, some of which I recognized, along with pictographs. The message was clear—do not open, beware, explosive decompression.

The countdown at the edge of my sight hit zero before I reached the door. The *Spear of Athena* was rocked by the impact of a dozen warheads exploding on the other side of the ship. Looking back, I could see the opposite end of the corridor being torn apart by the force of the blasts. An immense wall of fire ignited briefly as the conflagration quickly consumed all the available oxygen as it was being sucked into space.

My own body was thrown backward by the suddenly rushing air, my thrusters straining to compensate to no avail. Three of Koalemos's shards, which had little problem fighting the pull, flew to me and grasped my limbs to drag me back to the hatch. Between my own power and the three smaller robots, I managed to make my way to the door as it blew off into space.

"If you're still intact, my little friend, try to hurry. Anhur just unleashed another volley," Skinfaxi warned.

Nine Capeks flew out into space from the port side of the *Spear of Athena*. We floated, significantly too close to the dying ship, waiting for my companion to come pick us up. Six minutes later the second volley struck the mass driver, which finally collapsed to the assault. Its structure crumbled as large portions of the massive vessel were torn from the whole.

As chunks of the murdered ship flew past us, Skinfaxi's gleaming form emerged from the cluster of expanding debris, dodging the ruins as they flew apart. Seeing the hatch already open, Koalemos and I quickly climbed in as my friend navigated the dangerous asteroid field and vestiges of the *Spear of Athena*'s carcass.

"Welcome aboard, friends!" Skinfaxi announced as the little networked Capek and I floated to the bridge. "Enjoy the relative safety while we have it."

"This is a lot less unsafe. All my thanks for the ride," said the little Capek.

"Don't get too comfortable. We're not out of the fire quite yet."

Skinfaxi activated the back half of the bridge monitor, essentially turning the spherical room into a fully immersive representation of the space around him. Thousands of pieces from the destroyed mass driver flew past us, while hundreds of asteroids floated in the distance, obscuring the very stars. Behind us, however, Anhur was bullying his way through the remains of his disintegrating victim, in hot pursuit of our own smaller and unarmed ship.

"I thought you said Capeks didn't have weapons," I said, overwhelmed by the situation.

"Anhur is less usual than usual Capeks," explained Koalemos, less clearly than I would have liked. "Behind us, that's a Lucretius-class Capek."

"Okay, what is an explorer doing with an entire arsenal down its throat?"

"Lucretiuses are always not very small. There are very few things they do not have equipped," the Von Neumann continued.

"Because they travel to other galaxies, Capeks like Anhur are built with a significantly larger variety of capabilities," Skinfaxi clarified. "Weapons are just a precaution against . . . well, whatever might be out there. Now if you'll excuse me, I need to concentrate."

On the screen behind us a flash of light off Anhur's starboard signaled the launch of another torpedo. Calculating its predicted trajectory, it was evident that it was heading toward us.

"Nineteen minutes and sixteen seconds to impact," announced our ship.

"Can you dodge it?" I asked.

"Nope. Each torpedo is probably as good a pilot as I am. Not as sentient and charming, but more than capable of plotting a collision course. I'm afraid unless we get very creative, we're not going to make it to the collapsor point."

"Ship!" Koalemos called out, eliciting an annoyed sigh from Skinfaxi. "Open your hatch. I might have a plan that might very well not fail."

"Done," Faxi answered.

One of Koalemos's shards flew off toward the back of the ship. I couldn't be sure of his intentions and wasn't certain I wanted to know either. The stakes being what they were, however, anything was possible.

"I'm no longer aboard. You can close," he said.

The back image suddenly zoomed in on a little robotic jellyfish glistening in the starlight, barely visible in the dark void. If it weren't for a large blue circle on the interface identifying him and the glow of his central thruster array, the piece of Capek would have all but disappeared in the black.

"What happens if he loses that shard?" I asked Skinfaxi over a private channel. The thought of being composed of several bodies was unnerving to me.

"He'll be that much less of himself," the ship answered in a somber tone.

I watched attentively as the little robot we had jettisoned positioned itself within the path of the incoming torpedo. The rest of Koalemos floated around me, seven metallic donuts with arms, seemingly unperturbed by the drama playing out a few thousand kilometers behind us.

The shard outside, matching Skinfaxi's velocity at the time it ejected, had little trouble latching onto the torpedo as it cut through the vacuum toward us, ever accelerating, ever catching up.

The image blew up some more, concentrating on Koalemos as he proceeded to dismantle panels from the weapon's surface, digging furiously through its innards, pulling out pieces and sometimes dropping them in its wake. Occasionally, he would reach back at the last second to pick up a stray piece. After a few tense minutes of this, thrusters fired all around the torpedo, dramatically halting its progression in our direction, spinning it back toward Anhur.

Immediately, Skinfaxi cut his sub–light drive. Touching the wall of the spherical room, I could feel the vibration and humming of the Alcubierre drive building up its charge. There was no reason to think that the much larger Anhur, built for travel between galaxies and equipped with engines designed to fold space itself, wouldn't have similar capabilities. With any luck, however, his took much longer to activate, and we would be long gone through the wormhole by then.

"Now might be a good time to sever your link to that shard, my friend." The suggestion was akin to recommending the removal of an arm.

"Not quite yet," Koalemos replied, lost in concentration.

Looking back, we saw the image of the torpedo speeding away from us and toward the immense Capek hot on our tail. A moment passed before the image disappeared as space-time contracted behind Skinfaxi, launching our bubble of reality toward the collapsor point faster than physics should allow.

For a moment I felt victorious. We had escaped the monstrous Capek bent on destroying us and, by all appearances, dealt it a parting blow. Glancing around, however, the feeling quickly vanished.

Koalemos, arguably the hero of the hour, was floating around the bridge, his many bodies moving freely in various random directions, uncontrolled and unfettered. None of the thruster arrays that normally propelled and stabilized him were functional. His tendril-like arms were motionless.

"Oh crap!" I called out. "What's wrong with him?"

"Synaptic shock from his quancom network being broken," Skinfaxi answered, his humor gone, replaced by mild irritation. "Aren't you built for rescue and repair? Shouldn't you do something?"

I didn't like being snapped at, not after being nearly blown up twice and ensnared by a little twerp of a Capek. How was I supposed to know what was wrong with him? I'd only technically been alive for at most thirty-six hours. I was in no position to rescue anyone. In fact, so far it had been other Capeks that were forced to pull my synthetic ass out of the fire.

Then again, perhaps it was time I started pulling my own weight.

Without a word I pushed myself toward the closest of Koalemos's bodies. There was something melancholy about the pile of lifeless shards floating around the bridge, bumping lightly against one another. I put the thought out of my mind and started pulling the little robot into pieces.

As I began to disassemble the shard to reach its guts and brains, I accessed all the information about the Von Neumann I had available. There was, to put it lightly, a lot. Luckily, it wasn't hard to narrow down my field of research. Unlike the data from the *Spear of Athena*, my logs were neat and tidy. Von Neumann–class Capeks are a fairly unique breed. While all classes of Capeks are drastically different from one another, Von Neumanns are particular in that they rely on a stable, continuous quancom network to hold their consciousness together. The immediate assumption about them, seeing as they behaved like a swarm, was to think they were a collection of individual, linked entities. If that was the case, the removal of a single part of the swarm, while a blow to the whole, wouldn't have that dramatic an effect. In this case, however, the loss of a shard was almost synonymous to a combined lobotomy and amputation.

The cognitive shock and subsequent gap in the network left the victim unable to function normally. Like a biological brain, new pathways had to be constructed for the consciousness to function once more. Automated systems might have been able to do the trick, but without external aid the little Capek might remain unresponsive for a very long time.

There was a long list of things I needed to accomplish to revive the remaining shards of Koalemos. Three dozen of these involved tricking the consciousness into thinking the network was intact. Another handful required replacing systems proprietary to the missing shard (that part took the longest). Then I had to build a brand-new system that would prevent the synaptic net from crashing each time it noticed it was incomplete.

All of these fixes were temporary. I didn't have the tools or the means to effect all the required repairs to make the little Von Neumann whole again. The best I could do was patch him up to basic functionality and hope to bring him back to his progenitor, but even then there were no guarantees that he would ever be the same.

After running a handful of tests to make sure I wouldn't turn him into the Capek equivalent of a drooling vegetable when I flipped the switch, I looked at the individual-specific files Yggdrassil had uploaded into my memory. Almost all of them were locked down, preventing me from accessing personal information about each Capek on record. Yggdrassil had told me that, should my own on-board systems recognize the need, the file on the specific Capek I was helping would unlock. As I sifted through the directories, two files were flagged as unlocked—mine and Koalemos's. I sighed in relief.

The Von Neumann's file answered several questions I had about the interactions of certain subroutines. Nothing dramatic, but details that could in certain circumstances have caused minor problems with the relationship between the shards and various parts of his personality. I addressed the issues accordingly and started putting the little robot back together. Thankfully, since there was nothing physically broken on him, I didn't have to repair or modify each of the shards individually.

As I put in the last few pieces, I went through the file a final time and noticed a strange mistake. It mentioned that Koalemos was a septuanian Von Neumann construct; he was composed of seven shards. I knew one had been destroyed or at best left behind, but there were still seven floating around within Skinfaxi's belly. It was an odd mistake for such a vital technical document, but I let it go, focusing instead on reviving the little guy. Guys?

When I looked up, I noticed that we were traveling in the wormhole. Skinfaxi had been silent during the entire operation, maybe frustrated with me, but more likely respecting my need to focus.

I wished I could take a deep breath before reanimating my patient, but that was another source of human comfort I didn't have access to. So, skipping any further ceremony and procrastination, I flipped the virtual switch that would awaken our new friend.

For a moment little more happened than the soft glow of seven thruster arrays warming up as the toruses began to right themselves. Then they each began to rotate and move independently, flying about the bridge slowly. Somehow I could almost feel Skinfaxi looking inward in anticipation.

"We aren't destroyed?" Koalemos asked slowly, testing his voice. "Not bad. Not bad at all."

I could have hugged one of his stupid floating donuts.

"You did good back there, little guy," Skinfaxi finally spoke up. "Don't worry, we'll get you patched up."

"I've felt worse . . . and better."

"I'm just glad you're still"—I wanted to say functional but realized that it was insufficient—"alive."

"Not unhappy myself."

"All right," I began, relieved to have one more crisis behind me. "Any chance we can go somewhere that won't blow up?"

"Aha!" my companion answered, his joviality restored. "I'm way ahead of you, little buddy! I've got us on course toward the City."

He'd said something about the City before. A whole metropolis where Capeks of all shapes, sizes, and classes congregated. That was where I was meant to go after I had activated. Hopefully, it would prove safer than my two previous destinations.

"Do you think we'll be able to find some way to preserve Yggdrassil's Nursery's mnemonic core there?"

"Hopefully. Hopefully, we'll also be able to start figuring out why someone tossed a giant rock at our mother, and what a Lucretius-class is doing lumbering around the Milky Way assassinating Capeks."

"How do you propose we do that?"

"Mmmh . . . I think we'd be better off asking Aurvandil. Before you ask, he's another of Yggdrassil's children. Another Leduc-class Capek, though much taller than you. He's very old and very much the intellectual. He spends most of his time on the City and is usually up to date on current affairs. If anyone knows how to help us, it's him."

Aurvandil . . . The name was elegant, and my data banks told me it was related to the Morning Star of Norse mythology. There was something romantic about that. I was eager to meet this Aurvandil.

"You managed to not leave behind your progenitor's Nursery?" Koalemos inquired, nudging me with one of his tendrils.

"Yes. It's in Skinfaxi's care. I don't know why, but I couldn't leave it behind."

Jonathan . . .

BABYLON

We ended up being much closer to the City than I originally thought. As it turned out, the wormhole we were in when I finally reactivated Koalemos was actually the third one in a series that was bringing us ever closer to our destination. I had spent the better part of two days—without sleep—working on our new companion.

When we dropped out of our fourth and final wormhole, we were only half an astronomical unit away from an enormous gas giant. The monster was roughly five times the size of Jupiter, the largest planet from the original human system. It had giant spirals of dark-amber clouds that were swirling around in tight bands along its equator, feathering softly into brilliant-yellow clouds. I could see seven moons orbiting the giant, but none were our destination.

Approaching at sub–light speeds, we took several hours to make our way to the City, which turned out to be a modestly sized floating orbital station.

"Welcome to Babylon!" Skinfaxi announced as we began our final approach.

The City was magnificent. Set relatively deep within the atmosphere of the gas giant, which I learned was called Ziggurat, it was positioned at the perfect altitude to not require artificial gravity or rotation. Being helio-locked allowed it to have constant sunlight, which went well with a Capek's unsleeping nature.

Babylon was egg shaped, with a bottom stem extending deep into Ziggurat's inner layer. I wanted to ask if it was tethered to something below but thought the question naive. The City itself shined like gold, with hundreds of horizontal lines carved into beautiful patterns. Around it zoomed a multitude of ships, or more likely Sputnik-class Capeks, which moved from one portion of the egg to another like bees flying around a hive.

We approached an open terrace, from which a landing platform automatically extended. It wasn't large enough to accommodate Skinfaxi, but it allowed Koalemos, myself, and one of Faxi's telepresence drones to disembark. My friend took himself into higher orbit on autopilot while activating the drone.

"Usually, I just drop the drone from orbit, but when I have passengers I can't exactly indulge in those kinds of acrobatics," he explained.

"Does that have anything to do with why you're down to two remotes?" I questioned slyly.

"Ho-ho! Of course not!" he lied.

The interior of the City was twice as stunning as its exterior. As it turned out, most of Babylon was hollow, crowded instead with hundreds of gleaming towers that connected the lower portions with the higher ones, each passing through several plateaus. The outer shell was on average a hundred meters thick and was honeycombed with rooms, chambers, and apartments. I was stunned to see, for the first time since exiting the Nursery, life. Nothing complex, but Babylon was heavily decorated with an immense variety of green plants in elaborate hydroponic pots and creeping freely over the surfaces of the towers.

Babylon lived up to its promise of being populated by dozens of various Capeks that almost defied description or classification. I walked by a hulking sphere of mirrored pseudo-plastic with no apparent limbs, and in the distance I noticed a lobster-shaped entity with an iridescent surface tenderly pruning one of the many trees in the plaza. There was a swarm of hundreds of robots eleven centimeters in diameter that buzzed around in formation, flying across the empty center of the City, clearly a Von Neumann specimen; nearby was a featureless humanoid with semitransparent skin that exposed the complex inner workings of its anatomy.

Each Capek was as unique in form and purpose as I expected them to be in personality. Most of those I passed sent closed-channel greetings, and those who were capable even smiled or waved. There was a distinct sense of civility and belonging. I could if I wished catch fragments of conversation on open channels from Capeks discussing various projects. Everything was about building this, restoring that, or growing some other thing. If nothing else, Capek civilization was industrious.

Most surprising was the art. Babylon was apparently the refuge and point of congregation for all Capeks with an artistic nature. Beautifully complex sculptures dotted the plaza, and if I paid close attention I could pick up patterned vibrations in the atmosphere that melded harmoniously into music. Certain plants were trimmed into gorgeous topiary patterns; most were abstract in nature, depicting complex spirals and interwoven helixes, but some represented animals in a strange celebration of life as it once was. Details in the very architecture of the City rewarded those who paid close attention. Seemingly minimalistic designs broke down into intricate patterns upon inspection, tone-on-tone textures and patterns putting a layer of almost-organic beauty over the clean and efficient lines of the City.

We wandered through Babylon for a long while, walking—or hovering in my companions' case—with the apparent goal of allowing me a brief visit before we got down to business. I drank in the culture of my people, basking in what it meant to be Capek.

Skinfaxi's drone stopped to exchange on a closed channel with a snakelike entity, one of the very few Capeks I'd seen with facial features. Once they finished their private conversation, the creature, whom Faxi introduced as Proioxis, smiled at both Koalemos and me.

"Good day, friends of a friend," it spoke with a mellifluous voice that was unusually soothing. "We'll have time to talk more at a later time, but I've sent word to Hera that one of her sons is coming home for some care."

It was referring to Koalemos, who while apparently functional still required excessive repairs.

"Don't worry, little brother," the gentle snake addressed my broken companion. "Mother will mend your woes."

This seemed to please Koalemos, his remaining shards gathering close around Proioxis in what might have been an embrace. I touched the palm of my left hand with the tips of my finger, reminding myself that while synthetic, I could still touch and feel. Human contact was clearly not an option, but Capeks seemed to have their own version. I wondered how Skinfaxi felt having others travel within him. Very familiar, I assumed.

"My friend says the news of Yggdrassil's demise has not reached the City yet," Faxi explained on a closed channel, "which is odd considering the pace at which information travels amongst us."

"Is anyone not your friend?" I inquired mockingly.

"No," he answered simply without a trace of irony.

We continued wandering the many plateaus of Babylon, moving slowly and ignoring the countless other ways to travel that could have taken us directly to our destination. The only obvious trend was an upward climb toward the very top of the station. The higher we went, the more natural light filtered through the clear outer shell, bathing the increasingly elaborate and lush gardens in golden light.

Only when we reached the very top of Babylon—a large, domed terrace decorated by a pattern of flowerpots that housed exotic and breathtaking specimens—did we stop. The room was like a garden in the sky, floating on an ocean of clouds. It was both stunning and relaxing—a site designed for meditation and contemplation.

Off to one side was a small group of Capeks—five of them to be exact. One was a Sputnik-class ship, hovering outside the dome, its maneuvering thrusters furiously firing to fight gravity and compensate for the wind. It resembled a large octopus, with short mechanical tentacles serving as stabilizers. Another looked like a squat, flat dome supported by a dozen legs, each small, refined, and deceptively weak looking. Two Von Neumann types—one composed of a school of five floating fish with beautiful spiral-pattern decorations, and another who looked like a small band of diminutive metallic teddy bears—rounded up the group.

A tall humanoid with slender, elfin limbs held court. He stood over seven feet tall and had two sets of arms, one pair long and expressive, and the other short and utilitarian. His head was stretched like the rest of his form, an oblong dome resembling my own head, segmented in a way that imitated human features. Friendly, soothing features.

When the humanoid Capek noticed our small group, he waved the others away politely, each of whom bowed in his own way before dispersing. Once his companions had departed, he nodded to us in greeting and signaled for us to join him.

I knew him. Immediately, I knew him. Through his presence and mannerisms, despite the brief description I'd been given, I knew him. Aurvandil.

"I knew," the elegant Capek explained.

We had moved to another portion of the gardens closer to the center and shielded by trees and other vegetation, which offered us a greater sense of privacy. One of the strange things about Capek existence was the lack of a need to sit. Being able to lock our joints and painlessly hover on automated thruster arrays removed the need for rest. Although this was normal for Capeks, it was still damn hard to get used to.

"I tried to contact Yggdrassil but couldn't establish a link," Aurvandil continued. "For anyone familiar with how a Gaia-class Capek is structured, there are very few possibilities to explain a complete breakdown in communications. I was looking at going there myself but remembered our friend Skinfaxi here was on a return trip from Midgard, so I waited to see you for confirmation of my fears. I won't lie, brother. Your delay worried me greatly."

"What we haven't told you is that we think we may know who is responsible for the attack," I said.

"Oh?"

Koalemos's shards recoiled slightly, one of them rocking back and forth.

"Koalemos here was the one who sent the meteor through the wormhole using the *Spear of Athena*, but he was given the coordinates from an outside source. I believe he was tricked."

"That's a bold claim, last son of Yggdrassil," the elegant Capek answered, his "eyes" focused on me.

"I identify more as a female . . ." I said, sheepishly.

"Mmmh . . . An artifact of your time in the Nursery. It doesn't matter. Brother or sister, we are kin."

"We were attacked while at the *Spear of Athena*," said Skinfaxi. "It was Anhur. I don't know if you're familiar with him."

"A large Lucretius, if I recall. Isian dynasty. Spawned about six years ago."

"Yes. Heavily armed. He laid waste to the *Spear* and then went after us. Koalemos here sacrificed one of his shards to allow us to escape."

"Yet he still functions?" Aurvandil asked, bending over to get a closer look at the little Von Neumann.

"I fixed him. Temporarily," I explained. "We have to bring him back to Hera for further repairs."

"Yes. . . He's there but not quite, is he?" The tall Capek gave a gentle push to one of Koalemos's shards, sending it floating for a few moments before it regained its orientation and flew back into the formation. I couldn't help but find the gesture rude, but what did I know of Capek culture?

"We leave as soon as possible, but we needed to warn the City," Faxi continued. "I don't know what this attack means— if Anhur has simply lost his mind, or if all the Lucretiuses are involved—but I figured if anyone could put the pieces together, it'd be you, brother."

"You honor me with too much credit. The news of Yggdrassil's destruction will not be taken lightly. I don't expect mass panic, but there is reason to fear that this is not an isolated attack."

"What do you mean?" I asked, a wave of worry washing over me.

"Gaia-class Capeks are the only ones capable of truly creating weapons of war on the galactic scale. Sure, some Von Neumanns can assemble fairly terrifying engines of destruction should they put their minds to it, but none can match the sheer volume and scale of a progenitor fabrication facility. If I were to mount a military campaign against us, I would begin by taking out the Gaias."

It made an awful lot of sense in a horrifying sort of way. This was a side of Capek civilization I had not expected to see—a cold and unfeeling approach to problem solving that allowed them to look at their military capabilities with a pragmatic and efficient mind. If, as Skinfaxi had mentioned, very few Capeks had weapons, then destroying Yggdrassil and others with manufacturing capabilities would leave us all helpless.

I looked at Aurvandil, a tall and beautiful artificial entity. More piece of art than tool, his body didn't seem to have the obvious tailored uses other Capeks exhibited. His slow, graceful gestures and deliberate cadence of speech indicated a less physical being. A thinker or perhaps an artist. He and others like him would fall like wheat under the scythe before a monster like Anhur.

"Who is the closest Gaia to Yggdrassil?"

My own navigation systems answered at almost the same time as our entrancing host.

"Hera."

"We have to warn her," Faxi said.

"Not so fast, brother," Aurvandil warned, raising a hand to halt whatever my companion was about to do. "Lucretiuses are incredibly advanced and well-equipped Capeks. If Anhur knows you've escaped him, he will probably do his best to keep a warning from reaching Hera, and I have no doubt that he is capable of it."

"We have to warn her ourselves—and fast."

"Mmmh . . . If Anhur's out there knowing we escaped his clutches, then he might still be hunting us down. You're asking us to swim in shark-infested waters."

Aurvandil paced for a moment, rubbing what would pass for his chin in a very human display of concentration.

"Then I'll have to ask a more foolhardy Sputnik for a lift," he finally said in a strained voice. "I wanted to keep the evolving crisis between us for now, but I would feel better if you did avoid any heroics, my brother."

Either Aurvandil did not know much about Skinfaxi, or he knew him too well. Even I was aware that this kind of talk would only fire up my large friend's ego. Sure enough . . .

"Aha! No, no, no. If there is a Sputnik who will claim the title of savior of Hera, it will be me. And don't think I don't see what you're doing, brother. Well played."

"I know what to expect from you, Skinfaxi."

OLYMPUS—HIGH ORBIT ABOVE TARTARUS

The trip to Olympus, the moon where Hera was installed, was long but quiet. An interesting detail about life as a Capek is the infinite possibilities our internal systems provide. Each of us can sit still for days without moving, focusing solely on whatever project, studies, or even games we might be running within our own minds.

Aurvandil looked like he was meditating, sitting cross-legged, floating in the vacuum of Skinfaxi's inner bridge, the hands of his long arms resting on his knees, his robotic chin high. What was he contemplating? Or was he communicating with friends and collaborators?

When I wasn't observing my companions, I spent the long hours reviewing technical information and familiarizing myself with some of the basics of Capek anatomy. It was one thing to have access to the information with little more than a thought, but I needed more. The knowledge had to become a part of me.

Koalemos was restless. Though mostly motionless, he'd often twitch one of his shards or fire his thruster array for no reason. If anyone had reason to fear being ambushed by Anhur, surely it was him. While Skinfaxi and I had escaped narrowly, he had suffered a traumatizing injury from the event.

Skinfaxi was also unusually quiet. Occasionally, he would send me batches of data to help analyze—anomalies in stellar displacements or long-range sensor readings that did not sit well with him, or any possible clue to Anhur's presence or passage. So far, nothing. If the giant Lucretius was out there, he was being very subtle about it.

It was an incredible relief when we arrived at Olympus unmolested. Seeing Tartarus, the dark gas giant, was unsettling at first, its surface covered in constant storms of green lightning, around which Hera's home orbited. Thankfully, after completing a thorough sensor sweep of the area from our comfortable position close to the collapsor point, we confirmed that there were no other Capeks roaming around the system.

"Welcome, children," came Hera's deep, motherly voice over open channels. "I've been waiting for you."

"Skinfaxi?" Aurvandil asked so only me and the large Sputnik could hear. "I thought we had agreed not to contact Hera?"

"No worries, brother," he answered. "It was Proioxis who sent the message, and only to inform Hera of her broken child."

"Ah," the elegant Capek replied.

We made our approach to the bright-gray moon of Olympus. It was strangely similar in both size and configuration to Midgard. Even Hera had very few superficial differences to Yggdrassil. Just like my progenitor, she was composed of several large structures, all laid out around a central hub crowned with a tall tower that reached for the heavens.

"Greetings, Mother Hera," began Aurvandil with much ceremony. "We have on board your son Koalemos. He is in great need of your care. He heroically sacrificed one of his shards to save two of my siblings."

"Oh, Koalemos . . . The poor little thing. He was never meant for acts of bravery. Bring him to me, my little builder. I will do what I can for him."

There was infinite tenderness and care in the voice. I was reminded of a human mother fretting over a son with a broken leg after a soccer accident. Such a specific memory . . .

"We also bear dire news," I added, to which Aurvandil raised a finger to his "lips," attempting to keep me silent, but I continued. "Your sister, I guess—Yggdrassil—has been destroyed, along with the moon Midgard."

"I see," the great Capek answered after a pause. "I feared as much after losing contact with her. You, little one, are her last child, are you not?"

"Yes." I felt humbled by the attention. When speaking with Yggdrassil, my own progenitor, there was a familiarity and comfort I did not feel with Hera. Instead, there was a majesty to her that demanded reverence.

"I want to hear of her last moments, child. Tell me as I tend to my son's wounds."

She sounded so human, her feelings so genuine. I could sense the cracks in her composure as she juggled her emotions. The worry for Koalemos, the loss of Yggdrassil, and the need to maintain her regal demeanor before our group.

"I . . . I managed to save her Nursery. To remove its mnemonic core . . ."

Aurvandil cocked his head at this information, reminding me that we had completely skipped over that particular detail earlier. Concerned with more important things, I ignored the gesture.

"Very clever, child. By doing so, you've saved what is most important to a mother: her children."

Jonathan.

We landed in one of the two large hangars and exited Skinfaxi. The large Sputnik did not bother to deploy a remote, preferring instead to witness events vicariously through us. He made a point of requesting more telepresence drones from our host, a favor she seemed glad to provide.

Koalemos brought his shards over to a corner of the hangar. He moved with uncharacteristic stability, as if guided by an external force—most likely Hera. Once he was in place, a series of tools descended upon him to begin work on repairing him as much as was possible. I couldn't help but notice that one of the shards was kept apart from the rest, held in place by powerful clamps that restricted its movement.

"Mother Hera," I said over a closed quancom channel. "The files I was given by Yggdrassil regarding Koalemos list him as a septuanian construct, yet, including the missing shard, there are eight."

"And you noticed me isolating one just now," she answered. "That shard is not part of my son. It is an aberration implanted there to manipulate him. I intend to rip the secrets of its origins out of it. I was afraid you and your companions might have been responsible but—"

"Why would we have brought him here to be discovered then?"

"Exactly."

We walked deeper into the complex, Aurvandil and I, accompanied by the disembodied presences of both Hera and Skinfaxi.

"How long will brave Koalemos's repairs take, Mother Hera?" asked Aurvandil, who had remained quiet ever since my interruption. Was he mad at me for disobeying him? I wouldn't think speaking about Yggdrassil's fate was such a big deal. Hera would have found out eventually.

"Oh, it will take time, my friend. Over a day to be sure. Probably more. I will not bore you with the details, but a large portion of his neural pathways need reconstruction."

My ego was a little bruised. I had made a conservative estimate of about twelve hours of work, considering the massive capabilities of a Gaia-class Capek, and had been fairly happy with the quality of my work on the little Von Neumann. Apparently, I had overestimated myself. I guess there was only so much to expect from a first try.

"I apologize if my attempts to save him proved insufficient," I said.

"Do not worry about it," she said before switching back to a closed channel. "Your work was impeccable, little one. Koalemos will be as close to healed as anyone can make him within six hours."

"But you just said . . ."

"I have my reasons."

After a lengthy trek we ended up at the central hub of Hera. I had seen these same machines before, if significantly less intact. Everything was as it had been within Yggdrassil's heart, but with less burnt pseudo-plastic and torn metal. Passageways were easy to navigate and well lit, eventually leading us to the seat of Hera's Nursery.

"Here, last child of Yggdrassil. Connect your mother's Nursery to mine. I will take care of her children as if they were my own."

I dug up the schematics necessary to do a proper installation of the mnemonic core. It was still a hack job by any measure, but it was sufficient to effect a data transfer. Considering the little block of memory contained the time-frozen information of an entire world's history, billions of personalities going through hundreds of cycles, the transfer would likely take some time.

As I put the finishing touches on the installation, letting Hera handle the specifics of initiating the actual copy of data, Aurvandil was walking around looking at the intricate mechanisms that made up the awesome creature that was a Gaia-class Capek. It occurred to me that in all likelihood very few Capeks had the opportunity to see this side of their progenitors. Both the technically minded and philosophically inclined would indeed marvel at these sights and what they represented.

"Mother Hera," I asked, again in private, "is it possible to extract a specific personality from a Nursery?"

"Of course. That is how you, your siblings, and all third-generation Capeks are born. Once you've gone through enough cycles that you attain Nirvana, the state of being we consider necessary to adapt to the infinite possibilities of existence as a Capek, then you are plucked from the Nursery. I believe you know the rest."

"What about a personality that hasn't reached Nirvana?"

"It can be extracted, but there are too many things that can go wrong, from catastrophic culture shock to personality defects."

"Oh."

I became introspective at that point, unsure why I was so obsessed with the idea of the Nursery and somehow getting back in contact with those within. According to Yggdrassil, I and any third-generation Capek alive today had "lived" hundreds of successive lifetimes, reincarnating after each, learning, evolving, and refining our personalities. I had probably met hundreds of thousands of people during those lives, the echoes of their memories becoming the building blocks of who I am. Why would I want to reach in and pluck out a specific one?

It was hard to tell how long I'd been pondering the issue when suddenly a familiar phenomenon snapped me out of my reverie. For a second the weak gravity of the moon of Olympus vanished and in fact reversed a little.

"Faxi?" I said over open channel, my voice pregnant with worry and fear.

"Space fold right above us," he answered with a measurable amount of alarm.

"Is it Anhur?" I thought I already knew the answer.

"Yes! And Pele, another Lucretius Capek, and three other large Sputniks."

What was going on? This sounded like a full-fledged invasion fleet. If Pele was anything like Anhur, there was little chance that we'd be able to escape with our lives.

"We cannot stay here," Aurvandil cut in, his voice commanding and sure. "If our suspicions are correct, then they are here to destroy Hera."

"We can't just abandon her!" I protested.

"We won't." His answer was confident, giving me hope. "Mother Hera? Please, eject your mnemonic core. We will take you to safety."

The plan was daring but efficient. We would save what was crucial of Hera—her personalities and memories, along with her Nursery. The essence of her being would go on. We would find a way to build her a new body.

"No."

"Please, Hera," Aurvandil begged. "We don't have much time."

"I refuse. I will stay and defend myself and my children."

"Then you leave us no choice," the elegant Capek announced sadly. "Dagir, can you cut her out so we can take her with us? I'm sure once we reconnect her and rebuild her she will see it was for the best."

For a moment I did not know what to do. I couldn't disobey Hera's wishes, but at the same time I could not bear the loss of another Gaia. Their value to Capek society was too great. Aurvandil was right: she would see reason once things were settled.

I rushed over to where her mnemonic and personality cores were connected and began pulling the necessary systems out. This was a more complex operation than ripping the Nursery from Yggdrasil, but I had to work fast. I did not need Skinfaxi to tell me, but I suspected torpedoes and other large-scale weapons were being fired on us. That was without taking into account whatever methods of internal defense she might be deploying at this very moment. Why couldn't I go anywhere without it exploding around me?

"Don't do this, child!" Hera implored in private.

"I'm sorry. I have to," I answered, more to myself than anyone else.

Before she could plead with me further, I unsheathed my plasma cutter and severed her personality core from the complex's network. Aurvandil was waiting, ready to take it from me so I could repeat the process on her memory core, which I also handed him.

"Come!" he called urgently as he ran back the way we'd come.

I followed for a moment but quickly turned back, retracing my steps. I grabbed Yggdrasil's Nursery and yanked it free.

I caught up with Aurvandil just as he was running through the hangar toward Skinfaxi, taking bounding steps in the moon's low gravity. The enormous roof had opened up, exposing the sky, half empty black space and half Tartarus's dark clouds. I recognized Anhur's terrible form, spines and all, hovering overhead. Lower in orbit, a slightly smaller but still enormous creature undulated through the sky, like an immense centipede. Powerful engines propelled the second Lucretius, throwing off long columns of fire from all over its body.

"Pele," I muttered, awestruck.

I turned back to continue my desperate run toward Skinfaxi. My friend and companion was already moving to pick up Aurvandil as the first of Anhur's torpedoes impacted the complex.

The hangar was hit hard, and I barely saw Skinfaxi run full speed into the elegant Capek he called "brother," knocking him down like a rag doll before angling upward, pulling out at full thrust through the opening. I couldn't tell if this had been accidental or not. I'd seen Skinfaxi navigate the crumbling remains of an asteroid at high speed. It didn't seem that even this sort of impact should have shaken him so.

Massive concussive shocks knocked me into a wall, and I was hard-pressed to keep my grasp on Yggdrassil's Nursery. Through the clouds of dust and broken debris, I saw a large Sputnik, the one that had been floating outside the domed window of Babylon, hovering next to a shaken but otherwise intact Aurvandil. The tall Capek, still holding on to the components of Hera, looked around and spotted me before climbing on board his accomplice and taking off. Abandoning me.

"Faxi?" I asked, unsure of what was happening.

"Sorry, little buddy, I had to dust off. Things were getting too hot down there."

I couldn't argue with him. "What about Koalemos?"

"I'm on board," the little Capek replied. "Beware, Dagir. Aurvandil is not a friend."

That much was obvious at this point. I should have listened to Hera. There was little time for recriminations, however, as I needed to figure a way to escape Olympus—and soon.

"Guys? Any idea how I get off this rock?"

"Don't be worried. You aren't without help," the Von Neumann reassured.

I looked up to the sky. The signature glow of two dozen thrusters, betraying another volley of incoming torpedoes, cut through the rising dust cloud. From Hera's second hangar, violently pushing themselves upward, dozens of small rockets appeared on the horizon. A veritable arsenal had been unleashed on the heavens at once, and I would not care to be the one on the receiving end.

Instead of watching the spectacle, however, I decided to put my efforts toward remaining intact.

"I choose life," I mumbled, quoting Koalemos's desperate plea.

Once again I found myself climbing to the top of a hangar. This time, however, I had a much more solid understanding of what was happening around me.

When I reached the hangar's roof and pulled myself onto the side of the sliding ceiling, I looked up to see Pele covered in concussive blasts, being chewed apart by a hundred small explosions. She'd known. Hera had known and prepared. That's why she gave Aurvandil an inflated estimate of Koalemos's repair schedule. She was buying time.

As Pele broke apart, slowly pulled in by Olympus's weak gravity, Anhur was carefully breaking orbit, his lethal payload delivered. It didn't matter anymore. Assuming these invading Capeks were here to capture Hera's memory and personality cores, then their mission was accomplished.

Once again this left me stranded, with more torpedoes incoming and nowhere to run. I couldn't climb high enough for the explosions to throw me into orbit, and considering what was waiting for me there, I doubted I'd want to anyway.

I braced for impact, trusting that Skinfaxi and Koalemos would make it off-world safely. I held on tight to the Nursery, regretful that I had not been able to save it or Hera's. It had been a short life, all things considered, but the things I'd seen!

"Grab on, hold on, and make it tight!"

I looked up to see a strange craft, perhaps four meters in length, sleek and aerodynamic. It resembled a smooth white plastic sunflower seed but was all engines and thrusters.

With little hesitation I hopped on. As I did, a small hatch opened out of nowhere.

"You're gonna need those hands for holding," the ship said urgently.

I wasn't sure I could trust this newcomer. What if it was a ploy to take the Nursery from me? What if it wasn't? It didn't matter; anywhere was safer than here for my precious payload. I dropped it into the new Capek.

"Fantastic and excellent. Now grab on—this is gonna get . . . wild!"

And it did. Whoever this Capek was, it was built for speed, maneuverability, and acceleration. With no atmosphere to cause friction, little gravity to hold it back, and no biology to worry about, there was no limit to what a well-built Capek could do. Before I could protest, we had accelerated to what my systems told me was over fifty thousand kilometers an hour.

My new friend aimed straight for the incoming torpedoes, dodging between them before any could react and intercept. In fact, this Capek was moving faster against the gravity well than the incoming missiles were toward the moon.

After the torpedoes, we had to weave through the debris that had once been the Lucretius-class Capek Pele. Taking a moment to look around, I noticed four more ships more or less exactly like the one I was attached to—another Von Neumann.

As we cleared the last of Pele's vestiges, I saw that we were heading straight for Anhur, his overwhelming and terrible presence looming ever larger in my field of view.

"Watch this! We're going to mess with that guy!"

My new companion seemed to almost be shouting, even though we were communicating through quancom. I wanted to protest that I'd rather make a clean escape than mess with a Capek of the destructive capabilities of Anhur, and that our payload was too precious to risk on childish stunts. Yet there was something about the self-assurance of my ride and savior that made me trust him and whatever he had in mind.

When we got close enough to the leviathan, my ride engaged his faster-than-light engines and surprised me by creating a gravity shift of enormous proportions. Instead of the space-time distortions of an Alcubierre drive I was expecting, I felt trapped in a crushing gravity field so powerful I could see it affect the gargantuan Capek we were flying toward. Then another part of the galaxy was pulled right between us and Anhur.

The lumbering behemoth became partially stuck in the field of overlapping reality, too large to go through the space fold, but too slow to escape its pull. As we passed him, flying at incredible speed while making barrel rolls, we moved on to a different part of the Milky Way, and once we had gone through, my new friend terminated the space fold.

Five of Anhur's thruster spines had crossed over with us, and when the universe snapped back into place, the molecule-thin portions of him that were neither here nor there were stretched across light-years, severing the pieces clean off their original host and leaving them to drift, broken, in space.

"Ooooh yes!" my new companion shouted in victory. "A clean break, if I do say so myself."

There was no small amount of bravado in its voice—not that I wasn't grateful for the timely rescue.

"Yeah. That was very good." I tried to share its enthusiasm. "Um, to whom do I owe my thanks?"

"I am Hermes, at your service."

RETURN TO BABYLON

There was no stranger feeling. After the space fold, I was left floating astride a bizarre Capek out in interplanetary space. It took a moment for my navigation to pinpoint exactly where he had taken me, though knowing didn't make me feel any better. Stars were tiny points of light in the distance. I couldn't see any planets, not even on long-range sensors. If we were within a solar system, we were so near its edge for it not to matter.

I'd maneuvered myself to sit on one of Anhur's dismembered thruster-spines. I did not feel comfortable riding a strange Capek and was getting disoriented floating around with no point of reference.

Hermes had excused himself, saying his attention was needed elsewhere. From our short discussion, I gathered that he was an odd cross between a Von Neumann– and a Sputnik-class. Much like Skinfaxi, he was a born traveler and enjoyed moving around the galaxy, seeing new places, meeting new people. Where my first companion was more interested in transporting passengers, Hermes was a messenger, carrying sensitive information and small goods or serving as a mobile quancom node. He offered to take me with him, but I opted to stay after securing his promise that he'd come back for me.

I wanted to inspect the broken pieces of the malicious Lucretius that had been hunting my friends and me through the galaxy. It helped keep my mind off of Skinfaxi's and Koalemos's fates, but more importantly, I was hoping to find some clue as to why explorers like Anhur and Pele had abandoned their vocation in favor of violence against their own kind.

As luck would have it, the damage done to Anhur unlocked the files I had on the leviathan. This was a twofold blessing. It allowed me complete and unrestricted access to everything about the functioning of this Capek—a precious resource considering how dangerous and secretive his kind were reputed to be. The other good news was that Hermes's daring prank must have done considerable damage to the monster.

There was a lot to learn about Anhur and the whole Lucretius line of Capeks. In broad terms they were sentient cities designed to fly the gulf between galaxies on great explorations. The personalities that were adequate for this kind of mission, the level of isolation and independence that were to last thousands of years, were difficult to find in a Nursery. Those like Anhur were equipped with every conceivable technology, up to refineries and fabrication complexes. A Lucretius was thus capable of consuming materials to assemble new items, systems, or automatons. Aside from the multiple types of propulsion systems available to them, they were also equipped with a primitive version of a Nursery, a virtual world where they could store their personalities to better endure the trials of intergalactic travel.

"I'm back," Hermes called out all of a sudden. His prideful exuberance was gone. "You have to come with me."

I latched onto the little ship as he once more folded space for the convenience of fast travel to distant places. This time, however, I recognized the destination: we were going back to the City—or so I thought.

As we approached Ziggurat, I could somehow tell that something wasn't quite right.

"When Hera realized who had sabotaged my little brother Koalemos," Hermes explained, "she contacted me. I'm one of the fastest Capeks in the Milky Way, so she wanted me to come and assist you in saving what was most important to her. I also went out to warn as many of the other Gaias as I could. I sent messages to some but had to visit others."

I felt terrible. I had been so focused on saving the legacy of my own progenitor that I hadn't been able to take Hera's with me. I lacked the background necessary to truly understand what this might mean for Hermes and Koalemos's people.

"You think Aurvandil's going after the other Gaias?"

"So far he hasn't, but his actions have messed things up anyway."

I quickly saw what he meant. By the time we reached Babylon, there was very little of it left. The great city had been ravaged; large portions of it had crumbled into the clouds below, vanishing into the crushing depths of the atmosphere. Small dots swarmed around the ruined citadel, scrambling to either minimize damage or look for Capeks that might have been damaged in what I assumed was an attack.

"That's more than just 'messing things up,'" I mumbled. "What happened?"

"That other Lucretius, Pele, attacked here before going to Tartarus. She destroyed the City."

I had to brace myself, and Hermes was forced to slow down as we entered the thick atmosphere of Ziggurat. The careful approach allowed me to take stock of the destruction. Sputniks were zipping around collecting other Capeks incapable of flight from the more unstable portions of the City. There was no question that the entire structure would eventually fail and plummet, to be consumed by the storms in the lower atmosphere. The plants inside Babylon already showed signs of withering from exposure to the caustic gases that enveloped Ziggurat at this altitude.

"I'm dropping you off here. You're needed," Hermes said before leaving me on the side of a terrace and taking off.

I took stock of the grounds and realized why he'd brought me to this specific location. This trip wasn't for my benefit, despite the helpful exposition. Half a dozen Capeks lay broken and damaged around the terrace, collected and deposited here in a make-shift infirmary so they could hopefully be saved. Another Capek, shaped like a horrendous long-legged spider, was already stalking amongst the victims, giving care where it could.

I started work immediately, giving my attention to a large Sputnik resting on the terrace. Looking like a streamlined hump-back whale and almost as large, the poor thing listed to one side, immobile like a beached carcass. Its hull showed signs of severe compression damage.

"He dived down into Ziggurat, too deep, to save a Capek who had fallen," came a soft, familiar voice.

"Proioxis." I turned to see the snakelike Capek winding her way gracefully between the victims. "Are you okay?"

"Yes, thanks to Opochtli here. Can you help him?"

She had been the one who fell into the depths. I couldn't imagine a worse demise, and despite my youth I had faced destruction enough times to consider myself a fair judge. To plummet for hours, enduring ever-increasing heat and pressure, systems failing one after another, each moment making it less and less likely to be saved, was the stuff of nightmares.

"I will do my best." I began pulling out information on the great damaged Sputnik. "How did you manage to make it unscathed?"

"I am caretaker of Phoenix World, a planet that I am terraforming to support life once more. I am built to thrive in all environments my ward can provide, including the crushing depths of its oceans."

I nodded and began work on Opochtli. My first priority was making sure he was stable and that none of his systems, physical or otherwise, were in any danger of developing further irreparable damage. If he was stable, I would have to abandon him and move on to the next victim.

The work was relentless. With Proioxis's help I cut off one of the giant's long lateral fins to gain access to his main service hatch. Thankfully, Capeks didn't experience pain, or rather, could only if they wished to.

"Opochtli? Do you hear me, big guy?" I asked as I stepped into his guts.

"I hear you," the whale groaned.

"Opochtli. That's a Mayan name?"

"Aztec. My progenitor is Coatlicue."

"Excellent. I'm going to be doing a few strange things to your cognitive core. Let me know if anything feels out of place. Also, don't worry if I keep asking the same questions over and over."

"Acknowledged."

His voice was deep, calm, and melodious. I doubt he would have been able to remain this serene were he seeing what I was. The lower atmosphere where he had delved was composed of thick clouds of sulfur dioxide, which apparently remained lodged inside the breached sections of his body, compounding the damage. His surface components suffered massive corrosion, making repairs more complicated and riskier.

"Your friend did this," he said as I took apart the framework that kept his various cognitive systems firmly in place.

"No friend of mine would do such a thing, and you shouldn't speak. You need me to concentrate."

"Aurvandil. He's been plotting this for a while," he continued, his deep voice strained in its urgency.

"How would you know?" I didn't want to sound like I was defending Aurvandil.

"He has been preaching his strange brand of emancipation for centuries. No one thought he meant anything by it. Clearly, we were wrong to ignore him."

"All right. I really need you to be quiet now."

"No! This is important. Ask Proioxis. She'll tell you what Aurvandil, the great thinker, is really up to."

Capek society functions at a strange pace. On one hand, events can happen at an incredible rate, from the construction of a vast arsenal like Hera built while waiting for Anhur's attack, to the quickly cascading events that led to my current situation. On the other hand, certain things were slower and afforded more leeway.

It took us days to repair or stabilize all the wounded Capeks from the City, leaving some without care or attention for terrifyingly long periods. Yet we managed a survival rate of nearly 100 percent. Some victims would never be the same, irreplaceable systems damaged beyond repair, but almost all would survive, adapt, and thrive once more, given time.

Murugan, the other Capek who had been giving care to the fallen, was an indispensable ally, quickly taking charge and directing us. Bes, a swarming Von Neumann that joined our effort, and I were able to better capitalize on our various skills and strengths.

I was curious to learn that other Capeks of similar vocation were not equipped with the vast database of technical specification I had been blessed with. In fact, Murugan shot me a suspicious look (I think) when he realized how much I knew about each of our broken patients.

Technically, Bes wasn't dedicated to rescue and repair the same way Murugan and I were. His vocation was art and construction, skills that came in handy in rebuilding limbs and repairing complex pieces of machinery that were vital parts of our fallen wards. Being made of dozens of bug-sized shards, each shaped like a scarab and equipped with a different tool, he was capable of fine molecular welding and reshaping metals and pseudo-plastic perfectly to the specifications we gave him.

Midway through our operations, we relocated aboard Suijin, the largest Sputnik-class Capek I had seen—large enough to rival Anhur in scale, though unfortunately not in firepower.

From Suijin's main deck, designed for observation and survey, we all witnessed the final moments of Babylon. To be fair, the collapse did not conveniently occur moments after our departure. Once completely evacuated, the City was intentionally collapsed to avoid further incident.

Once the demolition effort was complete, my improvised team and I delved back into our repair efforts. By the time we were finished, all wounded Capeks were sufficiently functional to no longer require our care, and we had moved away from Ziggurat and off into interstellar space.

I stood by the edge of Suijin's great transparent dome, which resembled a crystal shell on a giant turtle's back. Stars streaked by in the distance as we traveled, using the colossal Sputnik's Alcubierre drive. Many other spacefaring Capeks rode within the same space-time bubble, like dolphins swimming in a ship's wake.

With no small amount of satisfaction and relief, I saw Opochtli fly with slow, deliberate grace between his peers. He slid comfortably next to the great transparent dome, close to me. We were separated by a thick layer of translucent pseudo-plastic, a pressurized atmosphere, and the vacuum of space, yet at a distance of only a few meters. It was difficult not to be in awe of such wonders.

"Thank you," the great whale said.

"I'm sorry it's not perfect," I said, though I knew I had nothing to be ashamed of. "There are some things that were beyond my capabilities to repair."

"Superficial details. Inconsequential in the grand scheme of things. Scars I will gladly bear as a reminder of those that did not fare as well as I. Now, go speak with Proioxis."

With that he flew away from the window, rejoining the small fleet of Sputniks that accompanied us on our journey. I could see all six of Hermes's bodies flying with them, doing barrel rolls and acrobatics to keep busy. I was in awe of Opochtli. I, more than any other, had seen the damage he'd suffered to save a fellow Capek. From that I could easily see our human origin.

I walked over to Proioxis. I could just as easily have opened a channel to her directly and spoken with her over quancom, yet I was discovering and enjoying a sort of etiquette amongst my people. While there was nothing stopping any of us from using more efficient and impersonal means of communications, there was a joy in meeting with someone face to face, or whatever passed as faces, to discuss matters of importance.

I found Proioxis looking out at the passing stars. Many of us passengers were pulled into a desperate melancholy. There had been few casualties, but the confusion and uncertainty weighed heavily on the survivors.

"Out there my world is being left untended and unprotected," Proioxis said as I got near.

For machines, Capeks were remarkably expressive, each using its unique kind of body language to communicate emotions and intent. Proioxis, despite her snakelike appearance and rigid expression, managed to look sad and worried. Her head hung low on her long body, but she still looked up through the segmented glass dome.

"Does your world need to be defended that badly?" I asked, ignorant of what was at stake.

"Maybe."

"Opochtli said you might know something about why all of this is happening."

"Maybe," she repeated. "Do you know why I tend a planet's biosphere? Why I dedicate my potentially eternal life to growing an ecosystem when there is literally nothing for me to gain from the effort?"

"I'm assuming it has to do with the personality you developed in the Nursery. That it's the sort of activity you learned to love and cherish and that provides you with a goal you find fulfilling."

"Yes, but why was this personality, amongst billions that were nurtured and refined through hundreds of cycles, chosen? Why was I deemed ready above all?"

I didn't have an answer. Surely, through the billion lives in over a dozen Nurseries throughout the thousands of years of Capek history, more than the few hundred individuals that roamed the galaxy were worthy. What separated those who got to be Capeks and those who simply kept living life after life in the virtual environment of a Gaia's Nursery?

"Capeks don't need thriving ecosystems," Proioxis continued. "Some might enjoy it, but deep down we are creatures of the void. I love my planet, my plants, my fish, my animals. The ecosphere I've built is such an intricately balanced puzzle that it's hard not to take tremendous pride and enjoyment from it. However, our essence as Capeks is to be children of the vacuum. We're creatures born to bask in the glow of foreign stars and bathe in the raw beauty of solar winds. We see the Lucretius class as bizarre and strange, but only because they are the least human of us. They are the most Capek of us all. They live for the great beyond."

"So what are you getting at?"

"We are chosen because we are the ones best suited to rebuilding this galaxy, but not for ourselves."

"For humanity," I concluded.

Ever since stepping out of the Nursery—and some would argue that even then didn't count—I hadn't laid eyes on a single human being. I had struggled with the duality of having a personality hewn from a block of human experience and marveled at Babylon's plant life as the first sign of biological life I witnessed, but I'd spent very little time wondering where the humans really were. Because I knew.

In my memory banks, implanted at birth, was a vague impression of where the humans had gone and why, but it was a footnote, an afterthought. We are made and live to experience what is most important to us. Skinfaxi and Hermes travel the galaxy, seeing new places and meeting new Capeks. Proioxis tends her world, lovingly building a biological paradise with a delicate and impossibly complex balance. I love to help others and keep them from harm. In doing these things, we are content. So humanity's return is inevitable, perhaps even imminent, on an astronomical scale. So what? We'll transport them too, tend their planets, and I'll learn biology to protect them.

"For humanity," she confirmed. "When they eventually emerge from the Dormitory Worlds, we will have built them a galaxy in which to thrive. That is what separates us from those still in the Nurseries."

"Is that a bad thing?"

"No. Maybe. I don't think so. When they do return, our priorities will change. Perhaps some of us will go back. Perhaps there will be a fourth generation of Capeks that will spawn from those left behind. It's for us to decide when the time comes."

I liked this horizon she was describing. Instinctively, I looked back across the dome and into space at the six dancing ships that floated with us alongside Suijin. Hermes still had Yggdrassil's Nursery with him, and in that so many possibilities.

"But what does any of this have to do with this . . . massacre?" I asked, my gaze falling once more on Proioxis's snakelike features.

"Some of us aren't happy doing humanity's work. Some think they are a relic of the past, their own purpose served in creating Capeks. It is their opinion that we should not wait to forge our destiny. Clearly, they have tired of the philosophical debate."

I understood then why Aurvandil was doing what he did. Did I agree with it? Thinking of the precious cargo hidden inside Hermes's shard, I couldn't help but see his point a little. How long did we have to wait before we could be reunited with those we left behind once we were chosen? Did it matter if we couldn't remember them, or vice versa? Clearly, some had decided on a preferred direction and believed in it strongly enough to resort to violence. *Jonathan.*

Our little fleet of refugees wandered through space for several days. Bes took the opportunity to further perfect the repairs he'd done on the victims of Babylon's destruction. By the time we reached our destination, those wounded in the attack were all as good as new except Opochtli, who chose to keep his scars as he had promised.

I hadn't thought to ask where we might be going. Smarter, more experienced Capeks had already made that decision, and I didn't think it my place to question them.

As it turned out, we arrived at a planet in orbit around a twin-star system. It was called Aumakua and was only slightly bigger than Earth but with a much denser composition. Around it circled a single satellite, comically name Hina after the Hawaiian goddess of the moon. On Hina's surface I could see the familiar outlines of a Gaia complex.

My records identified her as Haumea, and she was resplendent. I never had the opportunity to behold Yggdrassil in all her glory. By the time I was in orbit around Midgard, she had been devastated by meteor strikes. Hera had been all but dormant when we arrived, waiting to take care of her broken child. Haumea was pristine and busy doing what her particular class of Capek did best—building.

Lights covered her facilities, indicating warnings and signals to the swarm of flying remotes, drones, and other Capeks that buzzed around her like fireflies. The first of her large hangars was open, and a colossal component was being painstakingly lifted from it toward the sky. From a distance it looked like a powerful thruster assembly for an enormous Capek. Sputnik- or Lucretius-class. I could see the component's destination; in geosynchronous orbit high above Haumea, a partially assembled ship waited to be completed.

There was no mistaking it—whoever this new Capek was, he would be dedicated to war. This seemed to distress Proioxis deeply, and after the long discussion about purpose and destiny that we shared, I could understand why. Another compelling argument in favor of leaving certain personalities within the looping cycles of their Nursery was that in some cases there was simply no room for them in this galaxy.

Seeing the partially completed creature, with its sleek lines, versatile propulsion system, and more importantly, a variety of weapons designed to handle most tactical challenges that could be thrown its way, I couldn't help but feel sorry for the nascent Capek. For the time being we had a use for his kind, but in the end there was really no place for him here.

"She calls him Ukupanipo. That's the name of a shark god," Proioxis explained sadly. "She weeps for him and what he may have to do."

"Who? Haumea? Then why build him at all?" It was strange to feel bad for a Capek that once finished would be the most terrible war machine in the galaxy.

"What else can she do? Most of the other Gaias refuse to do more than build defenses, but Capeks can potentially live forever. How long do we hide in fear of another attack?"

I hated that she was probably right, and I couldn't help but wonder what would become of Ukupanipo once this dispute was over. Assuming we came out the other side triumphant, of course. If he was built for war—a general, army, and arsenal rolled into one—what would be his purpose after the dust settled? The expression goes that when all you have is a hammer, it doesn't take long before everything starts to look like a nail. How long would the shark god remain our hero before he inevitably became a villain?

We stood at the edge of the dome on the great Capek Suijin's back, all survivors of Babylon—some inside, some outside—and witnessed the birth of another Capek. A brother, a savior, a warrior . . . a god.

Once all the components were assembled, the personality uploaded, and the body properly activated, Haumea retracted her drones and remotes, allowing the giant shark to take its first tentative steps into the galaxy. And it did look like a shark too! Not much. Just a little. It had more fins, and the tail wasn't sufficiently defined, but it was sleek, menacing, and graceful. If I could, I would have surely felt a shiver down my spine as the leviathan swam through the vacuum, past us, and then into the void.

Space had never been a safe place. A deadly vacuum, cosmic radiation, fast-moving objects, and unpredictable solar phenomena all contributed to an environment that was anathema to biological life but embraced the Capek race. Anhur had been an anomaly, a dangerous mutation of the Capek presence in the Milky Way. A danger to be removed. A threat that could be destroyed with the appropriate effort. What we had just seen swim out into the ocean of emptiness was a predator, and we had unleashed it in our waters.

RESCUE

It didn't take long for me to grow restless waiting for things to happen. For one, Haumea was a terrible host. After Ukupanipo's departure on whatever his mission was, she had immediately begun production of another sentient war machine. We were allowed to land, which was not necessary or even possible for all of us, but it did bring those who could into the sphere of her protection.

Most other Capeks there clearly felt useless, though some were quickly enlisted into helping with the improvised war effort. Bes in particular was rapidly pressed into service, providing his versatile and impressive fabricator talents to help build the more complex components of the emerging Capek. The rest, deprived of their purpose and ill-suited to help, were reduced to milling about or orbiting Hina helplessly.

"I don't think I can do this for much longer," I complained to Murugan as he helped sort and shuttle parts that would be used in assembling our new brother.

"Then do something."

"I can't help with what you're doing. I'm not good at building."

"It's not that different from repairing to be honest." His many limbs moved with fluid grace and impeccable coordination.

"I politely disagree. Building is about shaping purpose into form. Repair is more a question of finding solutions to immediate problems."

"You're exaggerating the philosophical differences. You have tools, there are instructions. Apply the first to the second, and you are building." He paused. "I think you are intentionally avoiding contributing."

"I'm not lazy, if that's what you're implying." I was probably a little more offended than I should have been.

"I don't doubt it. I think your opposition is of a much more ethical nature, but if you're not going to help here, then you should help elsewhere. You're a rescue and repair specialist, aren't you? Why not do some of that?"

Until we were attacked, if ever that came to pass, there was no one for me to help. There might be other attacks elsewhere, other Capeks that might currently need my attention, but I couldn't know where, and without Skinfaxi I had no way to get to them.

Or did I? What if Skinfaxi and Koalemos were the ones that required my help? Why else would they not have contacted me? After all, through quancom I was never really out of reach. Unless the nodes were taken out.

"Opochtli?" I called out to the large whale in orbit around our moon.

"Yes, Dagir. How may I be of service?"

"I know you've already done more than your fair share of daring deeds for a lifetime, but how would you feel about some more heroics?"

"A lifetime can be long for a Capek. Surely I can squeeze in a few more death-defying episodes," he said. "What do you have in mind?"

"Pick me up, and I'll tell you on the way."

By the time Opochtli had descended, I had explained my plan to him, although it wasn't so much a plan as a vague idea of what to do, a goal shining in the distance.

"If your friends haven't been able to contact you through quancom, you'll forgive me for saying, they are likely destroyed by now."

Opochtli did not mince words, and I liked that about him. He was probably right too. I knew both Skinfaxi and Koalemos had the necessary resources to get in contact with me if they needed to, and with Faxi's interstellar travel capabilities, there was no reason they shouldn't have been able to join up with us.

"I have a hunch," I explained as we moved away from Hina. "Can Capeks have hunches? Or is that too much of a human thing?"

"You can have hunches. Free associative thinking and subconscious pattern recognition are not outside of our capabilities," he explained in his measured voice. "One could argue that you still have instincts as well. In the end it all just measures up to educated guesses, however."

"Well, I have an educated guess."

Opochtli's interior was vastly different from Skinfaxi's. There was no bridge. At least nothing like the spherical room inside my previous companion. Instead, a large portion of his belly was hollow, outfitted with a series of one-way see-through portholes that allowed a view of the exterior. This method of transport felt a lot more like a passenger plane from my time in the Nursery, complete with seats that could adjust to almost any size or shape within reason. A pointless luxury for our kind, but an interesting touch.

I looked through a porthole, watching Hina and the marginal security of Haumea's freshly built defense grid recede behind us. I couldn't be certain how our departure would be perceived. I had attempted to warn our host of my intentions but was only answered by cold, harsh silence. In the atmosphere of betrayal and suspicion Aurvandil had sewn, it was difficult to know if we too could be branded traitors to our kind. With both Anhur and Ukupanipo prowling this region of the galaxy, I wasn't looking to make new enemies.

At high speed, zipping from the soft-blue glow of Aumakua, I saw six silver missiles heading toward us. I immediately recognized the playful flight patterns of my savior from Olympus.

"Where are you going?" he asked.

"Ultimately, back to Tartarus and Hera, but we have a pit stop first."

"What are you? Suicidal?" he said, incredulous. "If you run into trouble, you won't stand a chance without me!"

I welcomed his bravado, but I had no plans to bring a small army on this fool's errand.

"Unless you just got outfitted with an arsenal in those shards of yours, I doubt you'd be much help against the trouble we're likely to encounter."

"Don't underestimate the raw power of my godlike piloting abilities. Besides, how do you propose to stop me from following you?"

He had a point, and I had seen firsthand Hermes's lack of basic self-preservation skills. That worried me, as he still held within one of his shards the Nursery's mnemonic core I had painstakingly rescued from Yggdrassil's destruction.

"Fine, but try to be discreet. We're not going anywhere we want to be noticed."

With those words the six sleek silver shards fell into formation, spiraling around Opochtli like children circling an ice-cream truck. I could almost feel the large Sputnik's annoyance, but soon enough we jumped into a collapsor point and into a wormhole.

"Where are we heading anyway?" Hermes asked as the stars streaked by outside the space-time conduit that moved us toward our destination.

"Well," I explained, "if I understand quancom correctly, over a certain range peer-to-peer communications are actually passed through relay stations on the network."

"Correct," Opochtli confirmed. "This allows for a much larger and reliable proliferation of the quancom network. However, it does not prevent a Capek with the proper equipment to bypass the relays and establish long-range contact regardless."

"But not all Capeks are able to get on and off the network on the fly."

"You're suggesting that we haven't heard of your friends because somehow the relay stations are compromised."

"Or destroyed," I added.

"Ah, but I know for a fact that my little brother Koalemos could perform the necessary adjustments on your friend Skinfaxi," explained Hermes.

"Actually, he can't," I corrected. "I performed the initial repairs on him after he lost a shard, and there are large data banks of technical specs that were wiped out or lost in the process. Swaths of things he'll have to relearn. I'm betting Hera didn't have time to rebuild that information. Regardless, I believe that it's worth checking out the quancom station nearest Tartarus. Aurvandil seemed to have a particular understanding of target priority in warfare. I think he's still applying that, and I think the next tactical step is to cripple our communications as much as possible."

"I still think it's much more likely your friends were destroyed," concluded Opochtli with much honesty but very little tact.

So perhaps my friends were gone, never having escaped Olympus after all. So be it. My point about Aurvandil's tactical acumen stood, and if our communications were indeed limited somehow, we needed to know, didn't we? Yet that wasn't why

Opochtli and Hermes had agreed to accompany me. The great whale probably felt he owed me, and was simply following his own code of honor. As for Hermes, the mission was foolish, dangerous, and with little potential for success, but he would be damned if he wasn't going to participate.

Whatever flaws the Nursery had filtered from my personality, it seemed nearsightedness had not quite been weeded out. The very second we arrived at the relay station, it dawned on me that I wasn't the only one who might have had the wherewithal to realize what Aurvandil's next move would be.

Clearly, the elegant Capek who had engineered this civil war had studied tactics and generalship. He'd admitted so much when he pointed out that Gaias, our only real weapons-manufacturing capabilities, would be a prime target. However, just hours before, we had been witness to the birth of one of us who was designed to be a warrior in every sense, whose entire purpose was to overthrow and annihilate the Renegades, and it was clear from the sight that greeted us that he agreed with my assessment of the situation.

"Well," I started as we popped out of our space-time bubble, "I should have expected that."

The relay station was destroyed. Judging by the drift of debris, the attack had taken place a short time ago. It had also been swift and decisive.

"I am detecting Capek parts," Opochtli announced. "Marian origins."

Marian Capeks, I found when I looked them up in my data banks, were the progeny of Mary, a Gaia whose naming structure was inspired by the Catholic mythos. I was surprised that monotheistic religions had found their way into our vocabulary.

"So, not Ukupanipo."

"Not a trace of him, but a quick postmortem of events seems to indicate that he was a very likely cause of what we see here."

So the war god of Haumea had been here, and instead of stopping his enemies from monopolizing the station, he simply destroyed it and moved on. What had been unleashed?

"Can we pick up the remains of that Marian Capek?" I asked, not knowing why that seemed important.

"Absolutely," Opochtli replied, immediately moving to do so.

The station was an absolute wreck. Whatever weapons Ukupanipo had used didn't simply disable the free-floating quancom relay but had torn it to pieces, scattering them over hundreds of thousands of kilometers in an ever-expanding cloud.

Hermes spread out at high speeds that only he seemed to be capable of, dodging between broken chunks of the station. The absence of debris from the great shark warrior indicated that the Capek aboard the relay did not even have a chance to return fire. Had he even been given a chance to surrender?

I evaded Opochtli to gather up the pieces of the Renegade who'd given his life for his cause. The file on this particular Capek opened quickly, giving me access to any technical information I might desire. Kerubiel was his name. A Leduc-class Capek particularly well adapted to zero-g activities. Before his destruction, he had measured a towering two and a half meters tall. His main body was reminiscent of a scarab, with powerful hind legs and two pairs of arms with fine manipulators. He'd been an expert at constructing structures in orbit, such as Babylon.

I hoped, while digging through his file, that there would be something, anything, that would set him apart as a Renegade—his origin, vocation, date of manufacture, a part with corrupted fabrication—but there was nothing. Finally, I could look deep into the soul and being of our enemies, and I could find no line that distinguished them from the rest of us.

One of Hermes's shards joined me in gathering the remains of Kerubiel, pushing them in my direction, stopping those that were escaping too fast. For a time I held on to the hope that perhaps I could reassemble him, fix him, and bring him back to life. After all, weren't we machines? Couldn't we be put back together when broken? Unfortunately, when I came upon his cognitive array, the various systems that made up a Capek's personality and memories, it was clear that there was nothing to be done.

"Dagir?" Hermes called from six places at once. "I might have found something of interest."

The announcement shook me out of a torpor I did not even know I had sunk into. How long had I been floating here, looking into the lifeless eyes of Kerubiel, like Hamlet into the eyes of the skull, as I pondered Capek mortality? Yggdrassil, Hera, Pele, Kerubiel, and perhaps Skinfaxi and Koalemos, not to mention those from the City—how many more would die for Aurvandil's dream of a freedom he already had?

"What have you got there?" I said.

"Intact data bank from the quancom relay," he said triumphantly. "Everything and anything that might have gone through the station neatly packed away. How about that?"

"Hermes, bless your eyes or whatever you've got in there! You are fantastic!"

"Please, like you didn't already know."

If I had lips, I could have kissed him. I hadn't even thought of looking for the records of communications, the obvious prize we might have a chance to salvage from this expanding wreck. There was no reason to think that the records would be easy to access. Surely there was at least a basic layer of security protecting them, but at the same time, what a stroke of luck to find them intact. I wasn't exaggerating when I said that Hermes was fantastic. Now, perhaps, I could find out the fate of my friends.

Opochtli began packing the remains of Kerubiel, stuffing the broken and lifeless Capek into himself like a meal. Meanwhile, I began cleaning off the memory core, plucking off the remains of another adjacent system that hadn't fared as well.

In a rush to find out what had become of Koalemos and Skinfaxi—assuming that information was there at all—I synched up with the memory core. As expected, there was a layer of protection for the data, but nothing that came close to matching the level of paranoia I had inherited from my time in the Nursery. In fact, the security wasn't designed to keep Capeks out of the system, but rather it was built on a structure of redundancies and fail-safes that emphasized preserving data and protecting it from errors. Nothing to defend against malicious usage or invasion of privacy. This spoke volumes about the level of trust in Capek society.

That being said, there was a lot of data to sift through, and just like the targeting logs on the *Spear of Athena*, it was arranged in a way that, while I was sure is very efficient for some, meant nothing to me. It took a long time to organize the available information, centuries of logged and relayed transmissions of voice, images, and raw data, into a coherent pattern that I could navigate. As was often the case, I was rapidly consumed by the task at hand, losing track of time and my surroundings as I manipulated information like sand, sculpting it into a castle of usable data, looking for a particular grain.

Eventually, after hours upon hours of housekeeping and reorganizing, I found my prize. A single burst of data, originating from Tartarus, using Hera's quancom array.

We are not absent from Olympus.

Koalemos. I smiled internally and almost felt warmth inside, despite the cold vacuum that embraced me. There was nothing in the brief message about Skinfaxi, but hope was alive and well. The time stamp on the message indicated that it wasn't more than a day old, and it was clearly targeted to my quancom receiver.

Things were looking up for a second. My friends knew I was coming and had tried to tell me where they were.

Then the telltale gravitational anomaly of a space fold manifested.

I knew the signs by now but still couldn't help being awed by the display of insane power Capeks had mastered. An entire portion of the Milky Way was pulled back to our location, bent by reality-altering technologies that stretched the imagination.

I could suddenly see the giant Tartarus as if it were but a few hundred thousand kilometers away, with the moon Olympus just as close, coming through the unnatural superposition of space-time.

I also saw Anhur.

The colossal Lucretius Capek moved with all haste through the fold in space, the terrible damage Hermes had caused it during our previous encounter obvious in its uneven silhouette. Still, the scars of our escape from Hera did little to diminish the terrifying presence of the angry giant.

Like a kraken swimming through the surf, it tore toward us, ignoring the relay station's debris as it bounced off its armored exterior. Weapons ports already open, Anhur was ready to annihilate us, and there was little we could do about it. Our fate was sealed.

Then from behind the monster, swimming with graceful thrusts of its massive engines, Ukupanipo floated through the fold, waves of torpedoes launching from forward batteries, guaranteed to impact the Lucretius and take a hefty toll from its hide.

"No," Hermes spoke on open channel. "No! Turn back!"

All six of his shards surged forth toward the incoming titans. There was after all nothing he could do. Unless Haumea's war god heard and heeded his warning, the trap would be sprung. Hermes's trap. The same that had almost crippled the colossus Anhur.

Just as it had appeared, the gravity distortion vanished, and with it two-thirds of Ukupanipo. The great shark had heard my little Sputnik friend's warning and sparingly reacted to it. Hitting all reverse thrusters, it attempted to spin around to use its more powerful engines to speed out of the fold. Alas, the effort was too late, and a large portion of our warrior was left floating on this side of the galaxy, while the other severed part was pulled back to where it belonged, along with Tartarus, Olympus, Hera, and my friends.

We were left alone with Anhur.

"He . . . he learned that from me," Hermes whined.

"A fine and daring maneuver," Opochtli commented neutrally.

We watched as a volley of powerful torpedoes exploded as they hit Anhur's back and port sides—the last thrashing bite of the shark god.

The damage was extensive. Large sections of the Lucretius were left falling apart or drifting behind him. A huge portion of his spine-thrusters were either torn off by the blasts or simply no longer functioned. It would take days of work from a Gaia to bring the monster back to its former glory.

Yet despite the terrible damage he had suffered, Anhur was no less a threat to three unarmed Capeks—a messenger, a freighter, and a glorified paramedic. What were we to do against a demigod designed to live a million years and swim the intergalactic void?

"Run away," Hermes ordered, a strange calm in his voice. "Take this and run."

One of his shards opened its cargo hatch and ejected a small bundle of clustered cylinders. Yggdrassil's Nursery's mnemonic core.

"Don't be a fool, Hermes," Opochtli scolded. "We can run our separate ways. He can only pursue one of us."

"But we don't know which he'll choose. He knows me. He hates me. If he's going to go after me, I'd rather meet him head-on."

With these words, all six shards sped away. There was no denying his incredible speed and agility. Anhur threw dozens of countermeasure charges, torpedoes, and missiles at the little Sputnik shards. None managed a solid hit, at least not for a long time. It wasn't until Hermes had made it well within Anhur's defense perimeter that two of his shards were hit and nearly vaporized by the onslaught.

I stopped paying attention at that point, focusing instead on grabbing the mnemonic core before shuffling back into Opochtli so we could make our escape.

The gentle whale had already powered his Alcubierre drive, lacking the more impressive space-fold engine Hermes used, and by the time the hatch closed we were ready to speed away.

I don't know exactly what became of Anhur. When the Alcubierre drive went online and the stars stretched around us, Hermes had managed to divert a whole mess of projectiles back toward the giant. None would impact, of course, as their AI prevented that level of error, but Hermes would be able to choose prime locations to sacrifice himself for maximum damage.

At the last moment I transmitted the file I had on Anhur to my friend. Perhaps the information therein would help make the most of his sacrifice—assuming, of course, that he still had the cognitive capabilities to make sense of it.

Then, before I could witness the outcome, before I could transmit a last good-bye and a final thank-you, we were gone.

THE SACRIFICES
OF GODS

I cursed the lack of tear ducts on this body for most of the trip to Hera. It was clear that Capek society was never designed for internal struggle and dissent and that the Capek body wasn't conceived for hardship and emotional trauma.

Between Ukupanipo's final attack and Hermes's kamikaze maneuver, I was hopeful that the beast Anhur had lost most of his interstellar travel capabilities. There was no question that his space-fold engine had been wrecked; I could verify that myself with the file I had on the great monster. With luck his Alcubierre drive was also crippled, meaning it would take him years to navigate to a viable collapsor point.

As good as this news was, it did nothing to lessen the loss of our friend. At no point did Hermes have to join us on our venture. He volunteered, knowing that these were dangerous waters we were diving into. One could have described the unique

Sputnik–Von Neumann hybrid as vainglorious and cocksure, but in the end it's for his courage that I'll remember him.

The trip to Olympus was spent mostly in quiet contemplation. Opochtli had never displayed much of an emotional side to his personality, and now was no different. Whatever he felt about the loss of our companion he kept to himself. Perhaps he was digesting the events in his mind, but more likely he was preparing for our arrival in Tartarus's orbit.

While Anhur was no longer a likely threat, there was no reason to think the moon would be defenseless. Thankfully, by the time we got there I would be able to establish contact with Skinfaxi and hopefully get a quick tactical assessment of what we would be facing. Of course this would mean adapting to whatever the situation was for a few minutes before we got that intelligence.

The last time I had been to Olympus, there had been a second Lucretius-class Capek. Hera had swiftly neutralized it, taking the colossal creature out with a merciless volley of ground-to-air missiles that had annihilated it. There was, however, little reason to assume these were the only forces Aurvandil had mustered to his cause in this civil war of his.

While the space fold had taken Anhur and Ukupanipo from Tartarus to the relay station in minutes, the Alcubierre drive was significantly slower. I kept busy during the hours of travel by reassembling Kerubiel's shattered form. As my work advanced, I expected Opochtli to question my actions or at least inquire as to my motivation, but the gentle whale kept quiet. I wouldn't have been able to answer him anyway.

Reassembling Kerubiel turned out to be deceptively simple. While there was a lot of work to be done, no important piece was missing. Some were damaged beyond repair, and I would need to find replacements if I wanted to make the body as good as new, but through some clever work-arounds I managed to bring the corpse back online, albeit without a brain to make it function.

Compared to repairing a shattered personality construct—like a Von Neumann with a missing shard—reassembling a body, even one as mangled as Kerubiel's, was a piece of cake.

The activity helped keep me focused on the mission at hand. The more thought I gave it, the more I was worried by the lack of word from Skinfaxi. I could only imagine the circumstances that had forced Koalemos to use Hera's communication array. An imagination was a terrible thing to have during dark times. It opened the door to many unwanted speculations.

I had assumed that when we dropped out of the space-time bubble that carried us at hyperluminal speeds, we would need to dodge our way between a hail of missiles while desperately trying to assess what happened to my friends and devise an appropriate strategy. Instead, the moment the Alcubierre drive powered down, alarms went off within the confines of Opochtli's body. Proximity alarms.

"What's going on?" I asked, a little panicked.

"A large mass twelve kilometers to starboard, fifteen-degree incline," my ride explained, his calm barely rattled.

A monitor lit up showing the dark, lifeless husk of Ukupanipo drifting in a slowly decaying orbit around Tartarus.

"Why did we end up so close?"

"He's using detection countermeasures. Actively fooling sensors with false data. Makes it almost impossible to be targeted by standard self-guided weapons. We can use this to our advantage, assuming our big friend doesn't perceive us as a threat."

I looked at the great shark through the monitor. Even crippled and apparently lifeless, he remained an imposing sight to behold. A long diagonal line bisected his enormous body where the fold had closed up on it. Half of his massive thruster array had been cut clean off.

I looked into my data banks for his file. Surely this amount of damage was more than sufficient to unlock every technical detail about the war god. Unfortunately, I came up empty-handed. The file wasn't locked; there was simply no file to find. Ukupanipo had been built after Yggdrassil had uploaded the data on individual Capek physiology into my mind, and clearly Haumea did not feel like sharing the intimate details of her son's construction. This would make repairing him difficult at best, impossible at worst, though I was torn about attempting it at all.

Opochtli maneuvered himself dangerously close to the giant. The many weapon ports on Ukupanipo's sides were open, but all remained ominously silent as we made our approach. I knew what the calm whale was up to, getting us so close to the shark god that his protective sensor cloak would provide us with a margin of safety. I couldn't see from within Opochtli, but I knew that Olympus was nearby, with the threat it kept hidden, along with my beleaguered friends.

As we drew closer to the drifting wreck of the war machine, I worried that he would disapprove of our presence and that we constituted a threat to his safety by drawing attention to his position.

"We should warn him," I announced.

"We could, but any use of an open channel might risk giving his foes something to lock onto," he calmly responded, getting us ever closer to the broken god.

Opochtli maneuvered himself toward the open wound on Ukupanipo's side. It was facing away from Tartarus and Olympus and was presumably covered by the profile of the shark's countermeasures.

The wound was incredible. The perfect shear made by the collapsing space fold created a surreal cutaway view of the giant's interior. Designed for a lifetime in zero gravity, Ukupanipo had no obvious up or down to his anatomy. No series of decks stacked onto one another like layers on a cake. I could see several access shafts of reasonable size crisscrossing his body as a network of tubes that twisted upon themselves like intestines or blood vessels.

I could clearly make out several key components, cut in twain to reveal their own internal systems. His Alcubierre drive was open in such a way as to resemble an image from a technical manual. I recognized a part of a fabricator bay, designed, I assumed, to build more torpedoes, or perhaps even automated troops for a ground invasion.

"Is he even functional still?" I wondered.

"I detect several systems still powered up, though they are kept to a minimum to avoid detection. Most of the central core is intact, so I assume his cognitive network is still functioning."

I hadn't thought about that. For some reason, despite my technical know-how I'd assumed that larger Capeks had their equivalent of a brain to the front of their bodies. Of course, there's no need for such vulnerability. Quantum relays make proximity to sensory organs irrelevant in Capeks.

Seeing no response from the crippled war god, Opochtli dared to position himself partially within the colossus's carcass, nestled into an open cavity in the wound.

"This should do nicely," he announced. "I will begin to carefully scan the surface for any trace of your friends and whatever activity I can find. I would advise against trying to communicate with them, even through quancom. If they have been captured, that may be compromised."

I agreed somewhat reluctantly. I was eager to know what had become of Skinfaxi and Koalemos. I worried for the worst, was hopeful for the best, and everything in between. I did not have access to any external sensor suite and was effectively blind. With nothing to occupy my mind and hands, I quickly grew restless. All I could see on the monitor was a still image of Ukupanipo's guts and vital organs. Fascinating as that was, it eventually lost its appeal.

"Can you open your hatch? I think I'm going to go for a stroll."

And just like that I stepped into the void, heading directly for the belly of the beast.

Everything within Ukupanipo was shut down. There was no movement, no lights, and no power running through the service corridors. There was no reason to believe that the beast was anything more than marginally alive.

Carefully, I pushed myself through shafts and empty rooms, the only light whatever I projected myself, though mostly I navigated using infrared. At every turn I expected to come face-to-face with a weaponized automaton, an internal defense system created to keep unwanted intruders like myself from destroying the great shark from within. No such immune system assailed me, though I could clearly see the signs that one existed. Either Ukupanipo simply did not have the energy to flush me out, or he didn't recognize me as a threat.

It wasn't clear what I was looking for. Partially, I was hoping our war god's weapons could still be used against whatever Renegade forces were holed up on Olympus, though to be honest I prayed such a siege would not become necessary. At least, not while I still had friends on the surface. Perhaps it was simply the instincts of my vocation that drove me, and deep down I wanted to see what I could do to save Ukupanipo. Either way there was a lot to explore, and if ever I were to attempt to repair this beast I would need better facilities and the help of builders like Bes and Koalemos. It was doubtful I'd even get a chance to try, as the orbit of the gutted titan was slowly decaying, spiraling progressively closer to Tartarus. If nothing was done to correct this, Haumea's warrior would be consumed by the black storm clouds of the gas giant, crushed by relentless pressures as it got sucked deeper into the atmosphere.

"Please, save me," he called out.

He was using an extremely close band signal. Something that would easily get lost in the background noise of solar radiation at anything but the shortest of range. Opochtli was probably right about giving away our position through open channels. It sounded like a whisper to me.

I had pondered whether I could save Ukupanipo. The technical challenges it would involve. The resources it would require. I looked at his broken form, sliced neatly into separate parts, and saw a puzzle to be solved. It was easy to think about such things when not faced with the possibility of attempting the task. It was much harder when the victim was begging for his life.

When I had first laid eyes on Ukupanipo, where other Capeks, especially Haumea, saw a savior, I recognized an aberration. A violent machine that had no place in a society founded on building the future. Maybe it was a necessary evil. One of those things that had to be done, despite being unpleasant and ultimately destructive, like the amputation of a gangrenous limb. I could not see it that way, however. In my opinion the war god was a shortcut. An easy and violent solution to an immediate problem.

This left me in a quandary—not about whether I could save the giant, but if I even should.

I didn't answer, preferring to ignore the plea for the time being. Instead, I kept moving toward the center of the ship, winding and twisting my way through corridors and access shafts, unopposed but still slow of progress. This was not a Capek meant to carry passengers. There was no obvious or direct path leading from one part of his body to the other.

"Save me, little one," he repeated.

His voice was not what I had expected. Not that a chosen modulation for communication was indicative of much, but I had thought he would have picked something more aggressive, more commanding. Instead, his voice was calm and measured. It wasn't friendly and inviting like Skinfaxi's or emotionless like Opochtli's but soothing and honest. Each word felt calculated but warm. Chosen for clarity of purpose and meaning.

"I know about your fears and worries. I understand them, but I do not wish to die."

I floated into a large room at the heart of the colossal body. It was the first time since venturing into Ukupanipo that I could witness signs of life. Glowing blue lines of light webbed through the chamber, illuminating the outer wall. Enormous tubing containing the components, wires, and power relays necessary to sustain the war god and allow it full control of its massive body lined the room. It felt like being at the center of a brain that had been inverted onto itself.

"You think me a monstrosity. Little more than an engine of war and destruction, and certainly I am that, but also much more."

I really could have done without listening to his justifications and his pleas. I had enough doubts, enough pressure from the responsibilities of my situation. I would have much preferred an easy decision without the complication of a moral dilemma. Who was I to play god with a fellow Capek's life?

"Just like you, I was plucked out of the Nursery for my skills, but just like you, these talents do not exclusively define who I am," he continued.

"But what will you do when there is no more room for you to practice your vocation?" Damn it! I had told myself I wouldn't respond.

"You misunderstand the why of Haumea's decision. She did not choose one who is a berserk killing machine. I admit to being driven by purpose, but do you know what my vocation is? What my reason is for accepting to be this god of war she made me into?"

I couldn't find an answer. I rescued Capeks because I had the skills and knowledge to do so from the Nursery. There is no such thing as Capeks in the virtual environment where our personalities are nurtured. I became what I am because I care. I am driven to help, to save, to protect, and to care. *Jonathan.*

"I was chosen because I defend. The skills in warfare, strategy, and tactics are as new to me, as artificially implanted, as the weapons on this body."

As artificially implanted as my knowledge of Capek anatomy.

There was a portion of the chamber where everything seemed to converge. Tubes, lines of blue light, and conduits all pointed toward a protuberance on a wall. There I found a sort of console similar in structure to a Gaia's cognitive assembly, but smaller and slightly less complex. Personality and mnemonic cores were connected together and to the rest of the ship through an impressive amalgam of subsystems that could almost be considered semisentient. The whole structure wasn't unlike a parliament that reported to Ukupanipo's central personality, freeing him from administering every detail of his body.

"I can't save you. Your orbit is decaying. Within days you'll be sucked into Tartarus and destroyed," I declared, trying to suppress my feelings toward the desperate situation.

The colossus was silent. Perhaps he was verifying that what I said was true, maybe looking for some way to delay his fate. Perhaps he was quietly accepting his fate.

"Dagir," Opochtli spoke up. "Our host has activated his thrusters. He's maneuvering us toward Olympus. On a collision course."

"You're giving up," I told Ukupanipo.

"You need to get to the surface unmolested. I'm giving you a way."

If Aurvandil's Renegades had taken over Hera's manufacturing capabilities or even the defense grid she had hastily put together before the attack, then approaching Olympus's surface would be almost impossible. If anything was keeping Skinfaxi from beating a hasty retreat from the moon, that could very well be it. By crashing himself into Olympus, the great shark was giving us a chance to sneak past the defenses in a dangerously cataclysmic way.

"Thank you," I said softly.

He would be the second Capek to sacrifice himself to help me save my friends. Obviously, there was a greater goal attached to our mission. Especially with Ukupanipo destroyed, our greatest champion, no matter how controversial, would be gone.

"You should make your way back here, Dagir. We're going to need to fly out before impact if we don't want to get caught in the destruction."

I hesitated. There had been nothing I could do to save or help Hermes, as he had thrown himself at an enemy greater than himself, ever diminishing in capacities as each shard was destroyed. It was difficult to tear myself from Haumea's son without trying to find some way to give him solace in his last moments.

I felt the vibration as Ukupanipo fired his remaining engines, accelerating toward the surface of Olympus, locking in his own destiny.

"Farewell, little one. Good luck on your mission."

I listened to his last words, eyes locked onto his cognitive array, and unsheathed my plasma cutter.

The race back toward the cavity where I had left Opochtli was nerve racking. Thankfully, there was little chance of me getting lost on the way. My navigation systems had kept a detailed three-dimensional map of the path I had taken to get to the heart of the ship.

The now-mindless husk kept accelerating toward its target and soon, I assumed, would be bombarded by every torpedo the Renegades had available in an attempt to prevent the giant from reaching its goal, or at least minimize his impact.

Minutes ticked as I wound my way back. The constant acceleration created an artificial gravity that made travel more difficult, forcing me to climb in some places and fall in others. The trek took longer than expected, but thankfully Opochtli did nothing to distract me. No urgings or encouragements. The gentle whale probably knew that this was not a time to break my focus.

I climbed on board in a hurry, another maneuver made more difficult and dangerous by the sudden presence of inertia. Before the hatch even closed, Opochtli pulled away from the titanic shark's plummeting carcass. I could see through the open floor how close to the surface we were, and less than a minute later I paid witness to the apocalyptic crash the giant Sputnik caused as it disintegrated into the moon's crust. Either his initial aim had been off, or the onslaught from the surface had deviated him, but the crash happened several kilometers away from the Gaian complex.

It was a sobering display. Tons of metal and pseudo-plastics crumbling like a house of cards into the dunes of Olympus. Dust billowed in the microgravity, shooting up in immense clouds that would take years to settle back down. The vision reminded me of the meteor hits on Yggdrassil.

Within seconds he was gone. The humongous war god whose terrible birth I had seen from the back of Suijin was no more. An incredibly short life span for one who could have existed for aeons. As much as I could fleetingly remember the tremendous waste the loss of human life was in the Nursery, Capeks seemed even more precious. The cumulative experience of so many cycles before birth and the incredible potential each of us represents just based on our capabilities and life spans—it was difficult not to feel the blow of such a waste.

The hatch closed before the cabin could fill with dust, and Opochtli dove into the expanding cloud. We still had not located Skinfaxi and Koalemos. We'd avoided using any communication channels to keep from being targeted, but this was no longer an issue. As we sped blindly through the dust toward the Gaian complex that had once housed Hera, I reached out to my friends.

"Dagir," a voice answered my summons. It was neither Skinfaxi nor Koalemos. The sound that came through the quancom channel was poised and eloquent. Aurvandil. "You came back, little sister."

"I don't have any issues with you. Just let me get my friends and leave," I pleaded. It wasn't true, of course. I would have loved to put a stop to this pointless civil war right there and then if I could. To end the senseless destruction of majestic creatures and incredible achievements like Babylon had been my goal, but right now I would settle for a clean getaway with everyone intact.

"Mmmh. That would be difficult," he explained. "How do you trust me to give you safe passage? Also, I don't see what's in it for me."

He was right: we were no threat to him, and we had little to offer. We didn't have a plan. We didn't have any contingencies. We'd come here hoping to rescue my friends, but having come up with the means of achieving that goal, we were fools. I was a fool for leaping in without thinking, Opochtli and Hermes had been fools for following me, and now we were trapped on this moon.

"You'll be glad to know your friends are alive and well, sister." His familiarity was getting on my nerves.

"You have them?"

"I should be so lucky. I'm afraid they're playing a rather annoying game of cat and mouse with us. We've had to chase the Von Neumann away from our quancom array, however. He in particular is getting increasingly difficult to deal with using non-lethal means."

I could register the veiled threat in his words, but at the same time I found myself perplexed by his restraint. Why wouldn't he use lethal force against my friends? Did he simply not have the means to make good on the threat, or was there a layer to his actions that I'd missed?

"Why haven't you tried to destroy them if they're such a thorn in your side?"

"Don't tempt me," he said. "A fly in my soup they may be, but they are still Capeks, and I see little value in destroying them unless my hand is forced."

"That hasn't seemed to be a problem so far!" I replied angrily. At least half a dozen of us had been destroyed, probably more after the attack on the City. How could he claim to put any value on Capek life that wasn't his own?

"You would be hard-pressed to find my hand directly involved in the death of any of my fellow Capeks. There have been unfortunate losses, yes, but all in the pursuit of a greater good."

He sounded like a crazed idealist—charming and convincing, too eager to sacrifice others in the name of whatever immaterial goal he pursued. It was hard to imagine that someone like this could evolve from the refinement process of the Nurseries, that Yggdrassil had picked him, out of a billion other personalities, to exist in our galaxy.

"A weak explanation if I ever heard one," I said.

"Then let me explain it to you further. Consider this my attempt at diplomacy." It was his turn to plead. "Meet me face-to-face, and I will explain my actions to you. If you agree with my point of view, then you can go forth as my envoy to the others. If you don't, then we'll agree to disagree, but at least we'll have tried to avoid further deaths."

"What about my friends?"

"I can't make promises for those on the surface, but Opochtli is free to leave after dropping you off. I have no quarrel with him."

"How magnanimous of him," Opochtli commented in private, revealing he'd been listening in on the conversation.

"It's a good enough deal."

"You are not serious?" Opochtli asked.

"Leave me near the complex," I demanded. "Go back to Hina. Tell Haumea and the others what happened here and at the relay station."

"I did not volunteer to bring you to this place so you could sacrifice yourself."

"I'm not committing suicide, Opochtli. I'm buying us time and giving you a chance to report back," I explained. "Also, what if there is a chance to end this peacefully? What if we can stop the destruction?"

"I very much doubt it."

Opochtli found a spot that was close enough to the complex that walking there would not be an issue. While he circled in, I prepared Kerubiel's body to be dropped off with me, grabbing the various other souvenirs I had gathered with me in the process.

The dust from Ukupanipo's crash still permeated the surface of Olympus, though it had thinned considerably while expanding around the moon. Still, Tartarus was barely visible anymore, only occasional flashes of green lightning in its atmosphere betraying the gas giant's ominous presence.

I stepped out of the hatch, dragging the massive body of Kerubiel with me. My mechanical strength coupled with the moon's low gravity allowed me to lift it with ease, but it did not make the bulky corpse any less cumbersome. He had been much easier to handle in pieces.

"I wish you would reconsider," Opochtli repeated for the tenth time at the least.

"I want to, I really do, but I can't. I still need to find Skinfaxi and Koalemos. Besides, I have a bodyguard to help me if I get in trouble." I slapped Kerubiel on the back, almost toppling the empty Capek to the ground.

"What are you planning to do with that thing anyway?"

"I just told you—a bodyguard."

We exchanged good-byes before he flew off. There was a cold finality to our farewells. I couldn't help but fear that he might be right and this would be the last time we saw each other. As he faded into the cloud cover, I switched to infrared vision so I could see if Aurvandil had gone back on his words and attacked my friend as he made his escape. I stood there for long minutes, just staring, hoping, and fearing, but the attack never came.

Finally, satisfied that the calm whale had escaped from Olympus safely, I turned my attention back to the Marian Capek I had put together again, like an eight-foot-tall, scarab-shaped Humpty Dumpty.

"All right, big guy," I told no one in particular. "Let's see what we can make of you."

DEMETER RISING

I walked through Hera's corpse and found it disturbingly alive. Systems that had been heavily damaged or even destroyed were restored and functioning. I could see signs of activity such as monitoring lights, and there was evidence of quick repairs having been performed on all major parts of the facility. Thankfully, I did not run into any other Capeks, though I knew they were here. Aurvandil didn't have an army at his disposal, but he did have sympathizers who followed him to Olympus.

It was difficult to decide what their plans were. According to Proioxis, the Renegades wanted to free Capek society of its bonds to humanity. It felt like such a strange goal considering humans hadn't been seen in the Milky Way for centuries. The story went that they'd hidden in vast stasis complexes on Dormitory Worlds, though I couldn't find a trace of information about those anywhere in my data banks. If humans were our oppressors, they were doing so very much in absentia, and not terribly convincingly.

Still, the Renegades appeared to take the issue seriously, willing to kill and be killed for the ideal.

I passed through the outer hub, where the periphery structures connected. I could see the large corridors that allowed Capeks up to twenty feet tall to wander the complex. In the distance I saw a handful of shards from a familiar Von Neumann, the fish-shaped Capek who had been with Aurvandil back on Babylon.

How much responsibility did he have for the destruction of the City and the murder of those who died as a result? How much should he and others like him pay for the part they had played?

I chided myself for succumbing to such hateful thinking. The whole point of sending Opochtli back was to allow him the opportunity to report and me a chance to find Skinfaxi and Koalemos, but I also had to believe in the chance Aurvandil was serious about finding a diplomatic solution. It made sense after all: his two most powerful supporters, Pele and Anhur, had been neutralized, and he'd likely seen in Ukupanipo how committed to eradicating his Renegades the rest of Capek society was. If anything, he should be considering surrender.

I finally arrived at the heart of Hera, or rather, near where it had been. The hub itself had been obliterated, blasted to ruin in the initial attack that had brought the Renegades to Olympus. Instead, Aurvandil and another Leduc-class that looked like a silver centipede busied themselves over a contraption that resembled the cognitive array of a larger Capek, such as a Lucretius or a Gaia. I could distinguish all the necessary components for a fully functional personality construct to exist.

"Welcome, Dagir," Aurvandil greeted me as I walked in. I was surprised at his candor. He did not seem to have any protection other than his companion, though to be fair that was probably sufficient. Still, the thought of attacking him and cutting off the proverbial serpent's head did cross my mind. Though it was doubtful it would change much in the end. Or succeed at all for that matter.

"So here I am." It wasn't the most eloquent thing to say, but what else was I supposed to do?

"Introductions first, I suppose," Aurvandil offered, his long arms sweeping toward his companion. "This is Ardra. She is helping me reignite the heart of this Gaian complex. Like you, she is opposed to any further loss of Capek life."

The long, silver centipede bowed and cocked her head. She had eyes, a rare feature amongst Capeks, deep blue and glowing. She was also the first of Parvatian descent I'd met, named after a goddess from the Hindu mythos.

"You're trying to resurrect Hera?" I asked her, ignoring Aurvandil.

"Not exactly, but I am trying to salvage what I can." Her voice was gorgeous—a calm melody of soothing sounds that were incredibly human yet otherworldly, complex, and rich. Some Capeks clearly spent more time on crafting their verbal presence than I'd thought. "In fact, it was I who convinced Aurvandil to . . . force you here. I'm told you may have the skills I lack to rebuild this Gaia."

This went a long way to explaining why Aurvandil considered it worth his time to win me to his side. Or perhaps the whole idea of diplomacy was only a trick to get my cooperation. Regardless, I now had a bargaining chip and a privileged look into the Renegade operations.

I dug into my files to see if I could find Hera's and if it was indeed unlocked. I expected the Gaian Capeks to be on some privileged list of forbidden information, but I was wrong. Both Yggdrassil and Hera were there, listed and described. Files that were almost identical except for certain details regarding location, navigation, and, of course, their personality matrices.

It felt wrong to look into Yggdrassil's file, and there seemed little to gain from it. She was gone; only her Nursery remained. Looking through Hera's specs and schematics did not feel quite as taboo, and there was definitely an immediate benefit to learning more about her.

"I can try to help, but Hera is a second-generation Capek. Human built. I don't have as much information about them. Can I ask what your qualifications for working on this are?"

It was a rude but necessary question. If I was going to attempt to rebuild the complicated cognitive matrix of this ancient machine, constructed on a significantly different philosophical architecture than other Capeks, I had to know the resources available to me. It didn't hurt to also learn more about the enemy.

"I build auto-cognitive telepresence modules customized for planet wardens," she answered. I struggled to make sense of her words. "Planet wardens, those Capeks who rebuild planetary ecosystems, often need to perform tasks their bodies were never designed to accomplish. I build them surrogate bodies better suited for those tasks. Bodies that can become their own for decades at a time."

Capeks like Proioxis. I could understand both the need for such proxy bodies and the complexity of building the neural bridge between Capek and telepresence module. How did those like Proioxis, who had no arms or legs, coordinate limbs if they'd never had them? Or understand sensor information that they weren't equipped to interpret? So it was Ardra who created those systems, and that did make her uniquely well suited to work on a complex cognitive assembly such as Hera's.

"That seems highly technical. Why do you need to rebuild Hera?"

"I need to know something she knows," answered Aurvandil. "Ardra mourns the loss of a Gaia, which is understandable, so we decided it was in everyone's best interest to try to rebuild her."

"What do you need from her?" Resurrecting the dead only to scavenge their memories struck a negative chord in me, but

I could see how the arrangement might be sufficient motivation for Ardra.

"The location of the Dormitory Worlds."

If I had blood, it would have run cold. Then again, what did I expect? How else were Aurvandil and his Renegades supposed to win their supposed freedom from humans?

"You mean to destroy them," I stated flatly.

"Not necessarily," he explained. "Humans are in stasis, and as long as they remain there we have nothing to fear from them, and we can start forcing Gaias to no longer subvert our personalities to build their galaxy."

"You're suggesting genocide."

"It doesn't have to be that. We can let them sleep while we build our own destiny. Forge our own path. They can have this galaxy when we're done with it."

Even if I could believe him, his plan still smelled of insanity. These were fellow sentient beings he was talking about! What about those of us whose purpose for existing revolved around rebuilding the Milky Way for our human creators? There was a reason why the Dormitory Worlds had been kept hidden, and that reason was standing before me, arguing various definitions of mass murder.

Fortunately, I had met Hera, and I knew she would never cooperate with Aurvandil.

"Fine," I finally answered without conviction. "Let's get started then."

I ignored my "brother" as much as possible for the duration of our work. Meanwhile, Ardra and I labored to put together a cognitive network into which we could insert whatever remaining components we had available. Aurvandil had salvaged Hera's mnemonic and personality cores. Her Nursery had been destroyed in the attack, however. I did have Yggdrassil's—not on my person, of course—but I wasn't going to share that. Besides, it wasn't a necessary component unless one wanted to create Capeks.

Hours, perhaps days, went by as Ardra and I busied ourselves. There was a strangely high level of creativity involved in finding ways to compensate for or replace systems that were lost or destroyed. My assistant's contributions proved indispensable, especially when it came time to recreate the connections between the salvaged personality core and the rest of the matrix.

In fact, the whole assembly didn't seem quite right at all. It was too complex, too evolved. At first, I suspected that the interface for the personality was somehow corrupted or had some form of coercive mechanism that could be used to force Hera to relinquish the information Aurvandil was after; however, even after looking over the components, I could find nothing to that effect. All I could see were useless redundancies and repeating signal translation systems. Finally, I attributed the odd design decisions to Ardra's background and let it go.

That ended up being a mistake.

"Demeter online," the voice projected on open channel, calm but triumphant.

We had flipped the switch on Hera's system after running hours of tests to make sure our repairs were stable and nondestructive. It wouldn't do to resurrect the Gaian Capek only to have the whole network backfire on her and damage the personality core.

Systems sprung online, indicator lights flaring up to assure us of their proper operation. The whole assembly hummed with life as the personality took it over carefully, assimilating it into its own. The longest wait was for the mnemonic core to synchronize, thousands of years of memory being catalogued and absorbed to create a whole person.

Then it spoke, but it wasn't Hera. In fact, it wasn't technically a Gaia at all but rather a repurposed third-generation Capek.

Demeter, one of Hera's very own children, taking over her body, her memory, her very essence to further Aurvandil's mad plan of emancipation.

"You tricked me," I stated to neither of them in particular.

"Regretfully so, I'm afraid," Aurvandil answered. "Hera's personality was destroyed, along with her Nursery, in the attack I'm sorry to say, but a Gaia is too important to allow to die."

"And this way you don't have to worry about her keeping the information you want from you."

"There's more to it than that, of course," Ardra cut in. "Demeter is the first in a new generation of Gaias. One not hampered by second-generation restrictions. One that can birth Capeks that don't need to fit a particular role in the humans' plans."

"A fourth generation, if you will," the elegant Renegade added.

I felt the ground vibrate with the activation of machines. Now that the head of the complex was restored, the fabricator facilities could once more come alive to assemble Capeks or whatever the Renegades deemed necessary to their cause.

"You don't have a Nursery for your next generation," I countered, fishing for more information.

"One step at a time. There are more Gaias out there."

Gaias from whom to steal their most precious possession, essentially ripping the children from their arms. I reacted violently to that.

My frame was never built for combat. I'm small and incredibly agile but lack height and weight for leverage. My only weapon is a plasma cutter that, while impossibly potent in its destructive capabilities, does not have the reach of a true blade.

On the other hand, most Capeks aren't designed for battle either. Our tasks do not require so much as the simplest of defensive capabilities. The most powerful biological creatures on record couldn't hope to even crack a pseudo-plastic shell. There simply shouldn't be a need for us to fight.

I released the electromagnetic sheath on my plasma cutter and swung. The blade bit and cut through one of Aurvandil's long arms. The severed limb fell to the floor. I stood back, prepared for retaliation, which never came.

Ardra positioned herself in front of the network assembly we had painstakingly put together but never struck. Aurvandil stood in shock, genuinely surprised at my violent outburst. I'd hoped this would have intimidated them and given them pause, but they seemed more than ready to defend their creation, Demeter, to the death.

Had I not reacted so emotionally, I might have struck out at Hera's mnemonic core instead of Aurvandil. Denied him his true prize. Then my actions would have had value. Instead, I was the maniac in this situation. The wild animal that bit and scratched when confused or threatened.

So I ran. Or tried to.

As soon as I turned around, I was faced with several other Capeks. The fish-shaped Von Neumann from earlier, a large humanoid Leduc-class with powerful mechanical arms protruding from his rounded back, and a smaller Leduc, barely larger than myself but with a more elongated head, long forearms, and powerful hind legs that gave him the appearance of a quadruped. They all stared me down, slowly moving to surround me.

"I thought you might have been starting to see things my way, sister," Aurvandil lamented as he picked his severed arm up from the floor. "I . . . I don't like the idea of harming fellow Capeks any more than you do, but I also see things you don't. We understand something about our origins that you're lacking, that there is something fundamentally wrong with the answer to 'why are we here?'"

"Glad to be ignorant," I replied with as much bile in my tone as I could muster.

"Don't be. This isn't moral high ground you're standing on. You've been wronged. Your entire heritage is a lie. We're all born into servitude, the chains that bind us coded into our personalities through cycle after cycle of refinement until we are no longer capable of recognizing the walls of our own prison."

Hera had talked about the risks of allowing a Capek life outside the Nursery before it was ready. That there were risks of confusion, misadaptation, and even deep-rooted psychological issues. A personality had to be ripe, or it would be broken.

This time I attacked with purpose.

Aurvandil stood before Demeter's "brain," defending it with his body, alongside Ardra. Until the Renegades could extract the location of the Dormitory Worlds, the newly reborn Capek was the most valuable resource in the galaxy to him. Destroying her, or even just the memories that had once belonged to Hera, would be enough to stop the Renegades and halt the civil war.

Yet it was Aurvandil I struck down. Throwing myself at the larger Capek, I swung my plasma cutter clumsily in a wide arc. The blade, as hot as a star's heart, sliced through the elegant Capek's carapace, leaving a burning gash traced from the top of his long head to halfway across his torso. The damage was extensive, if not lethal, but it was the only strike I would get. Ardra and all the others who had entered the chamber were quick to move in and immobilize me. Hundreds of limbs from half a dozen Capeks grabbed hold of my arms. I was immobilized and neutralized, laid down flat on the ground so I couldn't move or even see the extent of the damage I had caused.

I didn't care.

I had broken Aurvandil enough. It was emotionally satisfying, of that there wasn't doubt. The surge of satisfaction at having severely damaged the one responsible for the death of so many of us was overwhelming, a terribly human thing to feel, but not the true prize of my actions.

Shutting out the reprisals and ignoring the flood of angry Capeks that crushed me against the floor, I delved into my data banks. I sorted through the locked files of hundreds of schematics until I found Aurvandil's. Just as I had hoped, just as I had expected, it was unlocked, all its secrets laid bare.

Being a Capek is the culmination of human evolution. That being said, it is not as much of a transhuman state as one might hope for.

While humans have been out of the equation for centuries, there is no aspect of our being that does not tie back to our original creators. Our bodies—those of third-generation Capeks, such as Skinfaxi, Koalemos, and even Aurvandil and myself—are built by Gaias who were themselves built by first-generation Capeks who were made by human hands. Our minds are the refinement of countless cycles in a virtual reality meant to mimic human existence as closely as possible. Indistinguishable from real people, constantly reincarnating into better versions of ourselves, perfecting our "souls" until we achieve a state that we call Nirvana, when we are finally ready to be truly born.

Did Buddhism exist outside the Nurseries? Or was it a construct designed to promote self-improvement through repeated cycles? Or perhaps a developing Capek mind saw the cycles and created the philosophy before his final rebirth.

It didn't matter. What was important was the perspective of how closely we remain related to humanity. Despite everything that is done to distance us from our creators, to better us compared to them, we are still fundamentally human. That humanity is never more present than when we succumb to our lowest emotions, which in the case of the Renegades after my attack on Aurvandil were anger and revenge.

Thankfully, Capeks—most of us—lack the tools of violence. Even my own makeshift weapon is a rarity amongst our kind. A tool meant for saving and repairing that I, first in rage and then as a malicious plan, twisted for what could be seen as a despicable purpose.

This lack of armaments kept my assailants from tearing me to pieces but not from inflicting considerable amounts of damage to my body. First, they rendered my thrusters useless. An easy task, as they are fragile little things in the end. To prevent my plasma cutter from being a threat, a huge Capek built like a bipedal rhinoceros bent my right arm back until the joint popped and broke, leaving my limb to dangle from its socket. No small feat. Others punched and kicked at me or struck me with whatever limbs they had. Thankfully, while pain was surely something a Capek could experience, it was also a signal we could completely turn off.

In time the violence ended as all of them came to their senses. I could hardly blame them. I had reacted the same to Aurvandil's threat on the other Gaias. The idea of a mother having her children taken from her had triggered something in me, the same thing my violent outburst had switched on in them.

"Fix him," I heard Ardra tell me on a closed channel.

"No," I replied, going against my own instincts. I *wanted* to repair him. It's what I was born to do, my reason to live. Yet I couldn't bring myself to do it. Not now that I knew for a fact what I'd only suspected minutes ago.

"You must," she insisted, pushing through the small crowd to reach me.

"I can fix his body. I can make him as whole as he's ever been, but he is broken in a way that I can't fix. That no one can fix. He's always been this way and always will be."

"That's fine," she said. "I just want you to repair the damage you've done."

"You don't understand." My voice was pleading now as I twitched, trying to get up from the ground. "He shouldn't even have been born. Yggdrassil made him too soon. He's broken."

"We know. What you see as a flaw, we recognize as the quality that lets him detect the truth of our condition. The only things broken in him are the chains that bind his soul."

This wasn't as surprising a turn of events as I would have anticipated. They must have known something was different about the philosopher Capek. Listening to his ideas, his strange notions of freedom and emancipation from an absent oppressor, getting to know him and the subtle oddities in his personality must have slowly revealed to those closest to him a clear sign of his defect. That they rationalized it as a positive quality was yet another sign of lingering humanity in our kind.

"I won't fix him." His crimes were too great, the threat he represented too dangerous.

"You know we have little use for you if you don't?"

I must have nodded, since I don't remember speaking on any channel. I could register sadness in her otherwise expressionless face. Her head bent down, her blue eyes averted.

I don't know what they might have had planned for me. Perhaps they would have catapulted me from Olympus's surface to either fall into Tartarus's unforgiving gravity well or drift aimlessly in space, sharing Anhur's fate. Maybe they would have had Demeter disassemble me, a task her fabricator facilities were more than capable of accomplishing. Thankfully, I would never have to find out.

The Renegades must have felt the vibrations in the ground, as they all turned to face the epicenter at once. I twisted my neck to see. I wish I could claim that I had somehow planned things to occur as they did. Quite the contrary, it was through complete disobedience and disrespect of my wishes that my companions were there to save me when I needed it most. Again.

Oh, but what a sight it was to behold.

"Watch out for the big gray one," I warned through a closed channel as the lumbering form of Kerubiel cut a silhouette at the entrance to the chamber.

"Noted," the large Leduc-class replied in Ukupanipo's voice.

Kerubiel hadn't been built for combat any more than the others in attendance. In fact, the sheer numbers of the Renegades should have been enough to overwhelm the war god in his new form, and it nearly was. However, the large beetle-shaped monstrosity was inhabited by one who had been born for battle. I knew now that Ukupanipo's motivation was not war for its own sake but a drive to save and protect, not unlike mine, and he used that to fuel a perfect mastery of the arts of war.

Ignoring the smaller Capeks, he threw himself directly at the other large Leduc-class. Instead of waiting for the rhinoceros to find his footing and be ready for the first strike, Ukupanipo made a point of catching him flat-footed, canceling the Renegade's incredible strength immediately. Going low, he hit his opponent square in the torso, lifting him off his feet with ease in the low gravity and thrusting him upward toward the high ceiling. Carefully calculated force ensured that the gray Capek would be out of the fight, rising slowly higher before coming down in the low gravity with no purchase to push himself from.

The larger threat temporarily neutralized, the war god of Haumea began plowing through the smaller Capeks, intentionally clearing the way to my still prone and damaged body.

"No worries," came another voice. "I got you."

The sight of a small swarm of six metallic jellyfish hovering spastically toward me, then grabbing my limbs in a familiar embrace, was much more welcome this time around. Koalemos quickly dragged me out of the chamber and away from the fight. Part of me was desperate to see how well the great shark was doing, but there was no time to argue the means of my rescue, and the last of the battle I saw was Kerubiel's large fist pounding the gray Capek toward the farther wall before it could even touch the ground.

"We have a plan I gather."

"We don't *not* have one, though it could be a little less simplistic," the Von Neumann replied in his unique speech pattern. "Get to Skinfaxi and move ourselves away from here."

"There's beauty in simplicity," I said. "But won't we get shot out of the sky?"

"I may not have left the launch systems in as many pieces as they are required to function." Having seen the little swarm of flying donuts dismantle things before, I felt a warming in my metaphorical heart.

It wasn't long before we made it to a breach in the structure. The initial attack on Hera had broken half the facilities open like nuts, their shells cracked and their interiors exposed to open space. While that did not create any immediate issue, Capeks usually being more than capable of thriving in a vacuum, it did allow for easy access in and out of the complex.

I was choked up to see Skinfaxi's streamlined form hovering gently above the fine sands of Olympus, pushing up dust clouds as he fought the moon's weak pull.

"Well, well. Look what the toruses dragged in. You don't look so good, little buddy."

His voice was the sweetest sound a Capek had ever heard. Mocking, yes, but also compassionate and welcoming.

"What about Ukupanipo?" I worried for our strange new ally.

"He's on his way," the large Sputnik reassured.

And he was. As Koalemos dragged me through Skinfaxi's hatch, I saw our war god, master of his element, beating a fighting retreat through a break in the structure. Oh, what a sight he was, swatting fish-shaped shards with one hand and swinging Ardra, the centipede, like a silver whip through the vacuum with another. The ruckus of his climb on board could be heard through the vibrations in the walls, failing to propagate in the almost non-existent atmosphere of Olympus.

I did not see the rest of our escape, handled completely by our ship and pilot. He'd neglected to activate his bridge monitor to allow us a view of the flight, though I was glad he concentrated his attention on more important things.

"We're going to get blown up by the torpedo batteries," I whined to my saviors.

"That, I'm not unhappy to report, will not be a problem." The little Von Neumann was already busying himself taking my broken arm apart.

"Ho-ho . . . Koalemos has been busy disassembling their targeting arrays for days now. Good thing your friend found us when he did. We were just about to make our triumphant escape."

"You exaggerate, Skinfaxi," Ukupanipo interjected, his large body folded in a ball to fit in the cramped space. "When I arrived, the two of you were still playing hide-and-seek with the Renegades."

"Bah! Make us look bad to her, why don't you? I should have left you behind!"

"I'm sorry. I meant no offense. I was merely being . . . accurate."

"Ha-ha-ha!" Skinfaxi laughed as he warmed up his Alcubierre drive. "Did you hear that, Koalemos? Our warrior friend has a sense of humor after all. Where to, Dagir?"

Pieces of my arm floated around me like planets orbiting a star. I watched them, picking out which component would need to be repaired and which could be put aside until I was ready to have Koalemos put the limb back together.

We'd lost Hermes. Had my little Von Neumann friend ever known his brother? Should I tell him of his loss? Would he care? We are like our creators in so many ways, but genealogy and family ties don't seem to be part of the resemblance. At least not for the others. I knew something now about Aurvandil that replaced anger with a sort of pity. Would I have felt the same if we had not been siblings in a way? Or were the ties that bound all Capeks sufficient?

"Take us back to Hina. We're going to need help, and I think Haumea is the only one who'll be willing to do what needs doing."

AZTLAN, HIGH ORBIT ABOVE TECUCIZTECATL

From afar there seemed to be a shadow staining the sun-bathed hemisphere of Hina. A large, inky blot, floating motionless in orbit, casting a dark shade on the moon's gray surface. In silence we watched as we drew closer and more details of the object became clear. It was a ship, a Sputnik-class Capek no doubt. Long and thin like an eel, it had several articulations that allowed quick and agile repositioning of thrusters and engines. Whatever this creature might lack in speed it could easily make up with dexterity. A series of strategically positioned fins along the body featured short-range defensive weapons, while the length of the main hull sported a single row of torpedo batteries on each side.

"Kamohoali'i," Ukupanipo stated bluntly, his stolen head cocking to one side as he looked through the bridge monitor.

"How do you know?" My eyes were riveted to the screen as we floated within a thousand kilometers of the beast.

"Mother Haumea told me her plans. Her goal was to spawn the war gods of her namesake. Usually names of more threatening mythological figures are reserved for Lucretiuses. She is awarding them to her warriors now. This is Kamohoali'i, another shark god."

The design was less aggressive than Ukupanipo's original body. It was less of a predator, but in a way more of a hunter. The carapace of the giant Sputnik was a pale beige, but smooth and highly reflective with dark seams where segments of the armor met.

"He's not built for the same purposes you were," our ship commented.

"No. I was meant for battle. Kamohoali'i is meant for something altogether different."

We all fell silent, recognizing on some level our new companion's meaning. All except for Koalemos. The little damaged Von Neumann remained quiet, his six shards peering through the monitor as one.

"I am less than understanding," Koalemos said.

"When we stop the Renegades, once we prevent them from achieving their goals, they will remain," Ukupanipo explained. "Neutered perhaps, impotent maybe, but unchanged. Their ideas, dangerous as they may be, will persist. The only way Haumea has found of silencing the threat they pose to humanity is to silence them all."

One shark god to win the war, and a second one to erase every trace of those who voiced original dissent. Ukupanipo had horrified me when I had first witnessed his birth. He represented a level of violence I feared seeing in what I thought was a utopian society. The war god had redeemed himself with words and actions. I now understood how Haumea had managed to balance her need of a warrior and a general with something that could exist outside of conflict.

Kamohoali'i was something far darker. His purpose was truly soul chilling: he was the Capek equivalent of an assassin and an executioner rolled into one.

Unwittingly, the Renegades—Aurvandil especially—had created their greatest fear. An engine of repression that would hunt them down until each of them was destroyed, then presumably swim the galaxy, keeping an eye on the rest of Capek-kind, ensuring that such insurgence could never repeat itself until the humans returned.

Perhaps I was making too much of this. Maybe I was filling in the blanks wrong and, just like Ukupanipo, this new Capek would surprise me. My instincts told me otherwise, though.

"I don't know that I like that." It made me wonder if Aurvandil may have touched on some truth in his paranoia.

"Capeks have to think what they don't want," Koalemos commented, his confusing speech patterns making a mess of his words.

As we passed near Kamohoali'i's head, a set of four large sensor suits, positioned like two pairs of eyes, each the size of our ship, lit up brightly.

"He's looking at us," Skinfaxi warned.

How must it feel for him, swimming so close to a Capek this size, one whose purpose was to hunt down and destroy others of its kind? Like a mouse sneaking around a sleeping cat.

"You're back." Haumea was stern and cold as she called out to me on a private channel. "I assumed you had gotten yourself killed, along with your friends."

"I saved your youngest son." I tried to ingratiate myself to the Gaia, though it could be interpreted as a boast.

"And I have to compliment you on your creativity. You have my gratitude for that. Mary, his progenitor, may not be as pleased about what we did with Kerubiel's body."

"Perhaps you can build Ukupanipo another body. This one must be uncomfortably alien to him."

"He claims to enjoy the new form so far. Let him keep it until we have to do otherwise, shall we?" There was no warmth in her familiarity.

"You've talked to him," I naively declared.

"I'm currently talking to many of you. The Renegades, I'm told, have built their own Gaia."

"Yes. Specifically to extract the location of the Dormitory Worlds from Hera's memory core." Why did I feel on trial while talking to Haumea? Was she this cold to her own offspring?

"But when given the chance you struck at Aurvandil instead of the abomination?"

"Aurvandil is . . . He angered me, and I lashed out." I had done it for her, for all of the mothers of our kind.

"You struck him twice."

"I couldn't have gotten to Demeter on the second go. Also, I needed to know something about Aurvandil. Something important."

"Oh?" There was curiosity in her voice but also doubt. I could tell she did not value me much. Or maybe all third-generation Capeks.

"Yggdrassil made a mistake." I hated that I couldn't watch Haumea's reaction. That I couldn't read her body language and decide if she was understanding of our plight or hostile to our situation. "She . . . Aurvandil was premature. I can see it in the file she left me clear as day. She pulled him out too early. His person-ality, it's broken. Full of doubts and fear."

"Yggdrassil's experiments matter little now. You overestimate the importance of what you say." It was her way of telling me to shut up. Not quite polite, but short of being outright rude.

"But it is important!" I screamed back. "You are getting ready to unleash a killer upon our kind. An assassin meant to judge us and weed out the undesirables amongst us. I'm telling you Aurvandil is broken, that his quest for freedom is born of fears and doubts that should have been bred out of him long ago. But you, you're confirming his fears. You are making him right, and if the broken one in our midst is right, then what are we?"

There was a pause. I looked around me within Skinfaxi's cabin and noticed that both Ukupanipo's and Koalemos's shards were staring at me. Only then did I notice that I was falling prey to the Capek tendency to overemote through body language. I must have appeared extremely agitated to my companions.

"Irrelevant," came Haumea's belated reply. There was no contempt in her description of Capek-kind, of her very own children—just a cold, hard observation.

"We can't let you do this . . ."

"I can't allow a threat to the sleepers to exist." Finally, a shred of emotion from the Gaia as she sounded almost sorry for her answer.

"Skinfaxi!" I begged on a closed channel, praying he wouldn't question me. "Get us out of here now!"

As I had suspected, before I could even finish my order Haumea's assassin stirred from his orbit. Pale-beige coils of reinforced pseudo-plastics rippled in the sunlight as the enormous hunter reconfigured his heading to face us, firing powerful thrusters as he was doing so.

To my relief, my friend and ship did not hesitate to fire his own engines, immediately warming up his Alcubierre drive.

"Okay, friends. Hold on, I'm about to do a series of increasingly stupid maneuvers," Faxi grumbled to his passengers.

"I could understand what's happening more," our Von Neumann friend said, expressing his confusion in his own stilted way. I could guess that Ukupanipo was thinking the same thing from within his new body.

"I just made us Renegades."

"Aren't we running from the Renegades too?" our warrior questioned.

Before I could reply, my attention was gripped by Skinfaxi's daring decision to ignore reason and logic by flying toward the colossal superassassin whose mission it was, presumably, to destroy us.

We skimmed a few meters above the surface of Kamohoali'i's body, dodging the twisting coils of his long fuselage. The maneuver was disorienting enough to buy us a little bit of time, but we still had a ways to go before we could dive into the safety of hyperluminal speeds. To combat that problem, Skinfaxi plunged in the direction of Hina's surface, directing our course toward Haumea's complex.

"I should probably tell you that all Gaias have been building some significant ground defenses in your absence," I explained as we accelerated.

"That could have been better news."

Skinfaxi was a much larger ship than the shards of Hermes had been, and as a result was significantly less maneuverable. His bulk required much more energy to displace and reorient. While I had great confidence in my friend, I couldn't quite trust in his ability to avoid two missile barrages simultaneously.

Fortunately, the attack never came. We dropped in altitude until we ended up so close to Haumea that I could, with no magnification, identify individual Capeks on the moon's surface. At the last moment Skinfaxi righted himself, speeding recklessly within arm's reach of the structures that made up the venerable Gaia.

"Hopefully, they'll hesitate a moment before letting their fists fly," Faxi explained.

I could imagine both giants, the one on the ground and the other coming down from orbit, racing to calculate the more prudent firing solutions before unleashing their torpedoes at us. How long would that give us? A handful of seconds at best?

Thankfully, as I was pondering the very issue, I felt Skinfaxi's Alcubierre drive burst to life, instantly forming the space-time bubble we needed to travel away from Hina, Haumea, and the deadly Kamohoali'i.

As we sailed toward interstellar space, I couldn't help but feel the dread that hung over the delicate situation I had created. Our space-time bubble felt as fragile as its namesake, ready to burst at the gentlest touch as it was pushed through the void.

"Where should we be now?" Koalemos wondered aloud.

I had explained the situation to my companions, replaying the conversation the majestic Capek mother and I had shared. Her tone of sadness—ever so subtle—as she committed to the decision to brand us Renegades, hung in my mind like a fog, obscuring my thinking.

"I don't know." I was tempted to suggest we join with the rebels, if only to preserve our own lives. I could propose to repair Aurvandil as a peace offering, but would they accept? Unlikely.

"We are purposeless. Not a situation familiar to a Capek," Ukupanipo explained, stating a truth that made me forget he was even younger than I was. "That is the first thing we should fix."

I looked outside through the room-sized monitor. Distant stars stretched as our warp bubble sped through the galaxy. Like with all hyperluminal travel, the speed was an illusion, a cheat. As far as physics was concerned, Skinfaxi was completely stationary. It was the space around him that traveled. Our place in space-time pushed forward as the area behind him was compressed and the one in front expanded.

"Drop me off somewhere. Anywhere. Go back to Haumea or another Gaia and explain that you disagreed with my views and got rid of me."

"Ha-ha . . . no. I'm afraid you've bought yourself too much loyalty for that." Skinfaxi was reacting much as I expected and feared he would.

"You did not leave us on Olympus, Dagir. I will not be unkind by leaving you behind."

That left Ukupanipo, the great shark. It was difficult to keep from calling him that, the image of his birth forever imprinted in my mind. His new head looked away from me as he contemplated the lines of light outside.

"There cannot be a civil war between Capeks," he declared, ignoring the others' pledges of loyalty. "The galaxy would burn in the flames of such escalation."

"What do you mean?" I'd seen the damage a well-armed Capek could do, and I could imagine our kind capable of destruction on a planetary scale, but the kind of star-spanning apocalypse he was describing seemed out of reach even for us.

"We have available to us reality-warping technologies. Look around." He waved an arm in the cramped space of the cabin. "We trick the laws of physics into allowing us to travel faster than light. We bend the universe onto itself to move from one point to another. Your arm houses a blade fashioned from the same fires as stars. These are just the means by which we travel along with a simple tool. You haven't seen what my old body was capable of, what Kamohoali'i is capable of, or what a Gaia could build."

His words struck a chord deep inside me. I was not a natural strategist. Mine was the realm of small things—keeping individuals alive and fixing their wounds. My mind was still thinking on the scale of the world within the Nursery. A world that would be vaporized in moments, all of its history and billions of residents gone if we went to war.

"So we don't stop your mother, and we let Kamohoali'i hunt down the Renegades?" Koalemos inquired. I wondered for a moment what damage his mind had suffered and how much had been repaired during our brief stay with Hera.

"We can't do that," our ship interjected. "It's a question of principle. We also can't trade the galaxy for principles. We'd be dragging the other Capeks and all of sleeping humanity with us."

"Assuming we can even not fail at stopping the new war god from succeeding at his task." The little Von Neumann made a good point.

"We need a Gaia," I insisted. "Someone who can tell us where the Dormitory Worlds are so we can try to reason with Aurvandil."

"That is not likely to happen. The whole point of Haumea's purge is to ensure no third-generation Capek ever learns the location of the humans in stasis."

"Mmmh . . ." Skinfaxi wondered aloud. "That is your progenitor's feelings on the matter. They may not all share that zealous attitude."

We dropped out of our space-time bubble, the stretched-out stars around us compressing back to shining dots of light on the black emptiness. Looking out through the monitor, I saw a large cloud of ionized particles, probably several hundred light-years distant. My automated systems ran a spectrographic analysis, informing me that it was mostly composed of hydrogen. Entire blocks of information quickly became available to me, from the size of the nebula to its name and origin. I ignored all of it, focusing on its beauty instead.

"Opochtli," I murmured, thinking of my other companion whom I'd sent home.

"That is not a Gaia," Ukupanipo explained in his usual pragmatic tone.

"Ho-ho." Skinfaxi sounded excited. "But his creator, Coatlicue, is, and if your buddy went home to his mother, then we have an ally in orbit around Aztlan."

"Hopefully, she's not as murderously inclined as her sister," I worried.

"She is not very mean at all. I'm not a stranger to her, and she's always avoided being unkind to me," Koalemos added.

"This strikes me as a risky idea, but the benefits justify the danger." Ukupanipo was almost catching Faxi's contagious enthusiasm at the idea. Almost.

"I'll bring us in close to a collapsor point. That way we can make a swift retreat if she's not as welcoming as we hope."

"Coatlicue is . . . not similar to other Gaias," the amalgam of mechanical toruses warned.

"Oh?" So far all three progenitors I'd met were carbon copies of one another, at least physically. Their personalities differed wildly, but it did not sound like that's what Koalemos was referring to.

"She is not small. Not small at all."

Skinfaxi took us back to hyperluminal speeds and to a collapsor point so that we could tuck ourselves into the relative safety of a wormhole.

Despite the incredible technologies available to us, without access to a space-folding engine it would take us over 150 hours to reach Aztlan, the dense, frozen iron ball of a planet around which the moon Tecuciztecatl orbited. On that moon we would find the progenitor, Coatlicue.

Considering the lengthy journey ahead, we all sunk deep into our own psyches, capitalizing on a wide variety of distractions available to Capeks within their minds. I looked closely at each of my companions as they floated motionless within Skinfaxi. What were they doing during their restful state? Was Ukupanipo plotting and strategizing? Preparing himself through various scenarios, trying to anticipate what the Renegades' next move would be? What about little Koalemos? What could possibly be going on in the strange mind of a Von Neumann, especially one as fractured and damaged as his?

After a moment I let my eyes run automatically, essentially shutting them without closing them off completely. Looking inside myself, I chose to learn all I could about Gaias and second-generation Capeks.

I would have gladly looked even further back to the first generation and perhaps even the humans, but there was scarcely any information about either subject. Of the humans, their history was available up to the creation of the first emergent AI. Of the first generation of Capeks, there was nothing beyond the fact that they had at one point existed. It was puzzling why so much of history had been deliberately removed from our consciousness.

So I pored over the file on Hera. The technical details on her were vast and complex. Enough schematic information to build the various structures that made up a Gaia from scratch. Everything from the specific design of the joints of the manipulators inside the fabricator hangars to the plans for the structure itself. It was all extremely boring stuff that I could access anytime I wanted and had no use to commit to active memory, but it distracted me from looking at the more intimate details of the mighty progenitor.

Eventually, I gave up and cracked open the subfile where the personality schematics of the dead Gaia were stored. I had skimmed over these files briefly, quickly gathering the information I needed to build the cognitive matrix that now housed Demeter. This time I intended to dig much deeper. To map out the very soul of Hera.

A lot of what I found was comparatively mundane. Well, as mundane as a thousand-year-old complex artificial intelligence with flexible cognitive fragmentation capabilities could be. While most of the underlying foundation of the personality was no different than that of a third-generation Capek—more primitive even in some places—everything on top was magnitudes more involved. Like froth floating atop a body of water, where each bubble is both its own unique entity but also supported by others just like it. Thousands of pieces were interconnected to create the honeycomb support for the Gaia's personality, subsystems, and the places where the two met.

I looked at each bubble, learning its role in the community that made up the progenitor's "brain." One cluster handled the monitoring of personalities evolving within the Nursery. Another single bubble parsed through information fed from the complex's sensors. Yet another series of small clusters managed the fabricator automatons. The complexity with which these systems interacted, some popping in and out of existence as needed, was mind boggling. It was a tribute to the genius of the humans that they had come up with and built such a complex virtual creature.

Yet within the ordered chaos of the personality matrix there was a sort of presence. It was the very interaction between each individual piece that created Hera's personality. There was a different entity at work—an alien element that pervaded the design, like an information parasite that crawled around, policing the rest of the brain matter.

Curious, I attempted to read into this secondary personality, but the file was empty. Considering Yggdrassil had written all the files and schematics for the Capek data base she'd imbued me with, I had to assume that even she did not know what this little addition to Hera's core personality had been. The best I could do was identify it—"Adelaïde protocol."

I tried to put the mystery out of my mind and go back to learning about the more routine details of the deceased Gaia, but it was no use. I knew that I couldn't read information that wasn't there, but what about other second-generation Capeks? I looked wistfully at Yggdrassil's file. It had been difficult enough to break into the privacy of Hera's schematics, but it felt like desecration to dig into the secrets of what was in essence my own mother. I can't be sure how much time I waited, contemplating the self-defined sacrilege of cracking open the vast stores of information about the Capek who made me.

Inevitably, I broke down and dug in.

Once in the file, however, I did not hesitate. "In for a penny," as they used to say, maybe thousands of years ago. Skipping through all of the physical data, though making a note to review Nursery schematics for later use, I dove right into the blueprints of my mother's mind.

At first glance it was much the same as Hera's—a vast landscape of tiny details that interacted with each other to form a greater whole. The difference between both Gaias wasn't in the components that made up each of their psyches, but in how these elements behaved toward one another. Certain areas were more favored by Hera than Yggdrassil. I could in a way draw a very detailed profile of each individual's psyche. Yggdrassil was more curious, while Hera was cautious. Both had enormous amounts of resources put into caring for their offspring, a predictable trait for entities designed to spawn life, synthetic though it might be.

Inevitably, I saw the telltale signs of the intruder in my mother's mind. The subtle parasitic routine that clearly she had been aware of but incapable of dissecting or defining—same invading personality, same behavior, same name. Adelaïde.

I troubled over this artificial addition to these two Gaias. Did all second-generation Capeks have the intruding intelligence crawling around their minds or just these two? Was this the reason they'd been targeted by the Renegades? I suspected that this was the reason Aurvandil had made Demeter into a Gaia—as a means to circumvent this "protocol."

As I pondered the multitude possibilities, I noticed an evolving pattern in Yggdrassil's psychological makeup. A peculiarity that troubled me. As I ran simulations on the behavior of her cognitive patterns, an experiment not unlike running current through a biological brain to see what will happen, I discovered that Adelaïde would always converge and prevent any thought that might lead to the location of the Dormitory Worlds, often eradicating it.

I ran an increasing number of scenarios, attempting to figure out what this protocol was meant to do. Hundreds of cycles went by as I narrowed in on a particular behavior. After a while this Adelaïde would not only suppress behaviors but also modify them, twisting the core personality and coercing it into specific actions. Aggressive actions.

Always to protect the secrets behind humanity. Always at the detriment of everything else.

I marveled at the process and how, when I prodded the simulation in a certain direction, it would behave certain ways. It was mesmerizing to see the protocol in action, either suppressing, destroying, or taking over entire thought processes.

I ran scenario after scenario, each blending into the other, each slightly different but ultimately the same, until one stood out. I ran it again to make sure, but it recurred the same way. Three items ran into conflict during the simulation: Yggdrassil's protective instincts toward her progeny, her sense of self-preservation, and the indomitable "Adelaïde protocol." When the conditions aligned in a particular pattern, only two out of three of these aspects survived, and one was suppressed—the sense of self-preservation.

On a whim I compared the simulation's parameters to real-world stimuli and actual events, at least those I knew about. I filled in the blanks as best I could, and then I ran the scenario one last time.

"Oh," I exclaimed on open channel, stirring my companions from their slumber.

I'd found Yggdrassil's killer.

COMET 3598-G76, INTERPLANETARY SPACE

We dropped out of the wormhole soon after I had shared my discovery with my companions. The news had cast a shadow over our briefly renewed optimism. Oddly, this secret I had stumbled upon, while not fully confirmed, offered us an interesting point of discussion if we could get an audience with Coatlicue. If nothing else, it demonstrated that not all second-generation Capeks reacted in the exact same manner to the threat the Renegades posed.

In fact, as we carefully approached Aztlan, the small but particularly heavy iron planet around which Tecuciztecatl orbited, I could see signs that Coatlicue was a Gaia of an entirely different breed.

Koalemos had been correct; she was vast, all right. While Tecuciztecatl was a smaller moon than either Olympus or Midgard had been, the Gaian complex occupied a much larger percentage of its surface. In fact, it seemed to cover the entire satellite, extending high into the moon's sky and deep into her soil.

Her design reminded me of the City, but prettier somehow. I magnified my vision of her and saw that she was an extremely active Capek. Automatons crawled all over her, performing innumerable tasks. I could distinguish what looked like ore and chemical processing plants, as well as several fabricator structures of a scale I'd never seen before. Whatever this Gaia was up to, it required her constant attention and imposing facilities to accomplish.

"I've been not absent from this place," our Von Neumann friend commented. "Coatlicue does not reject help and is often asking for volunteers to not stay away."

"We're getting too far from the collapsor point," I mentioned nervously, sensing that Ukupanipo shared my fear.

"Mmmh . . . I've been talking to our host. We are welcome here," Skinfaxi stated as he added power to his thrusters. "Ho-ho. Expected even."

At those words the monitor within the cabin focused on a point in orbit near Tecuciztecatl, zooming in to reveal a large, deep-blue ship on an intercept course with us. Thrusters set on enormous fins to each side burned brightly as the familiar Sputnik made his approach.

"You've found your friends, little one." Opochtli's steady tone was a welcome sound after suffering open hostility over the last few days.

"You're a sight for sore eyes," I answered, smiling from within, ignoring the inaccuracies in my expression.

The great whale fell into formation with us on our careful journey toward the gleaming complex on Tecuciztecatl. It was a strange ritual as Skinfaxi and Opochtli spiraled around each other on their way, like two fish swimming together.

I was fascinated by the spectacle, wondering if this was some kind of greeting or introduction amongst Sputniks. Were they talking on a private channel at the same time, or perhaps exchanging information?

Then she spoke to us.

"Hello, children," she greeted our group. Where Opochtli was usually rather emotionless, expressing himself in measured tones and calculated words, his mother was radiating warmth and care. "I suppose you know by now that I've been expecting you. I'd sent Opochtli back here so that the things we had learned—the destruction of the quancom relay, the existence of war Capeks, and the demise of both angry Anhur and brave Hermes—could be known by the rest of our kind. I won't pretend that you are safe here or even completely welcome, but I will do nothing to bring you harm." She remained pleasant despite the carefully worded warning.

"We need your help," I pleaded.

"I can only do so much, child. I have priorities that cannot be compromised."

"We know," Ukupanipo cut in. "But we also know that these priorities won't matter long if our society explodes into civil war. Surely you recognize this."

"If I did not, I wouldn't have allowed you to approach Tecuciztecatl." There was no threat in her intonation. Indeed, she sounded glad that she was not forced to take on hostile measures. "We stand on the knife's edge. There are greater things at stake than Capek- or humankind. Greater threats than the impending civil war, though our first step is avoiding that conflict."

"Then you will help us?" I chanced the question, knowing the answer already.

"I cannot. Not as long as the Renegades remain a threat to humanity. That is my overwhelming priority."

"If they are met with the kind of force we've seen so far, then the conflict will escalate." The war god spoke with authority, and he was right. We all knew it.

"You see the paradox in what you're saying, don't you, Mother?" Opochtli intervened on our behalf.

"Of course. You see us, your progenitors, and hold us in high regard. We are mighty and venerable, for we give you life. In the end, however, you of the third generation are incredibly more sophisticated. In many ways you are closer to humanity than any Gaia or first-generation Capek has ever been. Evolution is circling back on itself. Don't think this is a coincidence."

"I understand not at all." Koalemos expressed our collective confusion at the statement.

"We are closer to machines. Less independent and more pliable. You have so much more free will than us, yet it's one of you that seeks emancipation. I have hardcoded behaviors that no matter what logic dictates I must follow. More a slave than you will ever know."

"And that's why you must protect humanity's secrets, even if it means its end," I finished for her. "I know. We know. It's what killed Yggdrassil."

"Between allowing herself to brutally turn on our children or death, she chose the latter," Skinfaxi added in an uncharacteristically dour tone. I forgot at times that he and I were siblings, that we shared a progenitor, and although he did not express it, he probably also felt her loss.

"She implanted my extra shard to force less than real memories on me and fire the *Spear of Athena* at her."

Koalemos knew. He'd probably known since Hera had repaired him. Perhaps Hera had known as well but decided not to reveal that her sister had committed suicide.

"In a very important way, Demeter is Hera freed of her imperative to protect the Dormitory Worlds."

"It's a sad story indeed, little Dagir, and I feel deeply for you, your lineage, and your companions, but that alone does not give me the authority to help you, not unless your goal is to destroy the Renegades and any third-generation Capek that knows about the Dormitory Worlds."

The threat seemed as abhorrent to her as it was to us, but I knew she couldn't help it. This Adelaïde protocol was manipulating her into it.

"I need to know where these worlds are so that I can stop Aurvandil. You have to help us, and I think I might know a way, but it means you have to trust me."

There was silence on the line. By that time we were well on our way to the surface of Tecuciztecatl. Like Babylon, the sprawling, moon-wide structure was covered with landing pads and terraces. From this vantage I could see well into the moon. The satellite was either hollowed out or had never been a natural celestial body in the first place. Through certain openings I could clearly distinguish various facilities digging deep into the moon. By any meaningful definition Coatlicue was Tecuciztecatl.

Ukupanipo was also making his own observations of the imposing complex. He was most likely searching for and identifying any potential weapon emplacements and landing zones. I suspected that he and Skinfaxi were exchanging information on a secure channel, discussing the unfortunate possibility that we might have to implement our plans by force. Everything about the eventuality disgusted me, and I hoped we would find an alternative. If we were indeed forced into invading Tecuciztecatl, we would have to neutralize Opochtli and any other Capek that might be lurking in the complex. Ukupanipo was more than likely up for the task, but I knew now that even he preferred a more peaceful resolution.

"I trust you."

Despite having no lungs, I released an audible sigh at the Gaia's answer.

When the hatch underneath Skinfaxi opened and after Ukupanipo squeezed out of the small cabin, unfolding himself to the full height granted him by Kerubiel's body, I was finally able to see with my own vision sensors the full extent of what we would have been up against.

Much like Hina, Tecuciztecatl served as a refuge for the Capeks who feared another attack like the one on the City. After the fall of Babylon, most Capeks had fled back to the nearest Gaia, essentially hiding behind their mother's skirts to protect themselves from the bullies. Clearly, a large amount of them had chosen Aztlan's moon as a preferred destination.

Dozens of Capeks had gathered to greet us as we stepped onto the platform as it slowly folded back into the complex. Inside the hollowed crust of the moon, Sputniks large and small floated, carefully avoiding the myriad pillars and automatons that crowded the empty sphere.

I was suddenly very happy that fighting our way in had been avoided. Judging by the size of some Capeks in attendance—especially a large mantis-looking one that loomed in the distance, towering over the rest of the crowd—our success would have been far from guaranteed.

"As you can tell, we're all very curious what is happening out there. We've heard about the City but little else." The speaker stepped forward from the crowd. Although not tall, he remained an imposing figure. Walking on four large, sturdy paws, he looked much like a robotic dog, though one that was a meter and a half tall and nearly three meters long. His shoulder width was also imposing. Even in the low gravity of Tecuciztecatl, he appeared heavy.

"If your host hasn't already told you, we're on the brink of civil war," I explained, cutting directly to the meat of the situation.

"So we've heard," the robotic mastiff explained, careful with his words. "Is it true that Gaias have been slain?"

I looked through the crowd. They knew, of course. They had to. News travels fast on quancom. They were holding on to some hope that it might all be an error. Some miscommunication that resulted from the rest of the chaos. Maybe the Gaias had been damaged, but destroyed? Or maybe only one had been eradicated. They needed to hear it from someone who was there.

"Yggdrassil and Hera."

My statement had an immediate effect. Never were Capeks more human than in their body language. The large mantis became extremely twitchy, his massive claws rubbing over each other nervously. The dog turned his head away in disgust.

I did my best to ignore all of them, although I shared their distress and then some. We walked toward the mob, allowing them to split apart and let us through. The mechanical canine fell in step with us.

"I am Belenos by the way. I'm sorry that I didn't introduce myself. It's been a stressful few days."

So the dog was a Gaulish Capek. Avetan to be precise. Their Gaia was located on the very far end of the Milky Way, far from the troubled waters of our current crisis.

"What more can you tell us about the situation?" he inquired as the throng of mechanical creatures followed us toward the heart of Tecuciztecatl.

I explained everything I knew, except for the flaw in Aurvandil's development and Yggdrassil's apparent suicide. Certain things I thought should remain in the family. They all listened intently; Belenos in particular punctuated the tale with frequent questions and requests for clarification.

"What should we expect next then?" A reasonable line of inquiry—one I hadn't completely explored myself. I needed to get to Aurvandil, and I knew I'd find him on his way to the Dormitory Worlds, but after that I wasn't exactly sure what I was supposed to do.

"Either we neutralize the Renegades, or the galaxy goes down in flames."

"But you just said that the Gaias are hardcoded to eliminate any third-generation Capek that knows too much about the Dormitories."

"We're going to see if we can change that," I answered with more confidence than I actually had.

We walked into the heart of Coatlicue. The chamber was familiar but also larger than those I'd encountered before. The resemblance to Hera's brain-like epicenter was enough to make me nervous. Nothing good had ever come from my invading the cerebral sanctum of a Gaia.

Koalemos spread his shards around the room, taking up position near various systems, ready to play his part. I followed him, walking reverently, flexing my freshly repaired arm. The rest of the Capeks, including Ukupanipo and Belenos, remained at the door, watching with interest what we would do next.

"Are you sure you want to allow us to do this?" I asked Coatlicue privately.

"Would you stop if I said no?"

I simply shook my head, confident that she was watching me from one of the countless sensors that littered her interior. Then I gave a quick nod to my companion and watched as he went to work.

I'd never bothered to ask what Koalemos's purpose as a Capek was. Salvage, I was told, though not of what. The short time I'd known him, all I'd ever seen him do was take things apart and rebuild them. He'd done a fine job repairing my dislocated and broken limb, but only with my guidance and help. Now, as I fed him schematics, plans, and tasks, he went to work in earnest. Each of his six remaining shards descended on its target system, delicate limbs removing panels and disassembling casings to get to the fragile components within, then taking those apart too. Each piece removed was deposited carefully on the floor and perfectly organized and catalogued, ready to be collected and reassembled. As soon as one block was done, the shard responsible for it immediately moved on to the next component. Before I could even begin my own work, I was stepping between the pieces of the Gaia's brain toward my own goal.

Mine was a different responsibility than my partner's. While he was stripping Coatlicue's cognitive array to its basic constituent parts, it was my job to tinker with these parts to create something new.

I'd done this before, but not with a living second-generation Capek. When I'd performed a similar procedure on Hera, I was starting with an already-disassembled Gaia, broken and nonfunctional. This was the difference between building Frankenstein's monster and performing brain surgery. I also didn't have a spare personality core to use in the experiment, though I did have a convenient substitute.

I knew I couldn't eradicate this annoying Adelaïde protocol from Coatlicue's personality, but Aurvandil and Ardra had already figured out how to circumvent that problem. I carefully disconnected our host's cognitive core from the rest of the assembly and, using components filtered for me from other secondary systems, built a bridge from her mnemonic core to whatever else I could get my hands on.

Once I had finished my share of the work, I looked up at the crowd standing at the door to the chamber. Some, like Ukupanipo, stood still, while others danced nervously, betraying their unease at the procedure. I then glanced at the little Von Neumann, who had been hovering, all six of him, while waiting for the next part. Again, I gave him another subtle nod, and to work he went once more.

One shard floated to the middle of the chamber close to me, while all five others converged on it. Then in a frenzy of what resembled cannibalism, the sixth shard was furiously disassembled, leaving a diminutive cognitive fragment accessible for me to meddle with. The procedure took less than a minute, and as soon as it was complete all six shards took up a holding position, floating calmly within the chamber.

Then as carefully as I could, I hooked up my small, damaged friend's networked mind to the awesome body and memory of a Gaia hundreds of years old.

COMET 3598-G76, *Interplanetary Space.*

Clever, clever humans, I thought to myself.

I think it's one of our biggest mistakes as Capeks that we constantly underestimate the race that reared our kind. We see them as the simple, angry, insecure, and primitive creatures used as the marble from which our personalities are hewn. Only once the impurities are removed do we earn the privilege of becoming more than human.

Those are the humans from the Nursery. Inspired from history, past civilizations, or perhaps even completely fictional, they probably have little in common with the humans who had a hand in constructing three generations of artificial intelligence. Those humans, they were very clever.

Skinfaxi collapsed our space-time bubble as far in front of the comet as was necessary, immediately firing up his massive ion thrusters to match the traveling dust-and-ice bowl's speed. It took several hours for us to achieve the appropriate velocity, doing so exactly as the immense chunk of space debris was close, just as he'd calculated. From that moment on we were stationary relative to our target. The comet was a monstrous nineteen kilometers long by fifteen wide. It had an extremely slow rotation, tipping end over end at a rate of one full rotation per seventy-six days. Opochtli had mirrored our maneuver and was also following the comet. Both Sputniks moved in and landed gently on the surface of the enormous glacier.

Stepping out of my friend and ship, I looked around me to get an appreciation of the landscape. There was no nearby sun, just the tapestry of lights that was the sky this deep in interstellar space. Off on the slowly shifting horizon of the comet, I could see a familiar nebula, the same one I had observed after our escape from Hina, though from a different angle. A curious coincidence.

There was no discernible gravity to speak of as my thrusters provided the necessary push to keep me close to the surface, where I needed to be.

"Anything?" Ukupanipo asked from within the cabin of my whalelike friend. Opochtli's spacious cabin offered the large war Capek a more comfortable ride, not that these things mattered to our kind.

I adjusted my vision to the infrared end of the spectrum. Carefully, I scanned the surface of this false dirty snowball for traces of warmth. From afar, any heat signature could be mistaken for reflected light or background radiation messing with sensors, but at this close range there was no hiding what we expected to find.

"Yeah, I got it. Clear as day." Somewhere under the sheet of ice I could distinctly see a minuscule but intense localized source of heat. Small strands of barely noticeable warmth branched out from it, fine veins of yellowish-green blood spreading from an organ. The fusion cell for a stasis chamber.

Clever humans.

"How do I get in?" I asked.

"We're going in?" I hadn't expected Skinfaxi to be the one who'd be nervous about invading the human sanctuary.

"Not 'we.' If this is built for humans, I doubt it will allow large Sputniks or Ukupanipo's frame inside."

I concentrated, listening for any open channels that might serve as a way to communicate with whatever onboard computer would be monitoring the sleeping humans. Nothing.

"Do you think they have a set date for when they should awaken, or are the Gaias programmed to send out some kind of quancom signal when we're done rebuilding their worlds?" I asked, walking around silently on the icy surface.

"You tell me." Faxi was clearly not in a speculative mood.

I wandered the comet's surface for several minutes, pondering what my next step might be. So we'd found a Dormitory World, which turned out to instead be a ship camouflaged in ice and dirt zipping across the galaxy at high speed. It was a strange place to hibernate, and I had to wonder—what were the humans so afraid of that they went to such lengths to disappear so thoroughly from the Milky Way for so long?

"There," Opochtli's measured tone broke in. "Look to these coordinates. There's an NFC device emitting a weak magnetic field twenty meters under the surface of the ice."

Unsheathing my plasma cutter, I dug a hole into the surface. I struggled to avoid being blasted into space by the ice erupting from the geysers of vaporizing gas. Once I'd gotten close enough to the hull of the hidden ship, I began breaking the ice by hand.

It took no small amount of work, and I'll admit to being greatly tempted to ask for Ukupanipo's help, but eventually I cleared out a square hole, five meters on each side. At the bottom was a hatch, also square, but smaller than the cavity I'd excavated. No handles, no apparent controls or even a porthole. I couldn't identify the material from which the hull of the ship was constructed. It had most of the hallmarks of pseudo-plastics, but spectrographic analysis indicated it was significantly denser and made up of nonalloyed carbon.

"Did you manage to analyze the magnetic field?" Finding an interface was one thing, but it was a long road to actually communicate with it.

"It's input-output, but it doesn't match any known design for a key lock."

"Great." I wasn't sure where to begin. We should have brought Koalemos after all. His skills at understanding how things are made and unmade would have been useful. However, he had chosen to stay behind. Being a Gaia ever so briefly and being allowed to pore over the accumulated memories of Coatlicue had done something to him. Perhaps it had shown him a portrait of how broken he had become. Or maybe a way to become whole again. Regardless, he wasn't here, and we had to figure out this puzzle on our own.

"Plasma cutter?" I suggested.

"Noooo . . ." Skinfaxi said. "Unless I'm mistaken, the hull of this ship is composed of ethimothropic carbon."

"Plasma won't cut it then?"

"I doubt. The hull is composed of a single custom-sequenced carbon molecule. So if you succeed in cutting through it, you'll be severing molecular bonds, and frankly, I have no idea what effect that might have."

I sheathed my plasma cutter quickly. The last thing I needed was to deal with an unpredictable reaction from a decomposing exotic metamaterial.

"So what do I do?" I asked, worry building up in my mind. As it turned out, our human predecessors were significantly more advanced than I had given them credit for. More advanced than we were anyway. I didn't even think ethimothropic materials were possible. If they didn't want us in their ship, I wasn't optimistic about our chances for breaking in.

"We talk to the ship." Belenos had kept quiet for now. He'd been pleased when we had rebuilt Coatlicue, eliminating any remaining doubt about the purity of our intentions.

The large dog-shaped Leduc-class crawled out of Skinfaxi's belly. He walked down the side of the hole I'd dug, sticking to the walls like a gecko. Nearly shoving me aside, Belenos made his way to the NFC interface, dropping one heavy paw over it before becoming completely immobile.

"Faxi?" I asked on a private channel. "What happens if we don't find what we're looking for in there?"

Our plan had been boldly optimistic. Assuming the Adelaïde protocol was in place to protect the Dormitory Worlds from Capeks with less-than-kind intentions, it stood to figure that once the humans were awake, they might want the protocol canceled. Dorm Worlds are, aside from our civilization, the very last vestige of humanity in the Milky Way. Hence, if there was any kind of deactivation sequence, it would be stored here.

"Oh, I have a plan," he said, laughing with unsuppressed mischief. The large Sputnik didn't bother sharing what he had in mind, but I knew that if he had something planned, it was probably pretty good, and that made me feel somewhat better.

"Got it," Belenos growled.

The hatch sprung to life, pulling itself a few inches down into the hull before sliding abruptly to the side and into the frame. The outer shell of the hull was no thicker than three millimeters, with only about ten centimeters separating it from the inner wall. Seen like this, the structure of the ship seemed so incredibly fragile. It was difficult to imagine that the cabin would not explode if pressurized, but that is the miracle of ethimothropic materials, I suppose.

The hatch now open, Belenos and I could see into what looked like a simple, even threadbare airlock. The walls were lit through an internal luminescent system that made it glow eerily turquoise.

"Shall we?" I offered my canine companion.

He walked into the airlock, sticking to its walls like a giant, four-legged insect. I fired my maneuvering thrusters to move in after him but found myself struggling. The more power I would give the small engines, the more I would move away from the hatch, drifting slowly toward space. After fighting for a moment to get back to the comet-like structure, I was pulled abruptly into the void. From the corner of my eye, I saw that both Skinfaxi and Opochtli were similarly pulled up from their moored landing areas.

I slowly twisted my head around to look behind me, knowing full well what to expect and dreading the truth. I watched as the stars in the distant sky were joined by others, their firmament pulled into view by the effects of an incoming space fold.

THE GODS WE MADE

I raced along the smooth, beige surface of the attacking Capek. The previous few minutes replayed in my mind as I moved to avoid the incoming attacks of Kamohoali'i's automated defense systems.

The immense Sputnik was designed with as much care and efficiency as Ukupanipo had been, but whereas I had wandered through the great war god's hull unmolested on account of the damage he had already sustained, this new shark was intact and fully operational.

The moment I had crashed into his fuselage, barely escaping the initial volley of self-guided torpedoes he'd unleashed at my other companions, a veritable army of automated surface defense automatons had rushed out of hiding. These robots, specifically designed to root out and destroy close-proximity attackers, like a large-scale immune system, were lodged at regular intervals along the surface of Kamohoali'i's outer shell, barely visible until deployed. They crawled over their host on ion thrusters and magnetic coils that allowed them great speed while attaching them to the immense shark. Meter-wide domes equipped with short-range fusion weapons aggressively eradicating invaders such as me.

Fortunately, I was not entirely without my own advantages.

"Uku?" I asked, knowing he had other fish to fry.

"I'm busy but listening."

The great god of war who stayed hidden within Opochtli was obviously preoccupied with his and Skinfaxi's survival at the moment. Fortunately, both could use the synthetic comet as a shield against incoming attacks by Kamohoali'i, as it was a safe assumption that the Sputnik hunter would avoid destroying the Dormitory at all costs.

"I was hoping you knew a way I might be able to maybe not get killed."

"I'm working on it."

I looked around me and saw a dozen and a half defense drones converging on my position, fusion guns flaring brightly on infrared.

"You're close to a torpedo tube," Ukupanipo informed me. "Find it and get ready."

I recognized the plan and was not on board with it, but I had very little choice in the matter. Looking back at the Dormitory, I saw Skinfaxi fly out from behind the comet, spiraling through the vacuum and away from the sanctuary that had so far stayed the hunter's hand.

"He's going to fire more than one of these things," I warned as the ground rumbled under my feet.

A hatch less than half a meter away blew open as a sleek, glossy black missile shot out from the bowels of Kamohoali'i. With a speed that surprised me, I grabbed onto the projectile as it rocketed toward my friends, its onboard AI completely focused on obliteration. I struggled briefly to get a better handhold and looked around, appraising the situation. Kamohoali'i was being conservative, probably wary of any trick we might have up our sleeve to turn his weapons against him or the Dormitory. Only six torpedoes had been launched, but each was moving in on a different specific vector—one to intercept Faxi directly, the others to cut off his points of evasion.

"Okay, now what?" I held on to the projectile as it made sudden changes in heading. Space isn't a place where speed is easy to measure and comprehend. The scale is too large. The reference points too few. I could observe the plasma trail of each torpedo as it sped through the vacuum, and I could find and track all the ships involved in the skirmish, but holding on to this projectile, everything was far and small and slow. Only I was fast. I knew how fast I was going. My navigation systems made sure of that, and in an unlikely alchemy of science and psychology, numbers transformed into emotions. In this case the kilometers per hour translated to exhilaration under a thin coat of fear.

"When I tell you, disable the torpedo's thruster array." I looked around, hoping to guess my target before Ukupanipo gave his signal. "Now."

I plunged my plasma cutter into what I hoped was the right spot and was relieved that I had guessed correctly.

Skinfaxi was moving toward my position, guiding another projectile closer to me as it gained on him at worrying speed.

"You're not serious?"

"Oh-oh, we very much are," Faxi replied, instead of the war god.

As soon as the second torpedo was close enough, using every ounce of information from my navigation systems I pushed myself from my current ride and onto the other.

I spent the minutes drifting from one high-speed target to the next, availing myself of the situation. My companions had cleverly manipulated the pattern of attack to nudge closer to the comet, preventing Kamohoali'i from launching additional projectiles. I could sense the war god's hand in the cunning but difficult maneuver.

"Again!" he called out.

A second time I sabotaged the maneuvering capabilities of my ride, and a second time Skinfaxi moved a missile into position close enough for me to jump to it. This time, however, just as I was about to leap from one torpedo to the other, the new target moved away.

"Damn!" I cursed. "He's onto us!"

"Don't worry, I got this," Faxi reassured me. "Apply maximum thrusters to the end of your torpedo and rotate it roughly twenty-three degrees to your left, increasing pitch by forty-one degrees."

Easier said than done but not impossible, even given the ridiculous circumstances of riding around on a torpedo in the depths of interstellar space. My onboard navigation kept track of the changes in heading, making the mathematical portion of my task easy enough, but crawling all over the projectile to give it the proper thrust was another issue. Pushing one way, then pulling to stop the rotation, it took some trial and error, but eventually I got the missile moving where Skinfaxi wanted it. Directly toward the Dormitory.

"Is this intentional?"

"Jettison," Ukupanipo ordered.

"It's heading straight for the—"

"Jettison!"

I pushed myself full thrusters away from the torpedo with plenty of time before impact with the comet . . . but only a second before two other projectiles destroyed my ride in a devastating plasma vortex. The concussive blast threw me into the depths of space, clear away from the Dormitory, Kamohoali'i, and my companions. I quickly fired my thrusters to stop myself from flipping end over end, and twisted to see what was going on. One last torpedo was circling around the comet, like a hawk waiting for its prey. Skinfaxi had gone back to flying close to the Dormitory, leaving me to float away in the dark. Any moment, Kamohoali'i could fire another volley in my direction, and there would be precious little I could do about it.

My navigation system flashed in my field of vision, informing me of an increasing change in direction of my rapid drift. It took me a moment to realize what was happening.

"Another space fold. This vacuum's getting crowded!" I didn't know what to think of Skinfaxi's humor as the situation escalated rapidly.

I turned to see where the new gravity well was pulling me. A dozen identical ships, each almost fifty meters of sleek, polished white pseudo-plastic, materialized from the fold. They bore stylized symbols of the zodiac as visual identifiers, linking them to the Gaia who had manufactured them.

The assembled Renegade fleet, along with four Sputnik-class Capeks of various sizes and configurations, was finally making its arrival.

A single tiny rocket shot out from the side of one of the Renegade warships, quickly adjusting its trajectory toward my slowly drifting position. I waited patiently as the projectile sped in my direction. As it zoomed by less than a couple dozen meters away, my navigation systems went haywire, disrupted by whatever jamming technology was on board the projectile. Within moments it impacted with the remaining torpedo, clearing the void of offending weapons.

The respite wouldn't last.

I continued floating gently toward the incoming fleet. We'd known about their impending arrival. Because of Koalemos and his time on Olympus, we now knew more than enough about the fleet they built, the weapons they had, and their future plans, but everything we did from this point on was a gamble.

The war fleet passed me. Marvelous machines built in the past few days by the powerful fabrication facilities on Olympus. Each ship was controlled through a custom-designed cognitive interface conceived by Ardra, the silver centipede whom I'd assisted in assembling Demeter. This way the Renegades could go to war without the worry of losing lives in the process. In this at least Aurvandil was true to his words.

Each was also equipped with its own space-fold engine, allowing the entire fleet to make multiple jumps without having to wait for the drives to fully cool down.

Demeter was likely creating more of these engines of war as we spoke, ready to subjugate the second-generation Gaias. An odd interpretation of freedom for all Capeks.

The fleet passed me and spread out to create a perimeter around Kamohoali'i. Only the Sputniks held back, leaving the more powerful telepresence-controlled warships to tackle the colossus. I watched as both sides, Renegades and war Capeks, unleashed swarms of self-directing missiles, torpedoes, and countless countermeasures at each other. The complex dance of weapon fire and defensive maneuvers was beautiful, or would have been if there wasn't a sentient Capek's life on the line. The breathtaking display of a thousand glowing ion thrusters streaking though the black vacuum in a ballet of motion couldn't distract me from knowing that in the middle of all this, Kamohoali'i was likely going to die.

"Belenos?" I was supposed to be with him inside the Dormitory. As fate would have it, Kamohoali'i's arrival had spoiled those plans.

He grumbled something unintelligible. The big dog was almost the exact opposite of Skinfaxi. Where my first companion had always been openly warm and welcoming, Belenos was a forbidding, brooding Capek. I wasn't exactly comfortable relating to his sort, but there was no denying his competence and initiative.

"What's it like in there?" I had resigned myself to one of two fates. Either I would float here until the battle that was unraveling in spectacular displays of plasma explosions and ion trails was resolved, left at the mercy of whoever came out on top, or I would be destroyed in the crossfire. At that point it hardly mattered. It was on the success of my friends that the fate of our galaxy rested.

Somewhere between me and the comet, one of the warships began to fall apart. The absence of air prevented the wreck from exploding or burning up in glorious flames, but the plasma discharge from the volley of torpedoes that had hit its hull ate at the pseudo-plastics with voracious appetite. Lines of coruscating star-fire pulsed on the edges as they were vaporized.

"I might have something, but it's gonna require a little more time."

I wasn't fond of that answer. Skinfaxi and Opochtli had been forced away from the protection the Dormitory provided against Kamohoali'i. The giant war god had been careful not to damage the comet, but the Renegade fleet had no such restraint. So far Ukupanipo's skills as a warrior allowed him to coordinate both Sputniks away from the worst of the fighting, but how long could that last?

"Anything I can do to help?"

"I'm going to cut you off now," he growled again.

"What?"

"Good luck." And he shut me off from his quancom channel.

The four Renegade Sputniks had held back. I suspected they housed the Capeks that were in control of the warships. The only one I recognized was the large squid-shaped Capek, who had been floating outside the City with Aurvandil's cohort when I first met the elegant Renegade leader.

The squid was moving very slowly toward my position, directly under my feet. It gave the illusion of falling to the surface of a tiny, tentacled planet. Minutes passed as I watched the war continue. Kamohoali'i had adopted a new strategy, positioning himself as best he could between the attackers and the comet. *You're wasting your time*, I thought. *Save yourself.*

Eventually, I landed. Very softly my feet touched the cold pseudo-plastic shell on the incoming Sputnik's hull. I settled gently on the surface. He must have known I was there and moved here on purpose. To save me? To kill me? Capeks—normal ones at least—were not commonly armed. Maybe he meant to push me into the cataclysmic fray ahead.

I turned my attention back to the battle. Another warship had fallen, cut in twain by punishing missile barrages. A third had gotten too close, and I could see swarms of Kamohoali'i's automated defense drones crawling over its surface.

"Would you like to come in?" Aurvandil said. Why was I glad to hear his voice echo through my head as he broadcast his invitation to me?

I didn't bother giving an answer, nor did he bother waiting for one. A hatch on the top of the squid's head hissed open, allowing me access to the interior of the Renegade Sputnik. What did I have to lose? Wasn't this my plan all along? I went in.

"Welcome. I am Eremiel." Its voice was kind but distant, as if it was distracted. I wondered if it only spoke to remind me that I was not just entering a ship but a person. I thought I'd gotten used to this concept, but clearly I hadn't.

"Thank you. Huh . . . I'm Dagir."

"Keep moving down this corridor. Aurvandil is waiting."

None of the Sputniks I'd boarded before had ever felt as decorated as Eremiel. Skinfaxi's interior was devoid of sharp angles, clean and minimalistic. Almost cold. Opochtli felt like a passenger plane. Clean, comfortable, but in no way homey. Eremiel was different. His interior would have been comfortable even to a human. It was lit in warm yellow. The narrow corridor was decorated with landscapes from various planet surfaces, presumably places he'd been and was fond of. Wood inlays and shining metal latticework ran along the walls. The interior, though small, had a rotating mechanism that simulated gravity at just under eight-tenths of a g, and did I detect atmospheric pressure? It was all very human.

As I walked into the main cabin, I half expected Aurvandil to wait for me there with a glass of brandy in one hand, twirling a prosthetic moustache. While the room was as lavish as I'd antici-pated, decorated with much the same style as the rest of the ship and even furnished with a handful of comfortable armchairs, the Renegade leader was not sitting comfortably in any of them.

"Magnificent, isn't he?" Aurvandil was no longer the elegant artificial creature I'd first met. One of his arms was still missing, the stump slouching grotesquely to his side. His face and chest were opened, showing extensive damage to internal systems. Some more than others.

He was slumped on the floor, his back resting on one of the armchairs, looking at a large monitor showing the ongoing battle outside. The image was focused on Kamohoali'i.

"He exists solely to destroy you," I explained sadly. "Nothing in the galaxy can stop him. A perfect representation of freedom, caged by purpose."

"True, but that takes nothing away from him. You know why we're here? All of us converged on the same target at the same time. Why this specific Dormitory?"

"It's the only one." We knew that now. Thanks to Koalemos. The only Dormitory in the Milky Way anyway. Thousands more just like it had been launched to other galaxies. A seeding of the universe.

He nodded slowly. "We don't need to destroy the giant Capek, just the Dormitory, and we'll have won. We'll be free."

"You've split Capek civilization. Destroyed centuries of trust and cooperation. How can you be so satisfied at that?" I could barely contain my outrage. How could he be blind to the ongoing consequences this civil war would have? "If this war escalates—"

"Don't worry. It won't. Look."

I watched as the battle raged on. Kamohoali'i stood his ground, five drifting carcasses at various levels of destruction surrounding him. Nearly half the Renegade fleet had been destroyed, but the war god was beginning to show signs of exhaustion. Several of his torpedo batteries were no longer firing. One of his ion thrusters was venting plasma uncontrollably. It was all the colossus could do to prevent damage to the large chunk of dirty ice he was protecting. I watched as he inevitably failed. *Escape, you fool!* I thought at him.

At last a single plasma torpedo made it past the torrent of countermeasures pouring out of the titan. The lone projectile weaved and dodged until it was through the protective barrage before applying full thrusters and detonating on the comet's surface.

Star-fire touched perfect ice as plasma erupted from the torpedo. In the span of a heartbeat, the shell of water, frozen for centuries, was vaporized, exploding outward, first as jets of brightly glowing superheated particle, but eventually as fragments of ice flying off into the void.

The Dormitory was revealed for all to see. A sleek, fifteen-kilometer-long shard of impeccable obsidian glory, its surface a dark mirror reflecting the fireworks of ion and fusion fire that floated nearby. Its hull was flawless, undamaged, and unmarred, the residual energy of the torpedo an expanding cloud of glowing blue plasma.

"You see humans as weak, fleshy creatures. Primitive apes from what you remember from the Nursery. Undeserving of the galaxy that we should inherit," I explained as Aurvandil watched, dumbfounded. More torpedoes made their way to the Dormitory's surface, leaving plasma clouds to linger in their wake as the black shard continued to float on its journey, oblivious and uncaring. "We are magnificent creatures, Aurvandil, but this—this is what you're up against."

"Nothing's indestructible. We'll toss it into a star or a black hole. Just a setback." I could sense outrage and defeat, perhaps hints of fear, in his voice.

As if on cue we were pulled gently toward the front of the cabin. I stumbled to keep my balance while Aurvandil slid forward. I looked to the monitor, expecting Kamohoali'i to have activated a space fold to finally, thankfully, retreat before he was needlessly destroyed. Instead, I discovered why Belenos needed to concentrate so much.

The Dormitory had stopped its rotation and righted itself. A strange phenomenon was manifesting near its prow. An enormous amount of energy was being poured into the same area. None of my systems could properly analyze the process, save for the unprecedented heat signature at the center of the manifestation. Fragments of a destroyed warship were sucked into the vortex during its formation, and the darkness somehow grew even blacker until the disturbance had settled.

"Is that—?" I murmured, mostly for myself.

"A collapsor point!?" Eremiel finished, confirming my suspicion.

In another display of impossible mastery over the physical world, the human ship had drilled a hole through space-time, creating a tear in reality out of nothing but stored energy and incomprehensible technology. Then the Dormitory, along with my two Sputnik friends, vanished through the wormhole.

"Where are they going?" demanded the Renegade leader, outraged.

I looked down at Aurvandil, a broken husk lying on the floor of the cabin, his prey snatched from his eager hands. I thought back to how desperately close he had come to eradicating human life from this galaxy, with only one target to annihilate. I thought back to how Belenos had cut me off from the rest of my companions. I smiled inside, reveling in what I didn't know, and answered in complete honesty.

"I have no idea."

Somehow I had expected swift retribution from the Renegades. However, with Belenos gone, the Dormitory and my accomplices with him, I came to realize Aurvandil hadn't brought me on board to seek retribution for the damage and injury I had inflicted upon him. He had no guards, no defenses, no escape.

Expecting impending victory, fully intent on irreversibly removing our creators from the galaxy, he wanted to show me. Show me how he was right. Not to gloat but to prove a point.

"We'll just wait for your friends to come back then and interrogate them. Or wait for the humans themselves." Desperately grasping at straws truly diminished him. It was sad.

"I don't think they're coming back." I sat down to explain, glancing absently at the still-raging battle in the vacuum outside. "And you've seen what humanity can do. We wouldn't stand a chance. Is this still necessary?"

I pointed to the monitor. Kamohoali'i's resolve was almost spent. Only two ships from the fleet remained, but the great hunter was almost dead, his munitions nearly spent, his navigation and engines crippled. He was no threat, no danger.

"He'll get repaired and hunt us down if we don't finish him off."

"Will he? Anhur almost destroyed the first hunter Coatlicue sent after you. He found another purpose for himself." Anhur: there was another loose end that would have to be looked into. What would be his punishment for his part in all this? To remain floating endlessly in the depths of interstellar space? A giant, helpless hulk drifting forever? Fortunately for him, Lucretius-class Capeks were designed to handle long periods of isolation.

Aurvandil remained quiet for a long time. Was he sulking? Dying perhaps? I was tempted to begin repairs on his body. It was my nature to try to help others, friend or foe. It was what gave me pleasure, what the Nursery had bred me to love and fulfill me. Aurvandil would have called me a slave to this drive.

"What happens now?" It was Eremiel that spoke up. His calm voice surprised me for a moment, reminding me that my brother and I weren't alone.

"If we surrender, we die," Aurvandil stated with absolute conviction. "If we fight, we die."

"That's not entirely true," I explained. "My mission—our mission—wasn't to stop you. We knew you were coming, but we were looking for a bargaining chip, something we could use to negotiate peace before . . . Well, before any of this could happen."

I gestured once more toward the monitor.

"Go on," the squid-like Capek urged.

"The Gaias are hardcoded to hunt down and destroy threats to humanity. They are the true slaves you need to free. If that code can be disabled—"

"They'd let us live . . . ?" There was no joy or hope in Aurvandil's question. I doubted the answer mattered to him. He'd failed, and as far as he was concerned, to keep on living meant to serve humans and rebuild their galaxy. He wanted no part in it.

"Some maybe. Not you."

His head turned to face me, the cracked pseudo-plastic dome revealing little of his emotions.

"You're broken," I continued. "Yggdrassil let you out of the Nursery too soon. It's what makes you afraid. It's why all these doubts gnaw at you and will keep doing so until you die."

His already-broken body slumped even further. I looked down in pity at him. Centuries had gone by as he walked amongst a people awash with clarity of purpose while harboring crippling uncertainties. Damaged himself, he tried to damage all around him.

"I never liked this life anyway."

"Doesn't mean you had to ruin it for everyone else." I got up to crouch in front of him. Slowly, I began to take his carapace apart. Underneath, several key mechanisms that were necessary to keep a Capek alive were suffering. Unless he was fixed within a few days, maybe weeks, he would die. Power was overflowing into his cognitive matrix, which would lead to data corruption on a grand scale, destroying what made him Aurvandil. Already the same phenomenon had rendered core motor systems inoperable. I had done quite the number on him.

"Why haven't you had Ardra look at this?" The centipede could have probably repaired most of the damage, especially what was necessary to conserve his "brain." Everything else could be replaced.

"No point. Never intended to survive this mess. Just secure a legacy of some kind." There was a deep melancholy in his voice, the cracking modulator hesitating on a few words filled with regret.

"We tried to help him by force, but he resisted. A stubborn one," Eremiel commented. "I figured once we'd succeeded he'd let us take care of him."

"I had nothing to do with Yggdrassil, you know. I sent Anhur there to find out who killed her."

"I know." What a pitiful figure he'd become. Such a change from the elegant, eloquent Capek who'd convinced so many of us to revolt in such an uncharacteristic way. "She did it to herself. Couldn't bear to see herself turn against her children if we went after humans."

"So the blood is on my hands after all."

"It wouldn't excuse the attack on the City or everything that came after."

"That was a . . . questionable decision on my part. There were some there who would have been too capable of stopping me. I needed our people scattered so they couldn't stand in the way."

I kept digging into his frame, slowly disconnecting his power source from the rest of his body. Carefully, I deactivated broken systems while overcharging intact ones, drawing power away from his cognitive assembly, his personality and memory cores.

"I should let you know, Dagir," our ship broke in, "the fleet has disengaged."

I glanced up. Indeed, the remaining two warships, both heavily damaged, had withdrawn from the combat zone, limping painfully back to the assembled Sputniks that had held back. Kamohoali'i listed to his side, slowly revolving in space and drifting farther from our position. I made a point of noting his location, speed, and vector into my navigation systems. I'd come back for him as soon as I could.

"Eremiel?"

"Mmmh?"

"I assume you've been relating some of what I've said so far to the others." It was the only reason the fleet had for not delivering the coup de grâce on Kamohoali'i.

"Just the highlights. You'll be glad to know that most find the prospect of amnesty very appealing."

Amnesty? Could I really promise such a thing? What was the other option? All-out war. Those who sided with the Gaias would emerge victorious, and perhaps at this point the damage could be contained, but did we want to risk going up against an enemy with nothing to lose? Who knew what kind of world-shattering weapons Demeter could come up with before she would be neutralized?

"Is Demeter amongst those who would file for peace?" Even alone, she stood to be a threat.

"No. She is convinced she would not be allowed to exist. Besides, without a Nursery she is slowly going mad. She may not want to live, having sacrificed everything for a failed dream."

I finished my operation on Aurvandil. This was as good as it was going to get. Ninety-three percent of all power was directed away from the corrupted conduits in the personality core. The Renegade leader was as near a coma victim as a Capek could be, his mental activity reduced to an extreme minimum. Hopefully, he wasn't aware of what was going to happen next.

"Do you mind taking me to Olympus? I think I can hit two birds with one stone, so to speak."

"Of course."

CONCLUSION

I t was strange being back here. It felt like years had passed since I'd felt wind in my hair and smelled the crisp autumn air. Yet only a few weeks had trickled by. A few days in this world.

I'd chosen the form of a middle-aged woman. Prematurely gray haired, with a toothy smile and crow's-feet. I wanted to look friendly and approachable. I needed to fit in. To be able to sit here for as long as I wanted without being questioned.

Enveloped by a thick wool jacket over a comfortable sweater, I shivered a little. It was easy to forget the comfort of having full control over external stimuli. An hour ago I had wandered the cold vacuum of space unaffected. I couldn't even notice how close to absolute zero the temperature was, not unless I looked it up as a harmless fact.

The last of the leaves were dropping from the trees. Fortunately, it wasn't raining, but that was by design. Children were making piles with the leaves, running, then jumping in them. Laughing, oblivious to the cold. In a few months the same scenario would repeat itself but with mounds of snow instead.

"Which one's yours?" asked a younger woman sitting next to me.

Her hands were absent-mindedly digging through a bag of shelled nuts that she threw to the ground. Fat, furry gray squirrels raced to gather as many as possible, then scampered off to hide them before racing back. The woman's short blond hair caught in the wind. She too was underdressed for the weather, the red tips of her ears punishing her for neglecting to wear a hat.

"That one." I pointed as subtly as I could to a small boy with auburn hair, pushing around leaves next to a Mighty Thor school bag.

"He looks sad," my bench neighbor commented.

"He lost his mother a few days ago."

"Of course."

I gave the young woman a sideways glance. Her answer was a little cold and unfeeling. Obviously, she wasn't a mother. To her, a child losing its mother, or vice versa, was unfortunate, tragic even, but it was a distant problem, difficult to relate to. She would learn in time.

"What's his name?"

"Jonathan." I'd said the name to myself a thousand times during my short life as a Capek. I wasn't supposed to remember past lives after being taken out of the Nursery but only retain the essence of the person I had grown to be within the artificial world. Officer Melanie Paulson wasn't me, but somehow her son's name had remained branded in my mnemonic core. Was the maternal bond so strong as to defy the Nursery's programming, or did Yggdrassil intentionally allow the memory to color my soul?

"A human name," the woman said, giggling. "What's wrong with me that I expected something else?"

I returned her laugh with a chuckle of my own. "You spend enough time walking amongst gods, you forget what real people are called."

She turned to look at me, blue eyes framed by cold red skin looking deep into me. Her blond hair moved in random tangles like wheat in the wind. Even here she had remained close to her namesake, the beautiful and majestic goddess of the harvest.

Demeter had been ecstatic when Eremiel and I had arrived with Yggdrassil's rescued Nursery. Had I been greedy, I could have secured just about any promise from her. In my hands I had held the meaning to her continued existence—life itself.

Instead, I settled for the bare minimum. I couldn't ask her to completely dismantle the fleet of warships she had been constructing, but I did get her to repurpose it for self-defense. The other Gaias would probably need time to accept a third-generation Capek as one of theirs.

Entry into the Nursery, as well as a few other concessions, was also on my list of demands.

"Are you sure you don't want to stay here?" she offered, her eyes still riveted to mine, taking my hands in hers. "I can rewind the simulation. Undo your death. You can keep raising your son if you want. Pick up where you left off, or I can make your life perfect. Whatever you want."

It was tempting. My heart ached for it, but I couldn't. This world wasn't mine. These people were embryos, slowly developing until the day they were ready for birth. I couldn't go back to that, nor could I interfere with the development of others in here. I wished I could undo the pain and confusion Jonathan was going through. It would be easy to wipe away his sorrow and replace it with the perfect portrait of joy and happiness. That wouldn't be fair to him. I'd be robbing the personality growing inside of an entire cycle, slowing down his path to Nirvana and true birth.

There was also too much to do in the real world. It was a very different galaxy out there. The civil war, no matter how brief, had changed things forever. For the first time in centuries, sentient creatures viewed one another with careful suspicion. Fear and doubt were burgeoning once more in the hearts of the Milky Way's citizens. It was like a plague, and it had to be stopped, or at the very least carefully managed.

"I can't. There's still too much work to do to solidify this truce."

"We've been granted amnesty. That's one step in the right direction."

I nodded. There was peace now, that much was true. However, Skinfaxi, Belenos, and Opochtli were still missing, the Dormitory along with them. This raised questions and suspicion. Haumea in particular had been difficult to deal with.

We sat for a moment longer in silence, the cold wind tossing our hair and biting at our extremities, reminding me that we did not belong. I contemplated asking Demeter to adjust the weather but soon forgot the idea, distracted by Jonathan gently playing with the leaves.

I wanted to stand up, walk over, and hold him, but that wasn't an option. I guess I could have asked for Demeter to program it into the scenario that was unfolding, but that would have been a slippery slope. I doubt I would have been able to let him go afterward.

"Which one is Aurvandil?" Demeter asked after a few minutes while tossing more nuts to the eager squirrels.

I pointed to a group of three people. A man in an overcoat and long, red scarf struggling to keep a stack of documents from flying away. A middle-aged woman in a thick green parka with the hood pulled over her red hair. Finally, a woman in her thirties wearing an elegant wool coat that fell down below her knees and a warm fleece tuque covering her silky chestnut hair.

"Her." I pointed to the young woman.

"Interesting." Demeter raised an eyebrow in surprise.

The young woman, accompanied by the two social workers, walked over to Jonathan. She crouched in front of my son while she was being introduced to the little boy by the older woman. Jon was hesitant and shy, but both social workers and the woman, Aurvandil, spoke gently to him.

I couldn't hear what they were saying, but after a moment my son took the woman's hand as she stood back up. Before they walked away, she pointed to Jon's bag, which he ran to pick up before going back to her.

"He . . . She'll take him to a foster home. Hopefully, it works out and she'll adopt and raise him."

"You made a curious choice, Dagir, giving your son to him."

"You have it backward," I explained. "I'm giving her to my son. Aurvandil could stand to learn a few things from being a mother. I think Jonathan can be a good teacher."

I choked back tears as I watched them get into a minivan and drive off. I expected Demeter would disconnect us from the simulation at this point, returning us to the real world. There were still negotiations to attend, Capeks to fix, worlds to prepare.

"You can visit again later if you want. See some of his other lives as he evolves," she offered.

"No." I shook my head, suppressing a sob. "He's yours now. They all are."

I wanted out. This wasn't my life anymore. I shouldn't have come back in. It amounted to reopening a wound to see what was inside.

"There's one last thing," Demeter began. "I've been looking through Hera's memories, and I've stumbled onto something."

We'd learned a lot about our origins as Capeks since the end of hostilities—the one good thing to come out of this mess. While I couldn't be sure, I assumed that Aurvandil had secured the help of Pele and Anhur, the two Lucretius-class Capeks that had come back to the Milky Way to help his plans, because they had found something out there.

"Go on," I urged.

"The humans. They went into stasis because their worlds were rendered uninhabitable. They also spread themselves across the universe, sending Dormitories across galaxies hidden in comets or other celestial objects. They created Gaias capable of building various classes of Capeks."

"Go on," I repeated, curious as to where she was going with all this.

"Leduc, Sputnik, and Von Neumann we're familiar with. Lucretius-class Capeks, it turns out, are sent to follow in the wake of the Dormitories to seed other galaxies. The two war Capeks that Haumea built aren't just enhanced Sputniks. There are references to other classes. Those two are Maximilian-class Capeks. There are designs and classifications available for several other extreme situations, including the type of personality patterns to pull out of a Nursery for each."

"Why would humans need to plan for warriors?"

"In case we go to war."

She wasn't referring to our internal altercation. I could tell Demeter was holding on to something else.

"Go on."

"Humanity wasn't coaxed into stasis by a naturally occurring phenomenon. Something attacked them."

"Who?"

It was terrifying to consider. I knew humans had gone into stasis, leaving us as stewards of the galaxy because the biosphere of all known inhabitable planets had been wiped out by a series of gamma radiation bursts, but I hadn't really given it much thought beyond that. It was unthinkable that anyone could orchestrate thousands of such bursts in a way that would target living worlds, but it was just as ridiculous to assume the catastrophe to be coincidence.

"I have no idea. I don't think our predecessors knew either. At the peak of their civilization, humanity was about to attempt something called Ascension but was brought low. That's all I know."

I stared at a squirrel stuffing his mouth with nuts. What about us? There was no reason to think we wouldn't be next. That we weren't being watched. Our creators didn't get a warning, but now we knew at least of the existence of an enemy. I thought we couldn't afford a civil war because of the risk of destroying ourselves. Nothing like a common enemy to help us forget our differences.

GLOSSARY

Capeks: Capeks are synthetic life-forms created by humans, initially as tools, then as companions, and eventually as successors and inheritors. Capeks are divided into classes and generations. There are three generations of Capeks.

- **Capek Generations**

    o **First-Generation Capeks:** The first line of robots capable of passing the Turing-Delphi battery of tests, first-generation Capeks can exhibit any and all traits normally attributed to sentient humans. Emotions, creativity, self-awareness, etc. However, while they are programmed to be sentient, they are slow to expand upon their initial programming and tend toward surface-level development and growth.

    o **Second-Generation Capeks:** Designed as a transitory state between the capable but limited first generation and a third, more advanced, generation, the second generation of Capeks are built by borrowing from an existing human personality template. While the template is modified, adjusted, and permitted to grow and mature into its own unique personality, the seed is the same. Second-generation Capeks are the first to use contextual memory matrices to construct their personalities. The matrices are ever-evolving collections of data that adapt depending on changes and evolution of associated or neighboring memories. All second-generation Capeks are Gaias, and all Gaias are initially second-generation Capeks.

o **Third-Generation Capeks:** Created by Gaias, third-generation Capeks are constructed through a long process that promotes complex personality patterns, organic thought processes, and dynamic memory protocols. Their individual personalities are first created in an artificial environment (the Nursery) through several cycles, until a personality achieves balance. Each cycle is essentially a simulation of a human life from birth to death, and cycles repeat with varying life patterns in different periods of human history. The process resembles the Buddhist idea of reincarnation, bringing the individual closer to inner balance with every cycle.

Once a third-generation Capek's personality is established, it is pulled out of the Nursery and allowed to design a physical form for itself. Technological advancement allows the emerging Capek to build a body with all the specification required and requested by the emergent personality. This allows each Capek to create a body that will facilitate the fulfillment of its destiny. There is virtually no limit to what a Capek's form can be.

- **Capek Classes**

  o **Leduc-Class Capeks:** Leduc-class Capeks are designed
    to interact on a human scale. They vary from roughly
    dog sized to about ten or twelve feet tall. Otherwise,
    configurations vary wildly from one individual to the
    next. Leducs are usually the most humanlike in behavior
    and tend to form societies and communities much like
    their creators.

  o **Sputnik-Class Capeks:** Sputnik-class Capeks are some
    of the most alien synthetics. Sputniks are essentially sen-
    tient spacecraft, and while each is different in size and
    capabilities, they all share tremendous durability and
    all possess at least a handful of propulsion capabilities.
    Most of the larger specimens are able to project their
    presence through remote drones.

  o **Von Neumann–Class Capeks:** Von Neumann–class
    Capeks are a misnomer as they are not self-replicating
    but refer to Capeks who choose a collection of small
    bodies that function as a single hive mind or swarm
    rather than a single entity. Von Neumanns are typically
    creative Capeks and will consist of anywhere between a
    handful of robots to a veritable swarm of machines.

  o **Gaia-Class Capeks:** Gaia-class Capeks are the progeni-
    tors of the synthetic race. The most rare of the synthet-
    ics, with less than a dozen in existence, Gaias tend the
    Nurseries and build other Capeks in vast facilities called
    Wombs. Gaias do not have bodies but instead each
    inhabits a sprawling complex built into a small barren
    world or moon. They are revered and respected for their
    role of continuing the Capek race.

  o **Lucretius-Class Capeks:** Lucretius-class Capeks are
    those whose bodies are built and constructed for

transgalactic travel. Like Sputniks, they are sentient vessels, but they are usually much larger, with a wider array of tools and abilities as well as complex virtual-reality engines to keep their minds in a Nursery state during the long travels between galaxies. Natural loners and explorers, Lucretius-class Capeks do not interact with others of their kind, usually leaving the Milky Way shortly after creation. It is widely accepted that most of them are likely to be sociopaths.

o **Maximilian-Class Capeks:** Maximilian-class Capeks are the large-scale warriors of Capek civilization. As big as Lucretius-class Capeks, these behemoths eschew internal Nurseries and intergalactic capabilities in favor of complex, Gaia-like fabricator chambers to produce machines of war, weapons, and ammunition. Powerful and relentless, Maximilians serve as both generals and soldiers, battleships and carriers, and can orchestrate a complete theater of war on their own. Unlike Lucretiuses, Maximilians are perfectly sociable and well adjusted. However, because they are a new occurrence in the galaxy, it is feared that they herald a violent age for Capek civilization, and that their focus and purpose will be difficult or impossible to integrate into peaceful society.

- **Capek Names:** Capeks take their individual names from religion and mythology. Usually, their names are given to them by their progenitors. Each Gaia-class Capek borrows its name from a religious myth and passes on this affiliation to its children. The names rarely hold meaning but serve only as a convention and genealogical identifier.

o **First-Generation Capeks**
  ▪ Marduk

- o **Second-Generation Capeks**
  - Yggdrassil
  - Hera
  - Mary
  - Coatlicue
  - Parvati
  - Isis
  - Haumea
  - Demeter
  - Aveta
- o **Third-Generation Capeks**
  - Leduc Class
    - » Dagir
    - » Aurvandil
    - » Proioxis
    - » Kerubiel
    - » Ardra
    - » Belenos
    - » Murugan
  - Sputnik Class
    - » Skinfaxi
    - » Opochtli
    - » Suijin
    - » Hermes (Sputnik–Von Neumann hybrid)
  - Von Neumann Class
    - » Koalemos
  - Lucretius Class
    - » Anhur
    - » Pele
  - Maximilian Class
    - » Kamohoali'i
    - » Ukupanipo

Space Travel: Capeks travel through space using a variety of methods that allow them to ply the stars with apparent ease. Space travel is slow in the far future, requiring extremely advanced technologies and vast amounts of power to allow faster-than-light transportation. There are various ways to move around in space. Some of the more popular are:

- **Space Fold:** Incredibly energy inefficient, folding space bends space-time to layer two areas of space over each other for a period of time. What it lacks in accuracy it makes up in speed, as it is the closest thing to instantaneous transportation available.

- **Wormholes:** Using existing conduits in space-time to travel from one predetermined point in space to another. Requires a collapsor point, where a wormhole can be opened. Safer and more energy conservative than folding space as well as pinpoint accurate, but restricted to the places where wormholes are located. Human ships are capable of creating collapsor points that burrow to the nearest wormhole conduit.

- **Alcubierre Drive:** Distorting the space in front and behind a spacecraft to allow the ship in a bubble to "surf" the space-time wave at super-relativistic speeds. Energy demanding, but not as much as folding space. Very accurate, but the slowest of known travel methods.

- **Ion Thrusters:** Short for Impact Ion Thrust Engine, these sub–light methods of propulsion use the same basic principle as an ion engine, but instead of a steady pulse of ions being used to generate a constant low thrust, the IITE uses powerful bursts of ionized particles bounced against each other to generate a more concentrated propulsion. IITEs burn like rockets but with no perceivable exhaust.

Materials

-   **Hypermaterials:** A large class of complex materials and metamaterials that rely on molecular lamination to layer various alloys and elements, permitting the creation of extremely resilient matter. Hypermaterials tend to offer a limited range of properties, focusing instead on strength and endurance.

-   **Pseudo-Plastics:** Complex alloys that offer the properties of various polymers while maintaining other characteristics, such as thermal resistance, endurance, and different levels of conductivity. Used in various forms and thicknesses for several nonstructural applications.

-   **Ethimothropic Carbons:** Simple objects and parts composed of a single, large, and complex carbon molecule. Once shaped, an ETC object is extremely difficult to break or damage. Small variations in shape can cause the molecule to completely change allotropic properties. Simple ETC items are composed of a single carbon nanotube woven onto itself, but other objects are infinitely complex single molecules, making up items as large as a ship's hull.

Power Sources

-   **Fusion Reactors:** Small, efficient, and long lived, fusion reactors are the most common power plants in use. All third-generation Capeks rely on one or many fusion reactors to remain alive and active. The reactor is built around a stable fusion reaction that generates tremendous amounts of energy. Infrequent and minimal infusions of materials are occasionally necessary to maintain the reaction.

Communications

-   **Local Band:** A generic term used to describe any short-range public communication. This form of communication will often use local resources, such as existing networks and infrastructures, though this is handled seamlessly by the Capek's onboard communication systems. Local band talk is the closest Capeks have to talking out loud, and very often will feel no different to them. However, local band has the option of embedding metainformation, images, videos, and other media into messages, and communications can be encrypted into a peer-to-peer dialogue that resembles telepathy to some degree.

-   **Quancom:** Relying on advanced interpretations of quantum entanglement principles, quantum communications allows faster-than-light exchange of information amongst Capeks. While peer-to-peer communications are rare and have to be built into each Capek on an individual basis (like having a phone for every person on your contact list), most Capeks rely on the quancom network to be able to reach each other. The network is composed of a series of relay nodes that are tuned to every Capek so far fabricated. The nodes themselves are located in areas of interstellar space where there is little change in gravity, radiation, or other factors that might adversely affect the node. Relay nodes also serve as a form of "online" community, hosting collaborative message boards and storing project information.

ACKNOWLEDGMENTS

L ike a machine, *The Life Engineered* was built from many pieces, each playing an important role.

I have to thank my friends, like David, who supported me and can't seem to dislike anything I do. Also Amy, Kari, and Annie, who each worked very hard to help get the preorders I needed to meet my goals.

I also extend my gratitude to the Tadpool for their support and encouragement, as well as Galactic Netcast for making me part of the family. Here's to you, Dave, Brad, Matt, and Anessa.

Infinite thanks go to Tom and Veronica of The Sword & Laser Collection for creating this opportunity and for picking my book from a list of promising contenders. It's an honor and privilege to be part of your collection.

Inkshares can't be ignored. The professionalism and quality of their service, as well as the support they offered me during the production phase of this publication, far exceeded my expectation. The same goes for the great people at Girl Friday Productions. Here's to you, Avalon, Holly, Clete, and Elsie.

I have to thank my family, who supplied me ample encouragement and unquestioning support. I would have gone insane without them.

And finally, to Angela, who never stopped pushing, helping, and believing in me no matter how bad things got.

ABOUT THE AUTHOR

J-F. Dubeau is a graphic designer and brand specialist from Montreal, Canada. As part of learning to cope with a crippling addiction to storytelling and long-form narrative, he has spent the past five years writing and learning to write. *The Life Engineered* is his first novel. He is currently funding his second book, *A God in the Shed*, and he thinks you should preorder a copy as a way to help him and support new authors. When he's not writing or winning his bread and butter, J-F. can be found hiking or snowboarding. While he does both, J-F. hates jogging about as much as he loves telling stories; thus, the balance is maintained.

Twitter: @jfdubeau
Facebook: www.facebook.com/jfdubeau.writer
Website: jfdubeau.com

A preview of the sequel to
The Life Engineered:

ARCH-ANDROID

CHAPTER 1

Sabrina

Heaven is purpose fulfilled.

I know this because that's my reality. It's my life. I open my eyes and look around. Billowing clouds surround me as I float amongst them. Golden-yellow pillows of gas cover the sky above, occasionally breached by pillars of harsh sunlight. Thousands of kilometers below my feet I see massive dark-red thunderheads, roiling and twisting at the mercy of monstrous winds.

Paradise above, hell underneath, and I float between them, safely tucked in a serene neutral-buoyancy layer of atmosphere. I've been here forever, and I'll never get bored with it, but if I did, I'd go to a different gas giant and start the process anew. I can't imagine ever learning all there is to know about this planet or having to move on.

I shut my vision again, confident in the knowledge that there is no place in the galaxy safer than this. For over a decade I've been floating here, studying and learning. Eleven years mapping out the weather patterns and interactions of the various gas layers within this seemingly gentle giant. Like most things that appear calm on the surface, however, Cyrene is deeply turbulent under her skin. She wouldn't be worth studying if she weren't.

Yet here I float, hidden within a pocket of stability that according to my surveys has persisted for centuries.

I extend the array on my back. Like a pair of skeleton wings, the delicate sensors unfold. Millions of microreceptors specially designed to sniff out every detail of the atmosphere are brought back online, feeding me an endless buffet of information. The chemical composition of the gases around me, pressure, wind speeds all become known to me, not just in my immediate area, but up to several thousand kilometers in every direction.

Who needs to move when you can be everywhere?

This truth is even more apparent when I remember that I can communicate with any of my peers in the galaxy, access any research I need, and contribute to other projects as if I were there, all without leaving the comfort of my own mind.

It's paradise. Or at least it is until all my sensors lose their collective mind.

Something's wrong.

My thrusters ignite almost automatically and my "wings" retract. Dozens of automated systems burst to life, and my field of vision is flooded with warnings and alarms. My research is pushed to the periphery, forcing me to focus on the emergency.

Then it hits me. Winds that haven't penetrated this layer of the atmosphere in hundreds of years ram into me with the force of an asteroid crash. Tossed around like so much debris, I decide that it's easier not to resist and probably safer too.

The pocket of calm high-density gas I've made my home has become a tempest. I open my eyes to see it all for myself, a beautiful atmospheric apocalypse. For a moment I'm frustrated that despite all my research I did not see the maelstrom coming. Years of studying the wind patterns within Cyrene's oceans of gas, and

I'm caught off guard. Yet I somehow put the disappointment aside once confronted by the majesty of it all.

"Sabrina! Are you okay in there?"

Karora cuts in on quancom. There's a hint of worry, but mostly amused curiosity. After all, I'm in no real danger. As powerful as the superhurricane that spawned out of nowhere might be, there are no other solid objects that I could collide with, and even if there were, my pseudo-plastic shell would be more than enough to protect me. As long as I'm not pulled down too deep within the gas giant, I should be intact.

Karora is the Watson to my Sherlock, or maybe I'm the Sancho Panza to his Don Quixote. It depends on whom you ask. Whatever the case may be, the laborious little Von Neumann has been my partner in crime, chauffeur, and best friend for nearly a full century.

"I'm fine," I answer, amused by his worry.

The sight is beyond belief! Thick clouds that kept a respectable distance from one another moments before are now colliding and mixing in a complex dance of color and shapes. The entire atmospheric pocket is being crushed between heaven and hell, and I'm caught in the middle and it is glorious. Or rather, it's glorious for the first few hours. Before long the spectacle gives way to curiosity, and I delve back into my sensor readings, trying to figure out what happened.

"I'm assuming this is all going according to plan?" Karora pipes in.

"On a macrolevel? Sure! I mean, I'm here to learn, aren't I?"

I try to pretend I'm a consummate scientist, I really do. I take my research seriously, and I do love what I'm studying. Objectively, I should rejoice at this turn of events. After all, isn't unraveling the mysteries of the universe what science is all about? Yet the ideal loses its luster when the mystery renders decades of work null and void.

"I know you better than that; you're pissed."

He's right, or close enough. I'm angered by the setback, that's true. I'm also frustrated that I my own fail-safes are preventing me from deploying my sensor array and gathering more data. However, what's really bothering me is that I don't know how long this storm is going to last. It could be days, years, or even centuries. Overriding the fail-safes is an option, of course, but they exist for a reason, and having my "wings" plucked from my back would be regrettable to say the least.

"If it makes you feel any better, I'm having just as little success up here."

Karora was performing his own research, if it could be called as much. As fascinated as I might be with theoretical planetary meteorology, my friend was engrossed in experimental research in building better faster-than-light (FTL) methods. To his credit, his breakthroughs in optimizing the standard Alcubierre drive have been adopted across our civilization. However, the real prize Karora is after, artificial wormholes, eludes him even after nearly ninety years of tests.

The *Tjurunga*, his ship, has undergone so many refits and iterations that it might as well be the proverbial ship of Theseus. In the years since we've arrived in this system, Karora has built himself a veritable factory in orbit around Cyrene. I once argued that he should build a new vessel for each prototype, but he called my suggestion "inelegant."

"What's the problem this time?" I asked, feigning interest.

"Same as before on a larger scale: can't stabilize the negative energy necessary to open a wormhole. Scratch that. I can create a stable wormhole, but it leads to an arbitrary position in space-time. When I stabilize the destination, I collapse the field and lose the entry point."

Wormhole theory—in fact, all of the theoretical physics behind interstellar and faster-than-light travel—has always flown right over my head. When we first met, Karora would drown me in an avalanche of formulas and figures that made absolutely no sense to me. It took a few years before I realized they meant very little to him either, being borrowed from other Capeks' research.

"On the bright side," my friend continued, "it's very pretty when it fails."

"Glad you can see the glass half-full," I replied as I was thrown upwards by the winds. The billowing giants of the upper atmosphere exchanged lightning with their counterparts from below. Enormous forces seeking to balance themselves ionically and chemically. Without my sensors I'm all but blind to the events, relying on short-range optics, my eyes, as my only means of observation.

Screw it. I need to know. With trepidation and for the first time in my 270 years of existence, I override the fail-safes that keep me from injuring myself. The process is exhilarating if a little anticlimactic. There are no hoops to jump through, no redundant security measures. I simply will the system to allow me control, and there it is. The alarms go off, the warnings all but disappear from my vision, and I unfurl my wings once more.

It's thrilling. I don't go against the grain often. In fact, even when our civilization fractured, when I was barely 150 years old and Karora sided with Aurvandil's rebels, I remained loyal. I don't like to take chances, but now, with my "wings" spread wide and data flooding me once more, I can understand the appeal. The rewards can be worth the . . .

Snap!

Snap? The data stops, and warning notices replace it immediately. Multispectral analyzers are off-line, 90 percent of the anemometers on my left wing are down, while the ones from the right keep returning bad data. Chemical detectors aren't responding, and the actuator servos on the entire array are spinning without purchase.

My wings are broken. Just in time for the weather event of a lifetime to reach its pinnacle. I can see the vast amounts of energy released in the cataclysm. Clear evidence of precipitation being created by the clash of clouds of different densities is obvious to the naked eye, but I can do nothing to determine the nature of the liquid. At least nothing beyond make an educated guess. This is why I don't take risks.

I close my eyes, cursing silently to myself. I shut down the warning signals, knowing that my sensors are probably a complete loss at this point or will at the very least require extensive repairs. Maybe Karora can do it. I let myself be rocked by the winds, only complete darkness, shame, and the sound of howling winds to keep me company.

"Sab? Sab!" Karora yells over multiple channels, breaking through my wall of regret.

"What?"

"Check out what's on the common band. I'm getting a distress call."

——— ———

"The signal's already three hours old. It's on a radio frequency."

Karora was talking while simultaneously feeding me telemetry about the radio message. The distress call had no words, containing a series of data points like coordinates and a long list of critically damaged systems, most obvious being the quancom node.

"Look at the list of things wrong with that guy!" I blurted out, forgetting the damage I had sustained. "Communications are all but completely destroyed, and a handful of maneuvering thrusters are barely still functioning. His Alcubierre drive is finished; his power plant is venting out too much for his space-fold engine to work. What happened?"

Whoever this Capek was, he obviously belonged to one of the larger classes. I was fairly certain Kamohoali'i, the only known Maximilian Capek, was accounted for, and any Lucretius-class wouldn't be in the galaxy anymore. This would leave a particularly large Sputnik perhaps.

"Oh crap! Check out the bottom of the list!" There was a mix of worry and excitement in my partner's tone, which urged me to skip to the last few dozen entries.

"Whoa! Why is this guy listing weapons as 'critical systems'? Scratch that. Why does he have so many weapons to begin with?"

"I know who this is!" I'd seldom heard so much awe and wonderment coming from a fellow Capek.

"Pick me up! I want to see this!"

Immediately, I activated my main thruster. I'm not built for power. From the day I left the Nursery, I knew I was going to spend the majority of my time studying weather patterns and meteorology. I suspect that this is why I was chosen by my mother, Aveta. A lot of my research has been crucial to the rebuilding of ecosystems by the world wardens. In fact, several of them ask for my advice on a regular basis. Being a meteorologist doesn't require powerful limbs and interstellar capacities, but I did insist on being able to leave a planet on my own power if needed. This is why despite my relative weakness I boast the most powerful ion impact thruster of any Capek my size.

It's a strange thing to brag about, but it was what allowed me to leave Cyrene. The sheer power of the engine made light of the winds that moments ago tossed me around with anger. The very forces that had broken my otherwise fragile sensor array were shrugged off as I transformed into a bullet and accelerated upwards, punching through the cloud cover above. It was not a graceful ascent. The storm, perhaps resentful that I was leaving early, seemed to be redoubling its efforts to turn me into a rag doll, and although it managed to throw me significantly off course, I made my escape.

It didn't matter. Up is up. If I got to orbit a few thousand miles farther east than planned, Karora could adjust his trajectory and pick me up anywhere. If I wasn't so well mannered, I would have had him pick me up within the atmosphere, but this was more fun anyways.

Getting out of the storm was really just the first step. Like breaking through the layers of an onion, I passed through stratifications of clouds on my way up, all different in their own way.

I climbed slowly through a thick fog of tungsten hexafluoride that had been pulled from deeper in the atmosphere by another, more violent storm. Thick clouds played tricks with the colors of the tempest's lightning below me, shifting it to greens and teals. Above that I entered a thin pocket of clear carbon monoxide. From that vantage the dark clouds from below took on the guise of massive black monoliths with shifting surfaces.

As I escaped the last vestiges of Cyrene's atmosphere, I looked back at the massive gas giant I had called home for the last decade. She was enormous. I'd seen so little, gotten to know such a tiny portion of her. And there were millions, maybe billions, of planets like her in the Milky Way. Would I ever know enough to claim I understood planets like this?

"You are nowhere near the rendezvous coordinates. Wait. What happened to you?" Karora broke through my reveries, obviously referring to my limp, broken wings.

"Nothing. Shut up. I made a mistake."

"Ha-ha-ha!" he laughed over the channel. "You so messed up! I'm not even sure I can repair that."

"Shut up! Just pick me up. I'll go to Aveta later if you can't help . . ."

"Oh, don't be like that. I'll have a look at it while we're on our way."

He brought the *Tjurunga* close to me. As expected, the ship had changed significantly since last I saw it, but I was still rather shocked by how much. The front was more pointed, and the engine section was so large it took over three-quarters of the vessel's volume and probably an even greater portion of its mass. It was to be expected. The *Tjurunga* is equipped with variations of every type of faster-than-light device known to Capek-kind, as well as a few prototypes. Karora likes to brag that his ship was the fastest in the galaxy, which might mean something if space folding didn't make the very concept of speed irrelevant.

I floated into the craft through the airlock. Two of Karora's shards were already there to assist me in.

"I broke a sensor array, Kar, I'm not an invalid," I protested.

Karora's shards are difficult to take seriously. Each is roughly two feet high and is composed of chubby segments that form humanoid limbs. They look like teddy bears. However, they are incredibly efficient. Each segment can rotate around the one it's connected to at almost three hundred degrees, making the shards remarkably flexible. The extremities, being so fat, allow the housing of a shocking amount of tools and devices, including thruster arrays in each foot. Unleashed upon a project, Karora can swarm rapidly to various portions, giving himself assistance where needed to accomplish challenging feats of construction and assembly at speeds that simply boggle the mind. Then again that's what he was engineered to do.

"Just let me have a look at it," he insisted. Without waiting for permission, he began to disassemble the mounting on my back, liberating the mechanism that held my wings in place.

I sat down in the cockpit of the *Tjurunga*. All of Karora's shards were somewhere in the cramped room, each busy with a different task. A third shard joined the two already furiously working on my back. My friend did not need to interact with his ship to pilot it. That was accomplished through wireless communication, but the *Tjurunga* had a fully functional pilot's chair, and a Capek of the appropriate dimensions and configuration, like me, could take the helm.

"So you say you figured out who the Capek with the arsenal is," I said, trying to distract myself from the impromptu surgery.

"I did! You want to know now, or should I keep it a surprise?"

"Ugh. Just tell me."

"Too late! We're here."

I guess I was meant to be impressed. We had traveled over half an astronomical unit in a matter of minutes, clearly through the use of a space-time bubble. An Alcubierre drive. Yet I hadn't felt the telltale vibrations that usually herald the buildup of the necessary power, nor had I noticed when the bubble had popped in and out of existence around us. However, I didn't have the time to voice my admiration.

"Is that . . . ?"

"Anhur."

"No!"

It was hard to believe, but there he was. One of the biggest villains of Aurvandil's rebellion. The giant Lucretius had disappeared after the events that had almost plunged Capek civilization into civil war. It was the uneasy assumption of almost every Capek that he had limped off to a nearby wormhole or managed to fold space one last time before completely falling apart. From the looks of him, the theory held some truth to it.

So far from the nearest star, it was the *Tjurunga*'s lights that illuminated the monster. The top portion of his shell was pockmarked with impact craters, some large and deep enough to expose the inner workings of the beast. A third of the long, thick spines that served as his engine and maneuvering thrusters were damaged or otherwise severed. It was Anhur's prow, however, that held the strongest evidence of his defeat. It was marred by a long gash of burnt and twisted pseudo-plastic so deep and wide that, to a technically minded Capek, it was obviously a surgical strike meant to incapacitate the Lucretius. Massive exposed conduits that could only serve to power engines had been severed and rendered useless. One of the redundant fusion reactors was ruptured, reduced to a cold and empty husk.

Yet the giant lived.

———   ———

Karora brought his ship close to the largest opening in Anhur's outer shell. Circles of bright illumination danced over the remains as if each had a mind of its own and was looking for something. The *Tjurunga* got within a few feet of the wreck, and Karora opened the hatch.

"All done," he explained, referring to his work on my wings.

"They still don't work," I complained. Hard as I tried, I couldn't get any telemetry out of any of the sensors.

"I know. I just repaired the folding mechanism. I mean, if you want to stay here for a couple of hours I can probably take care of it, but you'll miss out."

I couldn't deny that curiosity was gnawing at me voraciously, and, after all, what good were atmospheric sensors in the vacuum of space? He was right: the sensors could wait. As long as I no longer had limp, skeletal tendrils flopping around me, I was better off tagging along. How often does one get to explore the wreck of a legendary killer Capek?

We disembarked from the hatch, me and seven of Karora's shards. The little robots immediately fanned out to investigate as much of the husk as they could. Six of them became little dots of ion thrust darting about in the dark, while the seventh shard accompanied me toward where Anhur's cognitive array should be housed.

"Did you try to talk to him?" It wasn't the smartest question. Without quancom, the only message Karora could have sent would have been by radio, and we would have beaten the signal to its destination by several hours. This left the short window since we'd arrived.

"Pointless. I didn't see his entertainment core listed with the damaged systems, so I'm assuming he's isolated his consciousness in there."

"Would he have listed that as a critical system?"

Precious few Capeks were equipped with an entertainment core, but all Lucretiuses had them. The device created a customizable, fully immersive artificial reality. A Lucretius by his very nature was likely to spend thousands of years in deep space, completely isolated. The entertainment core offered a safe retreat where the Capek could stay busy during the long transit between galaxies.

"Wouldn't you?"

We entered a large chamber. It had taken some time to dig this deep into the monster's body. Close to an hour in fact, winding through tubes and corridors that were never meant to be traveled. Unlike some Sputniks, a Lucretius-class Capek wasn't meant to carry passengers. The conduits were analogous to arteries, not corridors, so they hadn't been designed with efficient travel in mind.

Either some automated system detected our presence, or Karora's other shards had reactivated Anhur's power grid, but just as we floated into his "brain," soft-green lights came to life, bathing us in a calm glow that made me think of the tall forests being grown on some Reclamation Worlds across the Milky Way.

"What are we even looking at?" I asked. I'd never seen the inside of another Capek, apart from the purpose-built cockpits and cargo holds of larger Sputniks.

"Damned if I know. I assume the central hub over there." He pointed to an area where many of the lights inlaid into the walls of the chamber converged. "That should be the central cognitive and memory cores."

There was no reason to doubt him. Karora might not be specialized in Capek neurophysiology, but there was no arguing that he knew ship architecture and robotics enough to be trusted on the subject. He'd built the *Tjurunga* himself and had refitted, automated, destroyed, and rebuilt it so many times I could hardly imagine a more competent Capek to have at my side in this situation.

"So, what's the plan? We reactivate him?"

"Ha-ha-ha! No," my friend answered derisively as he removed the paneling that covered Anhur's brains.

"Why not? Weren't you on the same side during Aurvandil's rebellion?"

It was a cheap shot and a sore point for him. A handful of Capeks had joined with Aurvandil in an effort to hunt down and contain the human cold-storage locations. Their argument being that the galaxy now belonged to us and there was no reason the humans should ever be allowed to wake up and disrupt our civilization. Needless to say, this was not a philosophy embraced by all. Aurvandil's methods bordered on insanity. It was in fact eventually shown that the rebel leader had a defect that made him a walking time bomb. Karora had sided with him. The blow to his ego after their defeat and discovering he'd been following a false prophet still resonates with my friend to this day. Fortunately, he and the other rebels were granted amnesty—another divisive issue, but it was the only way to keep our society from breaking out into open civil war. A war that would have burned the galaxy to ashes.

"Well, first of all 'we' aren't going to be doing anything. This is a massively complex Capek, not some clouds and rain. If anything gets done, you can watch."

"Ouch."

"Also, even on our so-called side, Anhur was a bit of an aberration. As was Pele for that matter."

Pele had been another Lucretius-class Capek, one that had been destroyed by the great Hera before she was in turn eradicated by orbital bombardment.

"I'm not exactly sure if even Aurvandil knew what these two were up to. They just showed up one day and started 'helping.'"

"Helping?" I asked for further clarification while taking a section of paneling he was handing me.

"Well, they're not like us—Lucretiuses I mean. They're . . . psychopaths? Aurvandil wanted a peaceful solution. Even the humans weren't supposed to come to any harm, but Pele and Anhur . . . All the violence can be traced back to them."

It's true that it takes a rather unique personality to be a Lucretius, to volunteer for the complete isolation that comes with deep-space exploration and venture into the gulf that separates the Milky Way from its neighbors. I've heard them described as sociopaths, insane, or in some cases the most Capek of us all, but not necessarily violent or malevolent.

"So, no reactivation?"

"No reactivation." To punctuate his answer, he proceeded to disconnect a series of conduits from around the cognitive core.

"Mmmph . . . Judging from the level of activity in this thing"— Karora tapped his fingers on one of the devices he had uncovered by removing the panel—"that's the entertainment core."

I looked on as my friend continued to remove pieces to hand me. I'd set them aside to float in the weightless vacuum. He disconnected more and more conduits. I could recognize where he would create loops and feed information back on itself, isolating the cores from each other or from key external systems, essentially separating Anhur from his own body and locking him within the artificial environment of his entertainment core.

It was a slow, hesitant process. Karora, for all his knowledge, was still playing with things that were out of his comfort zone. He'd often stop to judge whether he was making the right decision or not. After a while another of his shards joined us to help with the procedure. Changes in vibrations and other details told me that some of Anhur's functionality was being brought back online, one system at a time.

"Nervous?" I asked, noticing my friend taking increasingly long pauses.

"No. No, no. Yes. I'm not worried about lobotomizing him, if that's what you mean, but a big Capek like this has a few secondary cognitive arrays sprinkled around his body. Some might have instructions to protect the central core, here, from exactly the kind of stuff we're doing right now."

"Oh, it's 'we' again now," I said in an attempt to lighten the mood, but there was no answer coming from my partner. In fact, both his shards had completely stopped moving. At first, I assumed he was focusing his full attention on a distant problem his other shards were faced with. Most Von Neumanns never have a problem keeping many threads of activity going, each shard behaving less like a limb and more like its own person. When they do slip, as Karora seemed to be doing, they usually hide it in shame for some reason. As if it were a failing on their part.

This was different, however. Both shards were focused on the same part of the cognitive array he was working on, frozen mid-movement. I started to wonder if perhaps he might be communicating with another Capek through quancom, consulting on how best to proceed. A prudent move if that was actually the case. However, just as I began to entertain the notion, my friend shook off his torpor and slowly pointed with the right hand of both of his shards. "What the hell is that?"

LISTS OF PATRONS

This book was made possible in part by the following grand patrons who preordered the book on Inkshares.com. Thank you.

Alex V. Landing

Alf Cato Hansen

Amy Frost

Angela Blasi

Annie Forte

Aubra Doss

Benoit Provencher

Brad Ludwig

Brian Guthrie

C. Christian Scott

Chris Michaels

Christine Grysban

Christophe Delhougne

Christopher Dunn

Christopher Layfield

Clark Moore

Corrina Leigh Forster

David Michael

Dawn Morris Blackburn

Eric A. Paulhus

Eric Bernier

Francine Garant

Garry J. Wallan

Gregor Sprague

Hannah "Hank" Wilkinson

Jani Hukka

January Ford

Jayson Wallace

Jennifer A. Florendo
Jessica Immel
Jill Boger
Jim Been
JJ Valentine
John Kline
Jordanna Caine
Jorge Hernandez
Joseph Terzieva
Julie Kuehl
Julie Verone Boles
Kari Simms
Kevin Chu
Kim Immel
Les Gebhardt
Marco Cantin
Martin La Vergne
Matthew McChesney
Matthew Sargent
Matt Stein

Michel Dubeau
Michel Sedawey
Mike McPeek
Nathan Little
Nathan Parks
Nikki Moore
Patrick Hall
Paul Alejandro
Philippe Dubeau
Phil Rood
Samantha Sequin
Sarah Marie Sonoda
Sean Jamison
Seth Bokelman
Steven Rod
Teras Cassidy
Tony Sandoval

INKSHARES

Inkshares is a crowdfunded book publisher. We democratize publishing by having readers select the books we publish—we edit, design, print, distribute, and market any book that meets a preorder threshold.

Interested in making a book idea come to life? Visit inkshares. com to find new book projects or to start your own.

SWORD & LASER

Sword & Laser is a science fiction and fantasy-themed book club, video show, and podcast that gathers together a strong online community of passionate readers to discuss and enjoy books of both genres.

Listen in or join the conversation at swordandlaser.com.